SEX,
MURDER
AND A
DOUBLE LATTE

KYRA DAVIS

SEX, MURDER
AND A
DOUBLE LATTE

**RED
DRESS
INK**
™

First edition May 2005

SEX, MURDER AND A DOUBLE LATTE

A Red Dress Ink novel

ISBN 0-373-89519-4

www.RedDressInk.com

Printed in U.S.A.

For my grandmother Sophia "Sylvia" Davis,
a woman whose greatest dream
was to help those she loved realize theirs.

I would like to thank my agent, Ashley Kraas,
my editor, Margaret O'Neill Marbury,
and everyone at Red Dress Ink.
I also want to thank my friend Brenda Gilcrest,
and my mother, Gail Davis, for catching all my grievous
spelling mistakes, and Shawn Cavlin, along with everyone in
Doc Murdock's Writer's Group, for all their input.
Finally, I want to thank Alina Adams and Danielle Girard
for being such wonderful mentors.

 CHAPTER 1

"If Alicia Bright had learned one lesson in life it was that the more settled things seemed to be, the more likely they were to get messed up."
—*Sex, Drugs, and Murder*

The downside of writing sex scenes is that my mother reads my books.

Until I die I will be haunted by the memory of my mother confronting me after reading my first novel. She stood in the living room of my San Francisco apartment with one slightly arthritic hand resting on her robust hip and the other waving my book in front of my face. "I ask you," she said, "how can a nice Jewish girl write such a thing? It's not bad enough you should give me ulcers with all this talk of killing, but now you have to write about naked people too? I thought only shiksas wrote such things."

I somehow resisted the impulse to run and made the stupid mistake of trying to reason with her. "No, Mama," I said, "smut is nondenominational." But my mother wasn't satisfied with that, so she highlighted the scenes, took the book to her rabbi and asked him for his opinion of her daughter, the sex fiend. The rabbi, who in all likelihood was just slightly less mortified than I was, assured her that writing about sex between two consenting adults within a loving, albeit edgy relationship was in no way a violation of the Torah. After that my mother approached almost every member of the congregation, proudly showed them my book and said things like, "Can you believe this? My daughter the author. And you should read the sex scenes. Now if she would just do some of the things she writes about, I could be a grandmother already."

I don't go to that synagogue anymore.

Finding a new congregation was really the only way to avoid embarrassment, since blending into the background was not an option for me. With the exception of my father, I am the only black temple member that Sinai has ever had, which makes me pretty easy to spot. My nationality is an endless source of entertainment for the public. My skin is the color of a well-brewed latte (double shot), and while the mass of textured hair that hangs to my shoulders is frizzy, it's not exactly 'fro material, so people are constantly mistaking me for Brazilian, Hispanic, Puerto Rican, Egyptian, Israeli—you name it. I am spokeswoman for all people. Or at least all people with a slutty imagination.

I finished typing the details of my hero's and heroine's erogenous zones and switched scenes to the apartment of the gourmet chef who was about to be bludgeoned to death with a large toaster oven. How long would it take him to die? Ten minutes, fifteen…

I started at the sound of my buzzer going off and checked the time on the bottom right of my computer screen. Shit. My hands balled up into two tight fists. There's nothing worse than walking away from a keyboard while on a roll. I tapped *ctrl S* and walked to the entryway to buzz in my guests. I listened as the sound of heavy heels trailed by rubber soles pounded up three stories' worth of stairs.

"How are you holding up?" Dena gave my arm a quick squeeze before peeling off her leather blazer and draping it over a dining chair.

Mary Ann followed her into the apartment and threw her arms around my neck before I had a chance to respond. "Oh my God, Sophie, I'm so sorry! I've never known anyone who's done anything like that. I think I would just be a wreck if I were in your shoes."

I pulled away from the stranglehold and searched Mary Ann's blue eyes for some clue as to what she was talking about. "Okay, I give. Were you speaking in code or am I just so sleep deprived that the English language no longer makes sense to me?"

Dena raised a thick Sicilian eyebrow and seated herself on the armrest of my sofa. "You haven't turned on the TV news today, have you?"

"Well, I read the morning paper, but no, I didn't see the news shows. You know me, when I'm writing I sometimes tune out—"

"Tolsky killed himself, Sophie. They found him last night."

Okay, I was definitely sleep deprived, because there was no way that Dena had just said what I thought she said. "I can't imagine how this could possibly be funny, but I'm waiting for the punch line."

Mary Ann was on her feet. "Oh my God, I'm so sorry! I just thought you knew!"

I could hear the distant sounds of a siren screeching its warning. This was wrong. It was a misunderstanding of some kind. "I just talked to Tolsky *two weeks ago.*" I enunciated the words carefully as if by doing so I could help Dena and Mary Ann realize their mistake. "He said he couldn't wait to see my screenplay. He told me where he was going to film the movie. He told me where he was going to be next week. He told me which actors he was going to approach. Do you see where I'm heading with this? Tolsky was *going* to do a lot of stuff. He had plans. I may only have spoken to him a few times, but I know this was not a man who was planning on taking his own life."

"Well, he may not have been planning it two weeks ago, but he sure as hell did it last night." Dena nodded to Mary Ann, and continued, "I saw an *Examiner* downstairs in the lobby, it's probably in there."

Mary Ann tugged nervously on a chestnut-brown curl before hurrying out to retrieve the afternoon publication.

"You weren't close to him, right?" Dena asked. "You just met him that one time?"

"Yeah, just the one time he came up to talk to me about the possibility of turning *Sex, Drugs and Murder* into a movie. We talked about it on the phone a few times afterward. He seemed like a nice enough guy, maybe a little larger than life, but nothing that you wouldn't expect from a Hollywood producer.... Dena are you sure about this?"

"Oh, I'm sure, and if you thought he was larger than life, then wait until you hear how he chose to orchestrate his exit."

Mary Ann breezed in with the paper in hand. I'm in pretty good shape but it seems to me that after climbing three flights of stairs two times over she should be sweating, not glowing. I took the *Examiner* from her and read the headline, "Michael Tolsky Commits Suicide, Death Imitates Art." I placed the paper against the unfinished wood of the dining table and sat down to read.

"Right out of a movie…literally." Dena ruffled her own short dark hair and relaxed back into the cushions. "I don't mean to be disrespectful, but what a frigging drama queen."

I reread the description of his death. Tolsky had slit his wrists in a bathtub. The scene was right out of his film *Silent Killer*. He had even taken care to put vanilla-scented candles around the room, just as his character had done before his premature end. I tried to picture Tolsky lying naked in a pool of his own blood, his round rosy face devoid of animation. At our lunch meeting his presence had been so large that I had worried there wouldn't be enough room in the restaurant for the other patrons. How could things have changed that quickly?

"Of all his films, why recreate *that* scene?" I used my finger to trace a circle around the paragraph describing the incident. "I don't get it. In *Silent Killer,* it wasn't even a real suicide. It was a murder made to *look* like a suicide. Have the police considered that this might not be what it seems?"

"Read the whole article," Dena said. "There was a note."

Mary Ann nodded vigorously. "Mmm–hmm, a suicide note."

"Oh, good thing you clarified that one—I'm sure Sophie thought I was talking about a piece of music."

Mary Ann ignored Dena and continued to recite the information she had gathered. "He gave all the servants the day off—the maid, the chauffeur, everybody. I guess he was really upset over his wife leaving him. His blood alcohol level was like double the legal limit. I just feel so sad for him."

I focused on the headshot of Tolsky on the front page. So maybe he *had* planned it. Just woke up one morning and decided to check out. I probably should have felt sad for him too. Maybe I'd have felt more sympathetic if I had liked him more, or if I hadn't always considered suicide a cruel copout, or if I wasn't such a coldhearted capitalist bitch. What about my screenplay!

"You know, if he was so depressed about his marriage, why the hell didn't he try to win her back? She only left him a week ago. I mean, did he try flowers? Diamonds? Marriage counseling? Anything?"

"Would that have worked for Scott after you filed?" Mary Ann asked.

"No, but Scott was a freeloading, adulterous loser, that's why our marriage lasted less than two years. The Tolskys were married for twenty-five years, so obviously he had *something* going for him. You don't invest that kind of time and energy into a relationship, and then just roll over and play dead the minute things start to go sour." I winced at my own choice of words. "What I meant was…or what I didn't mean…you know what? This really sucks." I dropped my head onto the table and tried to suppress the frustrated scream burning my throat.

"Face it." Dena stretched her short muscular legs out in front of her. "He was a man of extremes, and when he got depressed, he did it in a big way. The whole way he re-created his movie scene was a pathetic but successful attempt to get everybody to sit up and take notice." She used her foot to gently steer my feline, Mr. Katz, away from her black pants. "This screws you up big-time, huh?"

"Damn right it does!" The chair screeched against the hardwood floor as I pushed myself back from the table. "He was just Mr. Enthusiastic about that project. Why did he even approach me about adapting my manuscript for him if he didn't plan on hanging around long enough to see a first draft?"

"And you know that people are lining up at the video stores to rent his films," Dena added. "If he could have just held off for a little longer, your little movie could have benefited from this postmortem media blitz."

"Gee, thanks for making me feel better about this." I squeezed my eyes closed and took a steadying breath. Let it go…there'd be other chances. They may not materialize for another ten years but that only brought me to forty. I might still be able to wear a size-six gown while collecting my Academy Award at that age. Sarah Jessica Parker was forty and she looked pretty good. I opened my eyes again and stared up at the halogen lighting above me. "Maybe I should put a rumor out that I'm terminally ill. Do you think I'd get another offer to turn my books into screenplays if I were facing imminent death?"

"Terminally ill doesn't count," Dena said. "Either you stop breathing or you'll just have to trudge along with the rest of us."

"Maybe I could do a Van Gogh thing and cut off my ear or something. That might get people's attention."

"Didn't do a lot for Van Gogh." Dena brought her hands to the back of her head in order to administer a self-indulgent massage. "From what I understand, it didn't even get him laid. Didn't his girlfriend break up with him after he gave it to her as a gift? She probably sent him a note in reply reading, 'I said ear*ring,* you idiot!'"

I couldn't help but laugh at that.

Mary Ann went to the kitchen and pulled a bag of microwave popcorn out of the cupboard. "Well, if all he wanted was to keep his name in the papers a little longer, wouldn't it have been easier to just make another movie?" she asked. Her eyes widened and she dropped the popcorn bag on the counter that divided the kitchen from the living room. "Oh my God, maybe it was an accident. Maybe he was shaving and he cut himself by mistake!"

If anyone else had said it I would have immediately assumed they were joking, but I knew Mary Ann well enough to be sure that the poor thing was totally serious. I bit down hard on my lip and tried to think about starving people in Africa, or the destruction of the rain forest, or anything to keep me from laughing.

Dena was not so kind. "I cannot believe we share the same gene pool. If anyone asks, please point out that you're my *second* cousin, and if you can fit in the 'once removed' part, I'd appreciate it."

"It could have happened." Mary Ann crossed her arms and glared at Dena. "He was drunk, right?"

"So he got into the bathtub and tried to shave his arms?"

"Well, maybe he had hairy arms."

"And he accidentally slit both his wrists? At which point, what...he thought to himself, 'Well shit, this sucks. I guess I'll wait for all my blood to slowly leave my body and if it still hurts after that point, I'll call 911.'"

"I don't know," Mary Ann said. "Maybe he passed out. Maybe he was embarrassed...."

"Right, that must be where they got the expression 'embarrassed to death.'"

"Okay, whatever. I still say it could have happened. If you'll excuse me, I have to use the little girls' room."

"Be careful you don't accidentally slit your wrists while wiping yourself."

"You are so crude," Mary Ann said as she made her way down the narrow hallway.

I finally allowed myself to give up the battle for self-control and broke into a fit of giggles. When I caught my breath, I unsuccessfully tried to give Dena my most stern look. "You were kind of harsh, weren't you?"

"I'm sorry, but there are times when her immense ignorance tries my patience. And what does she mean 'the little girls' room'? She's so fucking delicate she can't even call it a bathroom for Christ's sake."

I shook my head. I knew Dena loved Mary Ann in a big-sister kind of way. My mind wandered back to the time when a boyfriend of Mary Ann's had slapped her across the face. Dena had repaid him by breaking his nose.

Mary Ann emerged from the bathroom, an experience she seemed to have managed to get through without incident, and began to search my refrigerator for a more fattening alternative to the popcorn. She settled on a jar of peanut butter and a spoon. I eyed her size-four form enviously before refocusing on Dena, who was now examining the Blockbuster rental we had originally planned to watch. "I have a big shipment of vibrators coming to the shop first thing tomorrow morning, so if we're going to watch this we should do it soon."

Mary Ann made a face. "And you're embarrassed to be related to *me.*"

"Don't knock it before you try it. If those Neiman women you wait on started using vibrators, they wouldn't have to spend so much money on face cream to look rejuvenated."

I rolled my eyes. "Maybe Lancôme should make it their next gift-with-purchase."

Mary Ann started giggling and even Dena broke into a smile. She waved the movie in the air. "So should I put this in?"

I tried to muster up some enthusiasm for a movie night, but after reviewing the details of Tolsky's bloody death I no longer felt in the mood for Hannibal Lecter. Maybe I could use the rather vivid images floating around my head to add some realism to my crime scenes. At least that way I could feel like I was accomplishing something instead of sitting around idly after some razor-loving depressive screwed up my career.

I repositioned my chair so that I could easily address both of my guests. "Would you hate me if I ended things early this evening?"

Dena did a quick double take. "You want us to leave now? Thirty-five minutes for parking, Sophie!"

"I know. It's just that the whole Tolsky thing has kind of knocked the wind out of me. I promise to make it up to you next week. We'll do a double feature or something."

"Don't even worry about it, Sophie." Mary Ann put the popcorn and peanut butter back in their respective places. "It totally makes sense that you would need some alone time."

Dena let out an exacerbated sigh and reached for her sixties-style handbag. "Fine. I didn't even get to fill you in on the intimate details of my date last night."

"Anyone I know?" I grabbed the mailbox key before accompanying them to the lobby.

"No, new to the city. But I tell you, if last night was any indication, I'll be adding another notch to my bedpost by the end of the week."

Mary Ann's color rose, and I let out a short laugh.

"What, I'm not entitled to a little fun?"

"You're entitled." I paused by the glass door. "But if you keep this up you're going to have to break in a new post."

Dena grinned. "Hell, I'm already on the fourth one. Soon I'm going to need a whole new bed." She smoothed the lapels of her jacket and gave me an exaggerated wink. "If you really want to make tonight up to me, promise me that after you've finished with this manuscript we'll celebrate with a bottle of wine at the Bitches' Circle."

"Oh, oh, I want to come this time!" Mary Ann flung her hand up in the air like a schoolgirl trying to get her teacher's attention.

Dena looked at her through lowered lids. "You can't, you're not a bitch."

"I can be a...I can be mean."

Dena's shoulders sagged at the evidence of her cousin's impenetrable sweetness. Dena and I had been visiting our affectionately named Bitches' Circle periodically for the last fourteen years. It was a little spot in the Redwood section of Golden Gate Park Botanical Gardens that consisted of a cluster of benches surrounded by high brush. There was a small podium made out of a redwood trunk, from which we surmised that the area was either designed for poetry readings or séances, but Dena and I used it as a place to drink and get catty.

"You've taken Sophie's hairstylist." Mary Ann stuck out the lower portion of her heart-shaped mouth. "It's only fair that if he went, I should get to go."

"Marcus? Oh, please, that guy could put Joan Rivers to shame. You, on the other hand, could barely hold your own with Marie Osmond."

I stepped between the two of them. "I promise we'll invite you. Just practice your swearing." I took Mary Ann by both hands. "The word is 'bitch.'"

I heard the unpleasant sound of Dena's teeth grinding together, and I knew when the time came she would find a way to take me to our spot without the presence of any unwanted guests. But for now Mary Ann was pacified. She waited as Dena fished out her keys.

"Do we have to listen to Eminem again in the car? I just got a great new CD and I brought it with me…."

"We're not fucking listening to Britney Spears."

I held the door open for them and watched their backs retreat into the darkness. Why was I bothering with screenplays when two of my best friends were a sitcom ready to happen?

Before heading up to my flat, I inserted my key into my box and pulled out the mail I had neglected to pick up the day before. Fairly standard stuff—two credit card applications, one postcard from Macy's announcing yet another "biggest sale of the year" and…and what? I studied the last envelope as I absently closed the apartment door behind me. No return address, just my mailing info typed neatly on the front. Weird. I opened it and read the one-sentence letter. "You reap what you sow."

That was it. No greeting, just one typed turn of phrase. Okay, so we had moved from weird to downright freaky. Of course, I was used to getting a certain amount of fan mail from people who were a little whacked. Most of them were sent to me care of my publisher, but an occasional letter found its way to my home address, so this wasn't anything all that novel. Still, "You reap what you sow"? What the hell was that about? I looked over my shoulder and then laughed at myself. Who did I expect to find there, Freddy? It was just a stupid note—and it's not like it had been hand delivered. I rubbed my thumbs against the black letters. No reason to let a juvenile prank make me more rattled than I already was.

I went to the fireplace and tossed the letter in, along with a Duraflame log. Mr. Katz rubbed himself against my ankles as I struck a match and carefully lit the fire. The paper curled and twisted until there was nothing left but a pile of ash. I sat on the floor, pulled my knees to my chest and focused on the warm glow of the blaze. It should have been comforting, but I just wasn't able to push aside the feeling that a new element had entered my life. And for reasons unknown to me, that element was something to fear.

CHAPTER 2

"No one could say Alicia was all work and no play. She loved a good party almost as much as she loved a good fight."

—*Sex, Drugs and Murder*

It's funny how horrific events can spur a person to accomplish truly incredible feats, and that is exactly what Tolsky's death did for me. I, Sophie Katz, the woman who is known for perfecting the art of procrastination, had finished a book one week before deadline.

I pressed my foot up against the computer desk and propelled my wheeled chair across the room, my arms held high in a V for victory. My pet raised his head in mild curiosity. "I am sooo cool," I told him. "Hell, I'm better than cool, I'm responsible." Mr. Katz didn't seem that impressed, but then again…well, he was a cat.

Tolsky's apparent suicide hadn't sat well with me. Maybe I had written too many murder mysteries, but somehow the whole thing seemed too pat. I kept coming back to the fact that the screen death that had been recreated was actually a murder scene. It just seemed like that detail bore more significance than the police were crediting it with. But whether I was correct or simply imagining something out of nothing, it had inspired me to finish what could be my best book to date.

Although the letter I received the night I learned of Tolsky's death had undoubtedly been nothing more than a misguided hoax, it had disturbed me enough to result in quite a few restless nights. But as it turns out, that worked to my advantage too, because I had used all those hours I normally would have wasted on sleep to finish my book. So thank you, anonymous freak.

This required a celebration. This required a reward that was decadent and fitting the mood of the occasion.

This required Starbucks.

And this wasn't just a latte morning either. Oh no, this was a "Grande Caramel Brownie Frappuccino with extra whipped cream" kind of morning.

I threw on a pair of torn hipster jeans, a Gap T-shirt and a corduroy blazer, and was pulling on a boot when the phone rang. Oh goody, I got to tell someone else how awesome I was! Maybe I'd even get to share the joy with a telemarketer.

"*Hola,* Sophie the great, at your service."

Silence.

"Hello?"

Just a click, followed by a dial tone.

I put the phone down and started working on the other boot. "I hate it when people do that. How hard is it to say 'sorry, wrong number'?" Mr. Katz swished his tail in agitation. I guess for him that really would be a challenge.

The phone rang again.

"Oh, for God's sake." I snapped it up and cradled it against my shoulder. "It's still me. You have the wrong number."

Nothing. Not even a click.

"Hello? Is somebody there?" I sat up a little straighter and waited for a response.

They disconnected.

I pressed the hang-up button without putting the phone down.

It rang again. Three times, and then it stopped.

Who would want to prank-call me? The characters in my books got prank calls all the time, but my real world had always been blissfully prank-call free. I tapped my fingernail against the mouthpiece and waited to see if they would try again. After a few minutes, I gave up. Probably some bored teenager who had seen the movie *Scream* one too many times. I pulled my purse over my shoulder and stepped out of my apartment. As I was double-locking the door I could hear the ring. I didn't bother to go back in to pick it up. The SOB could call all day long if he wanted. I had a Frappuccino to order.

I headed on foot to one of the fifteen or twenty Starbucks located in my vicinity and when I arrived I decided that the experience wouldn't be complete without a *New York Times*. There was one last paper for sale on the rack by the counter and I could practically hear it calling to me, enticing me to spend the hours necessary to read it cover to cover, knowing the whole time that I had absolutely nothing else I needed to do. My fingers had literally grazed the first page when it was snatched out of my grasp.

I whirled around to see a six-foot-something brunette already scanning the paper with dark brown eyes. "Hey, I was going to buy that."

"Guess you'll have to buy another one." He spoke with the slightest foreign accent.

"In case you haven't noticed, there isn't another one. I had my hand on that paper, and you took it."

"So buy a *Chronicle*. I just came from New York this morning and I'm going to buy a *New York Times*."

"Well, if the *Times* is so damn important to you, you should have bought one in New York." He shrugged and started reading the paper again. "Hello. We're having a confrontation here. Look, I don't really care if you're from New York. I don't care if you're Rudolph Giuliani himself. That's my paper."

"Next in line, please," a voice called from behind the cash register.

"Are you going to order, or shall I go in front of you?" he asked, not even looking up from his reading.

"Oh. My. God!" This was not happening. No one was this big of an ass. I stormed up to the perky little blonde in the green apron.

"Hi. Can I take your order?"

"That guy just took my paper."

"Oh, um…" The blonde glanced around, trying to find someone else she could pass me off to. "Okay, sorry. So he took your paper?"

"Yes. I was going to buy it, and he took it."

"Oh, well, okay, the thing is…well, this is kind of my first day and this sort of thing wasn't covered in the training. Do you want to talk to a supervisor?"

I just stared at her for a moment. It was a fairly reasonable answer, but somehow I had been hoping that the blond Starbucks trainee was really a ninja in disguise and would knock Mr. New York senseless. But that didn't seem to be the case, and it was probably a pretty safe bet that her supervisor would also be lacking in the superhero department. I quickly reviewed my options. That didn't take much time because I had none. "Fine. Fine, fine, fine, fine. Just get me a Grande Caramel Brownie Frappuccino—and there had better be a lot of whipped cream to make up for this."

A customer with unnaturally red hair and a tie-dyed shirt who was being assisted at the adjacent register smiled and leaned over in my direction. "You know, my sister's dating a

Native American," she said winking at me conspiratorially. "I think you all have a really interesting culture."

Oh, I was so not in the mood for this. "Actually I'm Irish. I'm just wearing a lot of bronzer." I turned back to my cashier. "Could you make my drink now?"

The cashier wrote some illegible words on a paper cup and quickly entered my order into the register.

I looked back at the newspaper thief. He was watching... and laughing. The fucker was laughing at me. That's it, he was on the list. In my next book I would be sure that the first murder victim would be a dark-haired New York tourist and the police would find him bludgeoned to death in an alley behind a Starbucks with a *New York Times* shoved up his ass.

I picked up my drink and sat down at a table by the window that happened to have a discarded *Chronicle* resting on top. Although it was probably not the intention of its previous owner, it felt like the paper was left there for the sole purpose of further pissing me off. I pushed it aside and busied myself by mentally formulating the details of how I was going to whack the jerk who had just screwed up my morning. The task plus the extra dose of sugar and caffeine were just beginning to perk me up again when my desired victim strolled over to the table, winnings in hand.

"I read the articles I wanted to read. Would you like this now?"

Oh, this was too much. "No, thanks, I'm pretty happy with the *Chronicle*."

He gave me a little half smile and sat down opposite me. "Now, you obviously want it. You're not going to let your pride keep you from taking what you want, are you?" He pushed the paper toward me, and I unwillingly noted his hands...big, strong... God, I loved guys with hands like that, with the exception of this guy. This guy was a schmuck.

"Shouldn't you be out taking pictures of cable cars or something like that?"

"Oh, I'm not a tourist. I was just in New York wrapping up some old business. I made San Francisco my home a few months ago."

"Oh goody, another East Coast transplant moving to our wonderful city. How original."

He laughed. "Actually, I was originally a Russian transplant moving Israel and then an Israeli transplant moving to New York. So, you see, I've been condescended to by the natives of three continents. You're going to have to work a little harder if you plan on offending me now." He gently pushed the paper a little closer to me. "Take the paper."

I gave him my best glare but I couldn't quite keep my fingers from inching toward the publication.

"There are some really interesting articles," he said. "Corruption in the political world, greed in the business world—violence in the art world, all the usual sensationalism."

I begrudgingly took the paper. "Violence in the art world?"

"Mmm…it seems there's been a conviction in the KK Money murder trial."

I noted the headline on the front page. "It's JJ Money." JJ Money was a gangsta rapper who, seven months ago, had been killed in the exact same manner as one of his songs, shot in both kneecaps, once in the stomach and once in the head. Rival rap star DC Smooth, who already had a rather long criminal history that included a few assault-and-battery charges, had been tried for the murder and had now been found guilty, despite his continual protests of innocence, a detail I found a little odd. After his previous arrests he had been known to brag about his crimes. But then again, this was a different situation. This time his victim didn't just end up in a hospital but in a morgue.

"Well, I knew it was some letter of the English alphabet. The basic premise is the same, reaping what you sow and all that."

I nearly choked on my Frappuccino. "What did you say?"

"What, that the premise was the same?" he asked.

"No, the other part…you know what, never mind. Look, thanks for the paper. Now if you don't mind, I'd like to read it and enjoy my coffee by myself."

The man nodded and stood up. I couldn't help but notice his physique. He certainly spent enough time at the gym. He turned to leave, then paused and leaned over me, causing me to shift uncomfortably in my seat.

"By the way," he said, his Russian accent a bit more pronounced, "That's not coffee, that's a milk shake." And with that he walked out.

I stared at the door. Had he just insulted my coffee drink? Unbelievable! Everyone who had evolved passed the Cro-Magnon level knew that one should *never* make snide remarks about a person's weight, religion or choice in caffeinated beverages, which meant he was most likely a Neanderthal. A Neanderthal with really good hands.

I grabbed my drink and paper, and stormed home. At least my cat knew how to shut up and let me enjoy a few minor indulgences. When I reached my building, I struggled to retrieve my keys from my purse without putting down either of my two purchases. You never knew when a greedy tourist was going to sneak up and snag your periodical.

"Hello, Miss Katz."

The voice from behind startled me enough that I dropped my Frappuccino, spilling the beverage all over my suede boots. "Fuck!" I looked up from the disaster to see the pitifully distressed eyes of Andy Manning looking down at me.

"I'm so sorry, Miss Katz. I didn't mean to scare you. I just wanted to say hi. I guess I should go." He rubbed his massive head in a way that caused his fine blond hair to stick out in a rather awkward spiked configuration.

Everything about Andy was massive and awkward. He worked as the stock clerk at the corner market, and at six-seven and with a body weight that had to be well over the two-hundred-and-fifty-pound mark, he was pretty hard to miss. Andy also suffered from brain damage. I wasn't sure how that came to be. Alice, the market's proprietor, had said something about his being seriously abused as an infant. Whatever had happened, it certainly hadn't affected his disposition, which was one of the sweetest I'd ever come across.

I carefully extricated the sports section and used it to absorb some of the liquid penetrating my shoes. "No—I'm sorry, Andy. If I hadn't have been so preoccupied, you wouldn't have been able to surprise me. I didn't mean to swear." Well, I sorta had, but not at him.

He bent down and examined the mess. "I'm really sorry about your boots and your drink. Was it a Frappuccino?"

"Yeah, they're one of my favorite vices."

"I like them too. They're kind of like a milk shake."

The paper crinkled as my fist tightened around it. "Andy, I really have to go upstairs and see if I can salvage these. I'll see you later okay?"

"Okay, Miss Katz. I really am sorry."

"I know, Andy." I stuffed the soiled pages inside the now-empty cup and went upstairs.

Mr. Katz was spread out on the love seat, leisurely grooming himself. "Well, at least one of us is having a relaxing day."

The phone rang and I dumped my stuff onto the dining table in order to free my hands to answer. "Hello?"

No response. That was the last straw. "Listen, asshole, I don't know if you think you're funny or scary or what, but if you don't cut this crap out right now, my husband, who just happens to be a cop, is going to get his hands on the phone records and drag your juvenile butt to jail for harassment, got it?"

They hung up.

Ten seconds later the phone rang again. I picked up the receiver. "Oh, you are *sooo* asking for it."

There was no immediate response but I thought I could detect some background noise this time. It sounded like... Donna Summer.

A voice on the other end cleared his throat. "Honey, the only thing I'm asking for is world peace, the end of deforestation and a Miami beachfront property with a six-foot live-in housekeeper named Ricardo."

"Marcus." I leaned against the dividing kitchen counter. "Did you call before this?"

"No, but I'm guessing that the person who did, left you a tad out of sorts."

"Understatement, but it's not important. What's up with you?"

"I got a last-minute invite to an art opening for an artist named Donato Balardi. It's at the Sussman Gallery tonight. Want to come with?"

"That actually sounds fun. I've just finished a manuscript and I've been trying to celebrate, but so far I've been failing miserably." Mr. Katz blinked his eyes in what I took for agreement.

"You finished your book? Honey, that's great! Tell you what, I'll throw in dinner at Puccini and Pinetti to mark the occasion. My last appointment is at four but it's just a trim and style, so if we plan for me to pick you up at six-thirty I'll still have some wiggle room."

"Wiggle away. I'll see you at six-thirty."

I spent the rest of the day reading what was left of the paper and napping. It had been over a week since I had gotten a good night's sleep, and I had no intention of going out with saddlebag eyes. Knowing Marcus, he'd be fifteen minutes late, which was fine with me because I needed the extra minutes to do something with my hair. Tonight I would make Marcus proud, even if it killed me.

Several hours later, it was killing me. It was six-forty and I had been torturing myself with a blow-dryer and a curling iron for the last hour and a half, and my reward was hair that was big enough to intimidate Diana Ross. Marcus was so lucky; he had those short little well-groomed dreadlocks, and all he had to do was shave, get dressed and voilà—he was the next Blair Underwood. I was desperately searching my bathroom drawers for some styling product to fix the problem when the phone rang.

I rushed out into the living room to get it. "Hello?"

It was a hang-up. I stared at the phone. Either I hadn't been as convincing as I thought, or the person prank-calling somehow knew I didn't have a police officer husband. How would they know that? The buzzer jarred me out of my thoughts. My hand flew to my hair. "Damn it!"

I crossed over to the intercom. "Marcus, I just need another minute to finish putting myself together."

"In another minute, I'm going to have a meter maid in my face."

"Maybe you could flirt your way out of it?"

"Are you suggesting he's gay?" Marcus asked. "Honey, there isn't a gay man alive that would be caught dead in that polyester thing they call a uniform, and I'm not even going to get into that white scooter-deally they drive…. Oh shit, Sophie, he sees me! Oh my God, he's getting into the white scooter-deally… Run, Sophie! Get your little ass down here now!"

I kicked a nearby pillow with enough force to propel it across the room and send my cat running for cover. I looked over in the direction of the kitchen where the diamond studs I'd planned on wearing rested on the counter, and quickly decided against them. Considering the state of my hair, nobody would see them anyway. I did want to bring my cell phone, though. Funny, I thought I had left it by the earrings. The buzzer blasted again. Obviously I'd have to find it later. I grabbed my purse, and booked down the three flights of stairs to the entryway of my building. As I hurried out the door I saw the meter maid puttering toward us, less than fifteen yards away.

"Get in, get in, get in!" Marcus screamed from behind the wheel of his Miata, his eyes glued to the rearview mirror.

I jumped into the passenger side, and Marcus, without so much as giving me a sideways glance, put the car into gear and we were off, leaving the meter maid snarling in our wake.

"You know, you could have just driven around the block." I yanked my seat belt across my chest.

Marcus snapped his head in my direction for the first time that evening, a move that I assumed was a precursor to a snappy comeback, but the retort froze on his lips. "Oh my God, what happened to your hair?"

"Oh, well, I thought I'd do something different. Close your mouth and watch the road."

Marcus turned part of his focus back to the narrow street leading us toward downtown, but his eyes continued to dart in my direction. "You tried to use a curling iron again, didn't you?"

"Um…"

"How many times do I have to tell you…stay away from the curling iron. In the wrong hands those things are like deadly weapons. It's like that little Australian crocodile man always says—danger, danger, danger."

"Okay, fine, I look like shit. Point taken."

"You don't look like shit. The makeup's all good and the little camel suede halter dress, paired with the three-quarter leather is a look ripped right out of April's *In Style*. It's just the hair that's giving me 'Tina Turner in the eighties' flashbacks."

"Oh, come on, it's not that bad!"

"Well, it won't be in a few minutes. I'll fix it in the parking garage."

"You have hair supplies with you?"

"Never leave home without them."

I relaxed back into the seat. He brought hair supplies. Earth-shattering crisis averted. Unfortunately, that allowed my mind to wander back to the phone calls. It was pretty ballsy to crank-call after my last threat, even if the perpetrator didn't believe me. It showed that the caller was not just looking for an easy target to intimidate. In my book, *Sex, Drugs and Murder,* the bad guys had prank-called my protagonist and her roommate in hopes of determining when they were home. That way they didn't run the risk of running into them while breaking in. Could someone be thinking of breaking into my apartment? Had I remembered to close the kitchen window? The thing was almost impossible to close and I usually left it open a crack… No, I was being paranoid. The first part of my day had been hideous, and there was no way I was going to let a few phone calls ruin my night. I forced myself to think of a more removed topic that would hold my interest.

"Have you been following the JJ Money murder case at all?"

"And we're back in the stream-of-consciousness world of Sophie Katz."

"You know me, I'm all about keeping you on your toes. It's what gives me my edge." I made an attempt at a playful smile. "DC Smooth's appealing the verdict. I honestly think the guy is innocent. All the evidence against him is just way too convenient for my taste."

"As a mystery writer this is probably a hard concept for you, but in the non-MTV real world, people who are convicted of crimes are usually guilty."

"Come on, Marcus, what kind of black man are you? Shouldn't you be chanting 'Down with the system' and campaigning for the release of our unfairly accused brother?"

Marcus turned the car into the O'Farrell Street Garage and paused to collect his ticket. "You're not exactly little Miss Black Panther yourself. The only reason you're interested is that you think that if you tweak it a smidge you'll be able to use the case as a basis for a novel."

"I have no intention of tweaking anything. All I want to do is take what has been a very high-profile case, write about it and feed it to a voyeuristic society."

"God bless America." He slid his car into a spot on the third floor and killed the motor without bothering to remove the keys from the ignition. He shifted in his seat so that he could fully appreciate the enormous mass of hair weighing down my head. "We're going to have to pull it up in a braid thingy."

"A braid thingy? I don't get—"

"You don't have to 'get.' Just sit back and let me prove my genius." He pushed himself out of the car and came back seconds later armed with a wide-tooth comb, some ozone-depleting hairspray and a Tupperware container full of rubber hair bands and bobby pins.

Fifteen minutes later my hair was swept up into a sophisticated little braid and the few curls I had actually succeeded in creating were gently framing my face, keeping the look from going to severe. I examined myself in the side-view mirror. "I don't care if you are gay, I still want to marry you. I'll support you, do your laundry, turn my head when you bring home male companionship—all you have to do is my hair every day of the week and I'll be satisfied."

"Honey, the only thing I want to do every day of the week is Ricky Martin. Are you ready to eat?"

I took one last look at my reflection and allowed him to escort me to the restaurant across the street. We seated ourselves at the bar between a bearded man wearing a rather unfortunate Hawaiian shirt with pink palm trees on it and a woman who bore a disturbing resemblance to Prince, during his "formerly known as" period. Without bothering to look at the familiar menu, we ordered our prerequisite Cosmopolitans and a gourmet pizza to share. Marcus tugged gently on his locks as he watched the bartender mix our desired poison. "You're still coming to Steve's surprise party on Saturday, right?"

I nodded vigorously. "Like I'd miss an opportunity to eat chocolate cake. How's he doing anyway? Any change?"

"His T-cell count has gotten ridiculously low, but he's staying optimistic. He's going to be so excited to meet you. He's practically memorized every one of your books. I swear, girl, you are just the female John Grisham these days. Every client I have…"

Marcus's voice faded into the background as I studied a man on the other side of the restaurant talking on his cell phone. Maybe the prank calls had come from a cell. That would mean that the person could have been watching the apartment while making the call. But I hadn't heard any background noise, so they probably had come from someone's home or—

"Sophie? Have you heard anything I've been saying?"

"Hmm? Oh yeah, of course. You were talking about Steve."

"Yesss…about five minutes ago. What's up with you?" He paused to order a second round.

"I'm sorry. There has just been some weird stuff happening."

"Such as?"

"I've been getting prank calls. Five today. At least, five that I was home to answer."

"Oh, I hate those. You know how you deal with them?"

"How?"

"Heavy breathing. As soon as you realize that the person is prank-calling, start breathing heavily into the receiver. Trips them up every time."

"I'll try that." I swirled the remnants of my Cosmo. It must have been evaporating because there was no way I could have drunk it that fast. I thought I caught the pink-palm-tree guy casting me a disapproving stare. I swiveled my bar stool in Marcus's direction. "So what made you want to go to tonight's little shindig?"

A dimple materialized on his left cheek. "You know me. I am all about supporting up-and-coming young artists."

I gave him a sideways glance. "Uh-huh. There was a picture of the artist on the invite?"

"Mmm-hmm."

"He's cute?"

"Absolutely to die for."

"He's gay?"

"One can always hope."

"But you don't know. So it's possible that I stand a chance."

Marcus raised his glass in salute. "May the best man win."

"Or woman."

"Don't bother me with semantics."

We were presented with our pizza and I forced myself to wait until the bartender physically let go of the plate before tearing into it. Marcus must have been equally famished, because our conversation came to a halt as we devoured the pie at locust speed. I indicated to Marcus that he should eat the last piece. I was trying to lose five pounds and I had developed a kind of warped diet reasoning in which I don't have to count the calories of the food I eat if somebody else finishes it. It doesn't make sense but it does make me feel less guilty, so I choose to delude myself.

I sipped at my third drink while Marcus polished off our dinner. Alcohol was great for diets. If you drank enough of it, you didn't feel guilty at all.

Marcus checked his watch and grimaced. "It's almost eight. We want to be fashionably late but not late-late." He signed the charge slip and waited impatiently for me to collect my purse and jacket before hurrying me out of the restaurant and into the parking garage.

"You know, there's no way we're going to find a parking spot within five miles of the gallery," I said, "and the bus will practically take us to its door, plus it will be faster than looking for a—"

"Honey, you do not impress a man by showing up on a bus." His tone relayed the sympathy he felt for any woman who was so misguided.

"You never know, I mean he is an artist, a.k.a. a liberal eccentric. Maybe he prefers public transportation for the sake of the environment, or maybe he likes to rub elbows with all us common people who don't have cars or won't drive them for fear of losing our parking spots."

"Uh-huh." He tapped the face of his faux Cartier. "You need to close those little Mac-painted lips of yours and get in the car."

I grumbled some unflattering remarks and took my seat. I slipped my finger under the strap of my super-hip new platforms and caressed the forming blister. We would have to walk four city blocks at least—if we were lucky to even find parking.

When we finally did reach the gallery I was ready for a painkiller. Six blistering blocks. I peered through the crowd and eyed the little makeshift bar set up in the corner. Vodka always made a good pain reliever. Much more fun than ibuprofen.

Marcus shoved his wrist in front of my face. "See! I timed this perfectly. We are now officially fashionably late."

"Just like the artist." We turned to acknowledge a short little balding man who was standing close enough to eavesdrop. "Can you believe that this guy actually had the nerve to show up ten minutes late to his own opening? I know he's all the rage right now, but he still needs to show us collectors a little respect. Don't you agree?"

Marcus just stared at him blankly. Neither he nor I was a collector. We just wanted to pick up the artist. In the interest of furthering that goal, I asked the all-important question. "So which one is Balardi, anyway?"

I looked in the general direction of where the man was pointing. I put my hand on my chest and tried to keep from hyperventilating. "Marcus, do you see *that?*"

"Uh-huh, nobody could miss that, girlfriend."

The disgruntled stranger took his cue and slunk away to complain to someone else, as Marcus and I watched, slack jawed, as Donato Balardi worked the room. His black wavy hair grazed his shoulders, Antonio Banderas–Zorro style. He was slender, but the well-defined pecs visible beneath his silk shirt prevented him from looking slight in any way. His dark Latin eyes surveyed the room until they finally focused on us.

"Oh my God, he's coming this way!" Marcus dug his fingers into my arm. "I know he's gay, I can just feel it."

"No way," I protested. "God wouldn't be so cruel as to deprive the women of the world of something that beautiful."

He was upon us. If I reached my hand out I could actually touch those pecs. I summoned up my last bit of willpower and moved my gaze upward to his face. Sensual smiling lips, tanned skin and brown searching eyes looking at…

Marcus.

"Welcome, I am Donato Balardi."

Their handshake lasted way too long to be innocent.

Well, shit. Here it was, an enchanted evening: I had seen a stranger across a crowded room, he had walked to my side, and I was all set to make him my own—and instead he was coming on to my male hairstylist.

Sometimes I hated San Francisco.

Marcus and Donato (God, even their names sounded good together) were now fully engaged in some pseudo-conversation while they actively undressed each other with their eyes. I excused myself and headed for the bar—not that either of my two gentleman companions noticed. A friendly, relatively cute bartender (probably gay) greeted me.

"What can I get you this evening?"

"What cocktail has the highest alcohol content—?"

"Is this what you drink when you're not consuming coffee milk shakes?"

I spun around. There, smiling down at me, was the sexy Frappuccino-bashing Neanderthal from Starbucks.

CHAPTER 3

"She looked down at the shards of glass on the kitchen floor. Someone had been in the house."
—*Sex, Drugs and Murder*

"You've got to be kidding me," I said. "Are you following me?"

The Neanderthal let out a deep, rich, surprisingly *Homo sapiens*–sounding laugh. "Well I'm glad to see your ego's intact. No, I'm a friend of the gallery owner, Gary Sussman. We shared an apartment back in New York."

"Well how special for you." I turned my attention back to the bartender. "Vodka martini straight up." I refocused on my nemesis. "Well, you probably want to go reminisce with your friend. Don't let me stop you."

He extended his hand. Say what you like about his taste in coffee, you couldn't knock the man's hands.

"I'm Anatoly Darinsky."

"That's funny. I don't remember asking for your name."

"And yet I gave it." His hand remained suspended in the air. What the hell. "Sophie Katz." I placed my palm against his with a mixture of reluctance and curiosity. Yep, strong hand-shake. Maybe it was time to upgrade his status from Nean-derthal to Cro-Magnon.

"Katz…your father's Jewish?" Anatoly asked as he signaled the bartender to make him a duplicate of my drink.

"He converted for my mom."

"But Katz…"

"His last name was Christianson and my mother said she would rather choke on a hairball than be Mrs. Christianson so my father got inspired and they both changed their names to Katz."

Anatoly searched my face, undoubtedly looking for some hint of jest. "That's…interesting," he said.

I shrugged; personally, I still hadn't decided if the reasons behind my parents' name change were the result of creative thinking or indicative of a shared psychosis.

Anatoly tactfully let the subject drop. "So what do you think of Balardi?"

"He's magnificent," I said, stealing a glance at Donato, who was vigorously flirting with Marcus.

"Really? You're a big fan of spilled paint?"

"Spilled paint? What are you talking about—? Oh, you're talking about his *art*."

Anatoly made a little noise of disgust, which, in turn, perked me right up. It was always good to be able to annoy the people who annoy you, even if you had to embarrass yourself to do it. I examined the paintings on the wall for the first time and felt a little spark of shock bring me out of my haze of sexual disappointment.

"Oh God," I whispered. "It's awful."

I was surrounded by numerous canvases that Donato had apparently thrown a bucket of paint at. I squinted in an at-tempt to make the pictures more appealing. Who, exactly, de-cided that this was art? I could throw paint. In fact I was really good at throwing things.

I took a step closer to one of the pieces in an earnest effort to find some redeeming qualities. It was a big green splash
mark. I checked the title. *Verdi.*

"Ah, this one is my favorite."

I nearly spilled my drink down my dress. I hadn't realized
that Donato was behind me with Marcus, of course, right
behind him.

"I love your use of color," Marcus cooed.

I shot him a withering look, but he wasn't making eye
contact.

Donato, on the other hand, was watching me attentively.
He obviously expected me to say something.

I took a long sip of my drink. *Think, think, think.* "Um,
yes, well, it's very…it's very…green."

"Yes, exactly!" Donato grabbed my free hand and placed
it against his heart. "You understand. It's *green.*"

Now even Marcus looked a little embarrassed. I peeked
over at Anatoly who, still standing at the bar, was just within
earshot. He was having a ball. Hell, he probably hadn't been
so amused since the time I made a fool of myself at Starbucks. Donato, who still hadn't let go of my hand, was ea-
gerly waiting for my next artistic insight. But I couldn't
continue this conversation, not without saying something
that would get me thrown out. This called for desperate
measures.

"Have you met my friend Anatoly?"

For a nanosecond Anatoly's mouth hung open in a somewhat unbecoming fashion. Then he pulled it together
enough to slam the rest of his drink. Oh, this could be fun,
after all. "Donato, Marcus, this is Anatoly. He recently
moved here from New York. Anatoly, this is my friend
Marcus, and of course this is Donato, the man we've all
come to admire."

"His work," Anatoly corrected.

"What?" I had become distracted again by Donato's pecs.

"We've come to admire his work, not him, his work. We went over this, remember?"

I did a quick visual survey of the table being used as a bar. It wasn't quite big enough for me to crawl under. Fortunately Donato seemed oblivious to my humiliation.

"The two are interchangeable," he said. "To admire my work is to admire me and to admire me, is to admire my work."

"Yeah, you're a piece of work all right," Anatoly replied.

This time it was Marcus's turn to redirect the conversation. "So, Anatoly, how did you and Sophie meet?"

"We met at Starbucks. I let her read my *New York Times.*"

I felt my right hand involuntarily clench but I managed to keep a smile plastered on. Anatoly's eyes traveled down to my fist.

"She'll have another martini," he informed the bartender. "Mr. Balardi—am I pronouncing that right?"

"Donato."

"Donato, I'm curious about the blank canvas over there." Anatoly gestured to an empty canvas proudly displayed behind us.

"I'm so glad you asked this. That is my tribute to minimalism."

"Your tribute to minimalism." Anatoly spoke the words slowly.

"Yes, it is simplicity in all its purity."

"Uh-huh." Anatoly crossed his arms over his chest. "Tell me, Donato, do our tax dollars fund any of this?"

"Sooo, Anatoly, what part of San Francisco did you move to?" Marcus asked.

"I found an apartment in Russian Hill," Anatoly said.

"What?" My drink sloshed over onto my platforms. "But *I* live in Russian Hill."

"Well, this works out perfectly!" Marcus clapped his hands gleefully. "With you two living so close, I'm sure Anatoly wouldn't mind giving you a lift home."

"I thought *you* were giving me a lift home, Marcus."

"Oh, I am, or at least I was. It's just that…" Marcus transferred his jacket from arm to arm. "Well, you know I only have the two seats, and Donato is going to need a ride too…." Marcus' voice then dropped to a low mumble.

"I'm sorry, what did you say?" I asked.

Marcus sighed and stuck his hands in his pockets. "Donato took the bus here."

"I enjoy taking public transportation on occasion," Donato said. "It gives me a feel for the people who make up a city, the people I do not usually have opportunity to meet."

I was glaring at Marcus. He was engrossed in Donato's tribute to minimalism.

Anatoly shrugged. "I didn't drive here either, but I'd be happy to share a cab, Sophie—my treat."

"Really, that's not necessary."

"No, I insist. It wouldn't be right to force the artist to take the bus twice in one night. After all, there is a limit to how much time one can spend amongst the proletariat. And those people are known for their inability to appreciate spilt paint."

Well, so much for Marcus's attempts to avoid an explosion. But instead of taking offense, Donato just cocked his head to the side and smiled. "It is the rare individual who expresses his opinion when it is not popular to do so. I wonder if you would be willing to defend your views as vigorously as you attack others'."

"I wasn't attacking your views," Anatoly said. "I just don't like your art. Fortunately for you, there seem to be a lot of people here who disagree with me."

Donato laughed, and Marcus exhaled. "Yes, there certainly is a wide range of opinion in this country in terms of what is acceptable in the art world and what is not. Pity we do not see eye to eye, but I do appreciate your candor."

Anatoly nodded, but didn't smile. I was beginning to think

that the appropriate place for my drink was not down my throat but on his face.

Another patron approached Donato to question him about the source of his inspiration. He excused himself to give the woman a tour of his more complex pieces—those would be the ones with two colors.

Marcus took in Anatoly's brown shoes and black pants, and then surveyed the room for men more likely to swing his way. There was one man that stuck out more than the rest. Not because he was especially gorgeous but because he so obviously didn't belong there. He was no more than an inch taller than me and he wore his naturally highlighted brown hair pulled back into a high ponytail, which served to accentuate his goatee, groomed into a point like Lucifer's. He was wearing a studded biker's jacket and a pair of black velvet pants. I had to check the latest *GQ*, but I was pretty sure that wasn't the new men's look.

He strode over to *Verdi* and leaned in close enough that I felt the urge to remind him that this was a look-but-don't-touch kind of event. He leaned back again and shook his head with a deliberate slowness. "This is shit."

Anatoly took a large step forward. "I'm glad there are other people here who agree with me."

"Where's the social commentary?" the guy asked. "Where's the controversy? This isn't art, this is navel lint. A crucifix dipped in cow's dung, a black-and-white photograph of a man sticking his fist up another guy's A-hole. That's art. That's the kind of stuff that will make people stop and really think about their contrived Middle American sensibilities."

Anatoly stepped back again. So much for bonding with Velvet Pants. Disappointed, the stranger's head swiveled to Marcus in hopes of finding someone else sympathetic to his grievance.

Marcus made a little talk-to-the-hand gesture. "Don't look at me, honey—I draw the line at gerbils." He angled himself next to me in a manner that excluded Velvet Pants from our social circle. "How's your drink?"

I looked down at my glass. It was only half full now, but I seemed to be having a hard time keeping it from spilling. "I think I'm finished."

"Do you want to stay a while longer and get a better look at the train wreck, or shall we hail a cab now?" Anatoly asked.

"This isn't New York," I said. "You don't hail cabs here, you call them."

"Then it's a good thing I have a cell phone. Marcus, it was very nice to meet you."

I leaned forward to give Marcus a kiss on the cheek. "You owe me big-time."

"Free cut and style for the next three visits."

"I'm not hanging out, either," the goatee guy announced in case one of us cared. "See you later, Sophie."

My fingers tightened around the stemware. How many drinks had I had? But Marcus's expression assured me that he'd caught it too. The night was getting way too bizarre for my taste.

Donato came up to us again. "Ah, now I must show you the rest of my collection."

"Sorry, but your paintings reminded me that I need to pick up some stain remover to clean up the red wine that I spilled on my carpet," Anatoly said. "Although maybe it would be more profitable to pull up the soiled fibers and mount them on a canvas—for those art collectors who prefer texture."

That one left even Donato speechless. I definitely should have thrown my drink at Anatoly when I still had the ability to aim. As it was, it seemed the best course of action was to make a speedy exit.

"Thank you, Donato, your art is beautiful." I gave Marcus's hand a little squeeze before walking out into the cold.

Anatoly was close at my heels, so much so that when I whirled around to berate him for his latest impudence, he barely managed to stop in time to avoid a collision. The result was the two of us standing all of an inch away from each other. Old Spice. God, I love that scent. Without breaking eye contact, I became increasingly aware of his other body parts. If I took a deep breath, my breasts would press against his chest, and all he had to do was bring his hands slightly up and forward and they could secure my hips. His eyes finally left mine and lowered themselves to my lips.

He couldn't possibly be thinking of kissing me. He didn't even know me. And I hated him. He wasn't even fully evolved. I needed to turn away. Yep, that's what I'd do, turn away…in a minute.

Anatoly's mouth formed into a little half smile, and he leaned forward a bit more. Half an inch. "You were going to say something?"

I could feel his breath. Say something, right. I had turned around in order to say something. What was it? *Take me now, my Russian warrior?* No, that wasn't it. *Make me your love slave?* No, that was off the mark too.

"Well?" he said.

Anatoly still wasn't touching me, but damn if every inch of me wasn't responding to him.

Strength. Strength and resolve. I scrunched my eyes shut. "I'm having a hard time thinking. You're in my space."

Anatoly's smile broadened as he took a step back. "Is that better?"

No. "Yes." I dug my nails into my palm. "You really are a jerk, you know that?"

"As I explained on the day we met, if you're going to insult me you're going to have to be a little more creative than that."

"All right, how about this? You're an egotistical, arrogant piece of Soviet trash. You know, I didn't like the paintings in there either, but I didn't feel the need to criticize and belittle Donato in front of Marcus. The fact that you did just shows what a pathetic and scummy little prick you are."

Anatoly leaned back onto his heels. "That's definitely better."

For a minute or so we just stood there while he turned over what I had said and I tried to find a stable focal point.

"I'm not sure anyone can qualify as a piece of *Soviet* trash anymore, but you were right on all your other points."

Okay, I hadn't been expecting that.

"Donato rubbed me the wrong way as did that stuff he's trying to pass off as art, but that didn't give me the right to be cruel. I can be overly judgmental, it's a character flaw. I'm sorry. You're right, I'm wrong."

So now he'd gone and screwed up my first impression. I hated it when people did that. Plus, it was a lot easier to resist him when I thought he was a Cro-Magnon/Neanderthal. Now he was moving into the *Homo sapiens* category, which meant we just might be sexually compatible, and, considering how long it had been since I'd had sex, if I had to share a cab home with an extremely attractive, heterosexual specimen of *Homo sapiens,* with a slight Russian accent, no less… Well, I might do something unforgivable like knock him over the head with a club and drag him up to my apartment by his hair.

"If you'll still share a cab with me, I promise to be nice." The streetlight caused the shadows of a tree to play against his shirt.

Well, what kind of life would it be if you didn't take a few risks? "You'd better call a taxi now if we're going to get one within the next half hour."

Anatoly raised two fingers to his mouth and let out a shrill whistle that left me temporarily hearing impaired. "I *told* you, you can't hail a cab here."

But I was once again destined to look like an idiot because a cab pulled up right in front of us.

"This never happens."

"I'm sure it doesn't." Anatoly held the door and climbed in next to me as I gave the driver my address.

He seemed distracted now. I felt pretty focused. Granted, the things I was focused on were Anatoly's hands, but I was focused nonetheless.

"That man in the gallery, the one wearing the biker jacket, you knew him?"

"Thank God for small favors, no."

"How do you think he knew your name?"

"I don't know. Maybe he read one of my books. My picture's on the back cover."

"You're a writer?"

"Yep…murder mysteries."

"Really?" He repositioned himself so that he had a better view of me. "And the art lover back there, he's your target market?"

"Very funny." I pulled on a stray thread hanging from my hemline. "I don't know. I guess my target would be pretty much anyone who likes a good novel with a lot of action, suspense and sex."

There was a brief silence as Anatoly thought about that. "I like action, suspense and sex."

The driver must have turned the heat on because suddenly it had gotten very warm.

We were getting close to my apartment when the cab had to pull to the right of the narrow lane to make way for a police car. I visually followed the flashing red lights until it pulled to a stop next to two other police cars and an ambulance just a block and a half away from where I lived. "Something pretty major must be going on."

"I'll say." But Anatoly wasn't looking at the police cars.

When the taxi finally slowed to a stop, I literally threw some money at the driver and leaped out of the car with such velocity that I needed to grab hold of a lamppost to steady myself. Unfortunately Anatoly followed me out. The driver screeched away. He probably wanted as much distance from me as possible before I could think twice about giving him a twenty for an eleven-dollar fare. In truth the extra nine dollars would have been money well spent if Anatoly had just stayed in the car. I have never been very good with willpower. Recently I had resolved to limit my chocolate intake to one piece per week. It took me exactly a half-hour to break that resolution. And Anatoly was looking a lot tastier than your average chocolate bar.

"Shouldn't you have stayed in the cab until he got to *your* place?"

"Don't worry, I'm not going to ask to come up."

Damn.

"I just live two and a half blocks up, so I figured I'd walk. However, I was going to ask you what you're doing this Saturday night."

Uh-oh, he wanted to go on a date. It was one thing to fantasize about sleeping with him, it was a whole other thing to plan to spend several hours talking to him. "I have a prior engagement."

"Saturday afternoon, then. I've been here for a little over three months but I'm still not all that familiar with the city. You could give me a tour. Show me where all the good coffee shops are."

"That's a pretty long tour."

"Well then, just show me the Starbucks."

"That doesn't shorten it much."

He moved in a little. "I don't bite."

A little biting might not be such a bad thing. I took one more look at his hands. "Saturday at noon. You can pick me up here." I dug into my purse and wrote my number on an old business card. "Good night, Anatoly."

"Good night, Sophie." He slipped the card into his back pocket and proceeded up the street.

I watched until he had turned the corner. "Wow, he's even got a cute butt," I murmured aloud. I looked to my right where there were still rescue vehicles congregated. The excitement seemed to be around a little garage located on the first floor of an Edwardian apartment building. The dark and the distance made it impossible to see much. The paramedics were loading someone into the back of the ambulance. Was it a body bag? I instantly felt the alcohol I'd drunk begin to lose its grip. I was aching to get a closer look, but it was doubtful that the police would view my credentials as a novelist as enough to let me dig around a crime scene. I wrinkled my nose and went up to my apartment.

"Hey, Mr. Katz, you haven't been killing the neighbors again, have you?" Mr. Katz didn't make an immediate appearance. That was odd. He usually liked to greet me in hopes of obtaining a late-night snack. I spotted him hiding under a chair. "What's wrong, sweetie?" I asked, and tried to coax him out. The only time Mr. Katz acted like this was when strangers were around or when he had done something he knew I would be unhappy about. A horrible thought entered my mind. "You did use your litter box tonight, didn't you?" Mr. Katz wasn't owning up to anything, but he also wasn't coming out from under the chair. Maybe Friskies would be more persuasive.

I got up and noticed my cell phone on the coffee table. Well, at least that mystery was solved. I stepped into the narrow kitchen and immediately saw the source of Mr. Katz's agitation. One of the glasses I had left by the sink lay shattered on the floor.

"Is that all?" I bent down to collect the pieces. "How the hell did you knock it so far off the counter anyway…*ouch!* Damn it!" I sucked the blood that was dribbling down my finger. For someone who had virtually built a reputation on writing graphic violence, I really was a major wimp. I put my finger under the faucet and watched as the pink water flowed down the drain. Something was off. Why was I having a déjà vu feeling? I shivered a little as a cold wind blew in from the window in front of me. It was half open. Had I left it like that?

I heard the floor make a little creak. Someone was watching me. I slowly lowered my hand into the sink and clasped the dirty knife I had left there. I drew a quick breath and whipped around, knife outstretched, silently praying that whoever was behind me wasn't holding a more ominous weapon.

But it was only Mr. Katz.

From where I was standing I could see all of the kitchen and most of the living room. Everything was in its place. My gaze rested on the diamond studs I had carelessly left on the counter that divided the two rooms. The overhead light was hitting them in a manner that caused them to cast a faint rainbow on the cream tiles beneath them. They hadn't been touched. No sign of forced entry, nothing but a window that I had obviously forgotten to close, a broken glass and a cat with a suspiciously guilty look on his face. So why couldn't I bring myself to lower the knife? And why did this feel so damn familiar? It was like I had seen this scene played out in a movie or read about it in a...

I sucked in more air as the vision of my fingers typing the words flashed before me. I had written this scene. It was from *Sex, Drugs and Murder*. But that was insane. Besides, it wasn't as if Mr. Katz had never broken anything before. I had been forced to replace the vase on the coffee table three times in the last two years. If it hadn't been for the phone calls...and the note. Oh God, I had almost forgotten about the note. Could that be connected to this? I spread my feet a little farther apart for better balance. This must be what it's like to have a bad acid trip. You know that you've been given something that messes with your head, so you become unsure if your instincts can be trusted or if they are just the result of drug-induced paranoia.

The sting from the slice in my finger distracted me for a moment and I looked at the blood that had trickled onto the knife's handle. It was then that Mr. Katz made his move. In one fluid motion he leaped onto the counter, missing a coffee cup by half a millimeter. He proceeded to rub against my arm in a pathetic attempt to redeem himself as I tried to recover from the near heart attack his sudden activity had brought on.

I jerked away from the menacing fur ball and steadied the cup that was on the verge of suffering the same fate as the broken glassware. Culprit identified and caught.

"Stupid cat," I said, and threw the knife back into the sink. "No Friskies for you."

 CHAPTER 4

"There was no such thing as a slow news day. You could always count on the weirdos of the world to keep things interesting."

—*Sex, Drugs and Murder*

Just trying to follow the little black words printed in the next morning's *Chronicle* seemed to upset my equilibrium. I searched for some mention of what had happened in my neighborhood the night before, but as I expected, whatever took place had happened long after that edition would have gone to press. I might have found something out on the local news, but then I would have had to get up before nine. There was an interesting little article about Alex Tolsky. His daughter, Shannon, was convinced that her father was not capable of suicide and she was trying to lobby the LAPD to reopen the case, but to little avail. Even her mother believed it was a suicide, citing their impending divorce as the motive. That, coupled with the fact that Tolsky had a drinking problem and suffered from clinical depression, was enough to satisfy the police. Still, Shannon Tolsky was adamant.

A little voice inside me told me she was right. I reached past Mr. Katz for the scissors. Molded correctly, it could be a good premise for a future novel.

My eyes traveled to the kitchen window. It was open just a crack—exactly the way I had left it before going to sleep. Of course it was—why would it be otherwise? I had obviously forgotten to close it before going out with Marcus. Still, I would have sworn… I gently massaged my temples. My head hurt enough as it was, I didn't need to add to my pain by stressing out over nonexistent problems.

I pushed myself into a standing position and went to the bathroom to perform my morning ritual, starting with a marathon shower. Today had "mellow" written all over it. After all, I *had* just completed a book, which meant that I had earned at least a month of laziness. After getting myself cleaned up, I threw some kibble in a bowl for Mr. Katz, put on some dark glasses and went out to search the corner market for more artificial energy which I found in the form of a can of Red Bull. I smiled at the petite Chinese woman behind the register.

"Hi, Alice, just the drink."

"Did you hear what happened here last night?"

I slipped my sunglasses down my nose a bit to get a better look at the store's proprietor. She had the flush of someone who had heard something horrible and shocking and now couldn't wait to shock somebody else with it. "Does this have anything to do with all those cop cars and the ambulance I saw when I got home last night?"

"Yes. It's really bad."

I took my glasses off.

"You know Susan Lee?" Alice asked.

"No, I don't think I do."

"Oh, you know her. She's in here all the time. She's in her twenties, Chinese—she wears DKNY a lot."

"Oh, right, *Susan.*" I had no idea who Alice was talking about. She had just described half the women in San Francisco.

"They found her body in the Dumpster in her garage last night. She'd been strangled."

I glared at my hand that had somehow positioned itself dangerously close to the Mon Chère chocolates on the counter. "Any suspects?"

"They didn't say on the news. They think the body had been lying there for a long time. Hours maybe. Can you believe it? She was such a pretty girl, and someone just threw her in the trash."

Of course I could believe it. The Dumpster bit was right out of a B movie. Definitely not something I could use in a book.

"They interviewed her brother on TV. He just kept saying the same thing over and over— 'But I just talked to her, I just talked to her.' It was like he was in a trance. He couldn't think right."

I winced. How could I be so heartless? A woman had been killed and the lack of creativity of those who murdered her meant nothing to the people who loved her. All that mattered to them was that someone who was an intricate part of their existence had been taken suddenly from them, without even the chance to say goodbye.

Alice punched the price of the Red Bull into her register at a speed that indicated that she was not done talking. "Andy's taking it really hard. He's so sensitive, and I think maybe he had a little crush on her. Usually he won't take his full lunch break, but today I made him. I told him to walk around the block and get some fresh air. I even offered to give him the day off, but he said no. He never takes a day off. Doesn't matter if he's sick. He always comes to work."

I smiled and gave a slight nod of acknowledgment. I was only half listening. My mind had gone back to my window and the broken glass. But I was being stupid. If there had been a murderer in my apartment last night, why was I still in perfect health? Well, not perfect, but I'd have a hard time pinning my current condition on anyone other than my buddy

Smirnoff. I pushed my sunglasses back in place. Nothing like starting off the day with a few paranoid delusions. Maybe I needed a little chocolate to help bring me back to reality. Really…how many calories could be in one Mon Chère?

I silently gestured to Alice that she should add the candy to my purchase before handing her a few crumpled dollar bills and scooping up my items. "Be careful when you're locking up tonight."

"Oh, I will," Alice called after me. "And you be careful too. You never know what this crazy man might do next."

I gave a little wave over my shoulder in response. I stepped onto the sidewalk, looked down to check that I had zipped my purse, and boom, I had a head-on collision with the Jolly Green Giant. Or at least that's what I assumed upon impact. In reality it was just Andy. The corners of my mouth curled up.

"We've got to stop doing this," I said.

"Gosh, I'm sorry, Miss Katz!" Andy retrieved my dented beverage from underneath a newspaper stand.

"It was my fault—again. I wasn't paying attention to where I was going." I craned my neck back to meet his gaze. His eyes were even more bloodshot than mine. "Andy, I heard about your friend Susan. I'm really sorry."

Andy's face scrunched up to about half its normal size and his breath shortened into little gasps. I impulsively reached my arms out to him. His huge body collapsed against me, and I gently stroked his back. "Shh…it's okay, Andy. Shh."

"No, no it's not okay, I liked her. She wasn't supposed to die—I liked her."

"I know, I know. It's messed up, but she's in a better place now."

"Really?" Andy pulled back to use the sleeve of his plaid flannel shirt as a makeshift Kleenex. "You believe that?"

"Really." Maybe. I gave what I hoped was a reassuring squeeze to the portion of his arm that hadn't been soiled yet. "The best way we can honor her memory is to do everything we can to improve matters in this world so that things like this won't happen anymore."

"I don't want anything like this to ever happen again. Never."

It must be wonderful to be that naive. "Well, all we can do is our part, be nice to people, do unto others and all that jazz."

The two thin blond lines that made up Andy's eyebrows joined forces as he tried to figure out what the hell I was talking about. I tapped the top of my bloated Red Bull can with my fingernail. "Just be yourself and you'll be fine."

Some of the confusion and distress slipped from his countenance. "I can do that!"

"Yeah, you can. Andy, I've got to go. I'll see you later, okay?"

"Okay, Sophie."

I patted his arm again and started my journey to my Acura, which was parked somewhere near Siberia. As sick as it was, the morning's drama had actually put me in a better mood. I felt sorry for Andy, but I couldn't help but feel good about having been able to help him. Hell, the guy had even called me by my first name.

Of course, I would have felt even better if the murder hadn't happened so close to home.

Free Vibrator With Every Purchase Over $100
I didn't bother to suppress my laughter when I read the sign perched on Guilty Pleasures' front display table.

Dena emerged from the back of the store wearing a pair if black boot-cut pants and a Castro long-sleeved shirt. Considering her small size, the bold abstract on her top should have overwhelmed her. It didn't. She gave me a quick hug before gesturing to the sign.

"What can I say? When you're right, you're right." She shrugged. "So are you here to shop or visit?"

"Visit," I said absently as I toyed with a penis-shaped water bottle. "Do you have time for a short break?"

"Barbie, I need you to watch the floor while we go in back."

A Puerto Rican woman with heavy black eyeliner and dressed in a kind of dominatrix-style vinyl outfit looked up from straightening a stack of crotchless panties and gave Dena a cheerful smile.

I followed Dena into a small office connected to her stock-room. "That woman is *not* named Barbie."

"I don't care if she wants to be referred to as the Cabbage Patch Kid, that woman knows more about sex toys than any other employee I've ever had. It's like she has a Ph.D. in erotica." Dena removed a stack of invoices from a padded folding chair before offering it to me and seating herself at her desk. "So what's up?"

"I met a guy."

"A guy you want to date?"

"Uh-huh."

"Glory hallelujah, it's a miracle! My God, Sophie, if you had gone any longer on this celibacy kick of yours, I would have staged an intervention."

"I can only imagine what that would have looked like." I fingered an odd-looking Beanie Baby with five legs that had been left on top of a small filing cabinet. Wait a minute. "Dena…your Beanie Baby seems to be rather…um…excited."

"It's not a Beanie Baby, it's a Weenie Baby. I'm going to put them out tomorrow. I know they're going to blow. No pun intended. So tell me about your new love interest!"

"Well, he's not perfect. He doesn't appreciate Caramel Brownie Frappuccinos."

"Sophie, I'm going to let you in on a secret…there are a lot of people who don't appreciate Caramel Brownie Frappuccinos. Hell, I give him ten points just for not frequenting Starbucks. That place is a fascist corporate monster."

Dena has an odd point system that she uses to rate men. I have never figured out what the scale is, but the men I've dated in the past were clearly on the low end. "Sorry, he frequents Starbucks, he just doesn't buy Frappuccinos."

"Okay, five points." She tapped the number five on her desktop calculator.

"He does have an accent."

"What kind?"

"Russian."

Dena turned back to her calculator and pressed Plus Five.

"Yeah, it's very slight—you have to listen for it—but the way he says certain words…like when he pronounces his name, Anatoly, it's really very sexy."

"Anatoly…I like that." She added, three more points.

"Mmm. Anyhow, he's somewhere in his mid-thirties, about six foot, dark hair, brown eyes, very physically…fit." Dena raised her eyebrows before adding fifteen. "And he's got the most incredible hands I have ever seen—you know, big, strong, and just a little rough."

"Shit, you're turning me on just talking about him. Twenty points for the big hands. I think we're up to an overall score of forty-eight. That's a new high for you."

"Yeah, he's definitely eye candy. I wasn't sure what I thought about him at first—personality-wise he's a little rough around the edges."

"I thought you just said you liked it rough."

"*Hands,* Dena. Rough hands."

"Whatever." Dena turned away from the calculator and swiveled back and forth in her wheeled chair. "Look, the guy obviously does it for you, so when are you going to jump him?"

"Do you ever bother even pretending you believe in traditional courtship?"

"It's hard to spout puritanical ideals when you own a sex shop. You didn't answer my question."

"I'm going *out* with him this weekend. He's new to the city so I'm going to play tour guide for a day. You know, ride the cable car, go to the top of Coit Tower, all the stuff

I openly denounce as beneath me but secretly long to do…
then maybe I'll jump him."

"Sounds like fun." Dena's smile changed to one of mis-
chief. "Hey, the guy I'm dating just moved here too."

"Right, I remember you mentioning him…the 'notch in
your bedpost' guy."

"Yes! Sophie, he's sooo fucking hot. Easily scores over fifty
points. He's intelligent, has a goatee, works as a bartender
in the Lower Haight, so you know he makes a mean martini, plus he just has a different approach to things, you
know? He doesn't automatically conform to all the dictates
of society."

"In other words, he's a sociopath."

"Funny," Dena said. "He is not a sociopath. He is perfectly
sane…or…he sort of is. Okay, I'm sure there are some people who think he's a little crazy, but they just don't get him.
He's just…different."

"Oh my God, you're dating Michael Jackson."

"I am not dating Michael Jackson. Besides, it's not like he
has long conversations with his cat or anything like that," she
said, and graced me with her most antagonistic grin.

I responded by giving her the finger.

She laughed and checked her watch. "He's supposed to
meet me for lunch in a few minutes, so if you hang out you'll
get to meet him."

"Oh, I can't wait for this." I repositioned the Weenie Baby
so that he was balancing on his two heads. "Speaking of bizarre things…"

"We weren't."

"Okay, sorry, that came out wrong. I just want to tell you
about something weird that happened to me last night."

"Does it involve some kind of sexual foreplay with your
Russian love god?"

"No."

"Oh."

"I came home last night and there was a broken glass on the floor."

"Uh-huh, so your cat knocked over a glass." She glared at the overhead fluorescent light that had begun to flicker. "He's always knocking stuff over. Maybe if you didn't feed him twenty-four–seven…"

"Yeah, yeah, yeah, okay. Dena, it was the way the pieces were scattered…it almost seemed like the glass was dropped in the middle of the room."

"What are you saying? Do you think someone was in your apartment?"

"I don't know."

"Was anything taken or out of place?"

"No."

"So you think someone broke into your flat, dropped a glass and left?" Dena was wearing an expression that she usually reserved for Mary Ann.

"Right, it doesn't make sense, I know that. But here's the thing…do you remember my book *Sex, Drugs and Murder?*"

The condescension disappeared. "The broken-glass-in-the-kitchen scene."

"You do remember."

"It was the first indication Alicia Bright had that someone had been in the house."

"Exactly. Of course, that's stupid."

"It's at least highly unlikely."

"There's more."

Dena swallowed visibly and waited for me to continue.

"I got a note in the mail a little over a month ago, no return address. It was typed, and it contained just one sentence, 'You reap what you sow.' And then last night, before the whole glass thing, I got a whole bunch of prank calls. The person calling didn't say anything threatening. He—or she— just called and hung up."

"Okay, that's it. You need to call the police."

"And tell them what? That someone sent me a note in the mail that is, for all intents and purposes, perfectly benign? That I got a few hang-ups? Or that I found a broken glass in my apartment that may have been knocked over by my cat?"

Dena pressed her palms into her thighs and studied the discarded price tags on the floor. "All of the above?"

"Dena, I told you this because I wanted you to calm me down and bring me back to reality, not so you could further bolster my paranoia."

"Sophie, if there's a chance that someone is stalking you, the authorities should be alerted."

"Great, now we are both being paranoid." I ran my fingers through my hair, inadvertently tearing it as I went. "Look, I even cut my finger when cleaning up the glass, the way Alicia Bright did." I held up a bandaged finger for Dena's inspection. "Do you think *that* was planned too?"

"Okay, I get your point." Dena chewed her lower lip. "Still…"

"Dena?" Barbie peeked her head through the door. "Your maaaann is here."

"Oh good, I do get to meet him." I stood up and waited for Dena to do the same.

"Sophie…"

"Dena, it's fine, really. It was the cat. Now come on, you have an introduction to make."

Dena put her hands on her hips and paused for a moment as she tried to figure out what her next move should be. Finally she shook her head in defeat. "Fine, I'll let it go for now. Let's have you meet Jason Beck." She took my arm and guided me onto the selling floor, and there he was.

Mr. Velvet Pants.

 **CHAPTER 5**

"One look at Kittie's car told Alicia that there was more to the story than she was letting on."

—*Sex, Drugs and Murder*

"No, no, no, no, no, no, no." Dena did a quick double take. She had every reason to be offended—I was being rude—but what the hell was she thinking?

The freak smiled. "Sophie and I met last night," he said. "I ran into her at a gallery south of Market."

"A gallery?" asked Dena. "I thought you were…"

"Going to participate in the vampire games? I did, but I was a little early, so I crashed an opening. It wasn't worth the effort. The stuff being exhibited was the kind of shit people buy to match their thousand-dollar couch. No message at all."

Okay, we needed to back up a bit. "The vampire games?"

"Right, let me explain that one." Dena slipped between Jason and me in an attempt to ease some of the mounting tension. "Once a month a group of people—"

"Vampires," Jason corrected.

"Right, okay, let's call them vampire *people*." Dena folded her hands under her chin. "Anyhow, a whole bunch of vampire people get together and act out some kind of vampire story. It's often based on a novel or a movie."

"Have you read much about vampires?" Jason asked. He stepped to the side so we could have a full view of one another again.

"I've read *Dracula* and *The Vampire Chronicles*."

"Then you know a lot about the creatures of the night. I often get to play the part of Dracula."

"Really."

"Yes, I am Dracula."

You are insane is what you are. I examined Jason's current ensemble. The velvet was gone and in its place were a pair of black suede jeans, a white dress shirt with the breast pocket not so carefully cut off, and the motorcycle jacket from the night before. Dena was right, Jason had a different approach to things.

"Last night, how did you know my name?"

"Well, when I was at Dena's place I was looking through her bookcase and noticed that she had several titles from you, which sort of threw me off 'cause Dena's not the type to buy into that whole bestseller thing. She's more an Anaïs Nin type than a Jane Austen chick. So I got curious and flipped one open and saw your autograph. You wrote a pretty detailed message, so it stuck in my head. I recognized you from the picture in back."

Dena shook her head. "I don't remember that."

"You were in the shower," he explained without bothering to move his eyes in her direction. "I know I came on a bit strong. When I'm in vampire mode I can be a little dramatic."

"Understandable." Not.

"I got one of your books this morning. I just started it."

"Oh? Which one?"

"Your first one. *Criminally Insane*."

"Always good to start at the beginning. I hope it's not too 'Jane Austen' for you."

"No, I'm sure I'll like it." He brought his hand up to stroke Dena's back. "She and I have similar tastes. Although, as a general rule, I'm not all that into fiction."

"But you do like books about vampires."

"Yeah, but I'm not so sure they're all fiction."

"Well." I tried to choose my words carefully. "Parts of many novels aren't. The writers tend to use a lot of accurate historical references."

"Yeah, but that's not what I'm talking about. Come on, you read the books. You had to have stopped sometimes and said to yourself, 'Man, these characters are so real—too real.' It must have crossed your mind that some of those guys are really out there—that the immortals exist."

"I'll concede that some of the writers who wrote on the topic are talented enough to bring their characters to life on the page, but I'm pretty sure it stops there."

"And why are you so sure of that? Because our current western Judeo-Christian ethic says so? You need to broaden your thinking, Sophie. Open your mind to the bizarre."

I looked over at Dena. She had become very busy rearranging her glow-in-the-dark condom display. "Okay, Jason, for the sake of argument, let's say there really are vampires. Does the fact that you are so involved with this—this vampire subculture mean that you want to become one of them?"

"I would be open to it. Vampires aren't inherently bad. They drink blood because they have to in order to survive. We, on the other hand, slaughter chickens and cows because they taste good. So ask yourself, which one of us should be wearing the black cowboy hat?"

I had to admit I was moving from irritated to amused fairly quickly. I decided to dispense with the standard etiquette I would normally observe upon meeting a new acquaintance.

I leaned against a display table and stuck a thumb through my belt loop. "You really are weird, you know that?"

"Yeah, but I got your attention, didn't I? Crazy beats the shit out of boring."

I laughed. I was beginning to like him. So he was schizophrenic, he still had a certain *je ne sais quoi*. "So what are your feelings on Santa Claus?"

"Sophie, I know you just stopped in briefly to say hello, and I wouldn't want to keep you…." Dena took her attention away from the condoms long enough to stop an impending conversation about the existence of Rudolph.

Jason didn't seem the least bit perturbed. It probably wasn't a stretch that he had met up with other people who had difficulty accepting his creature-of-the-night theory. "Okay, I'll get going. Dena, I'll see you later, and Jason…it's been interesting. Have a good lunch—or are you on a strictly liquid diet?"

"For now I'll settle for sucking the juice out of a red grapefruit."

He could laugh at himself. That was good. Dena rewarded him with a light kiss and then turned her triumphant smile on me. "I'll see you later, Sophie. Oh, I almost forgot, I have to do inventory Sunday. Can we move movie night to Monday? I've already cleared it with Mary Ann."

"No problemo, I'll see you Monday." I turned to leave.

"Hey, Sophie," Jason called after me.

"Yeah?"

"You'd make an awesome vampire. Exotic features with supernaturally white skin…that would be cool."

"Thanks, but I'm kind of digging the whole mortal thing right now. I'll see you two later."

I left the store and looked both ways down the sidewalk as I tried to remember where, exactly, I had parked. There was a man sporting a scarred face and a rather obtrusive gold chain peeking into the store window, clearly hesitant to enter.

"You should go in, it's a good store," I assured him.

Glazed eyes stared silently back at me. He used his finger to pick some food out of his teeth. Lovely. That was the problem with owning a sex shop. Most of Dena's customers were fairly respectable, but at least once a day she had to deal with some heroin-loving scumbag looking for a public place to whack off. I considered going back in and warning Dena, but the man turned around and wandered off before I had a chance. Gross, but harmless. I left to find my car. If he did go back, Dena could handle it. After all, she was now being backed up by the power of the living dead.

By the next morning I was physically in much better shape than I had been twenty-four hours previous, but I was also intensely anxious and confused. I approached the mirror and turned from side to side, then turned my back to it and tried to do some kind of contortionist move with my neck so I could review every angle. In a half hour Anatoly would come to pick me up and I had just changed clothes for the eighth time. I was now wearing black boots, jeans, a black V-neck shirt and a leather jacket. "I don't know, maybe this neckline is a little too low," I mumbled to myself. I struck a couple of poses to ensure that my boobs would be contained in any position I might need to assume. "What do you think, Mr. Katz? Does it look like I'm trying too hard?"

Mr. Katz was busy making a nest out of a discarded wool sweater. I picked up the fitted gray turtleneck that I had tried on three tops earlier. "But what if he wants to kiss my neck?" Mr. Katz licked his fur suggestively. "I didn't say I'd *let* him kiss my neck, but it would be closed minded of me to completely eliminate the possibility." I looked in the mirror again. This was just going to have to do. My hair couldn't take another shirt change.

There was a knock at the door. Mr. Katz lifted his head in alarm.

What kind of jerk shows up a half hour early for a first date? I didn't even have my makeup on yet. I should have trusted my first impression of him. I had a date with the last living caveman.

The knock came again.

"All right, I'm coming." I gave Mr. Katz a "why me?" look and headed for the entryway. "Which one of my idiot neighbors let you into the building anyway?" I asked before throwing open the door.

"Oops." It was one of my idiot neighbors.

"Sophie, I didn't know you had such a high opinion of us." Theresa Conley wasn't going to let that one slide. But then again, letting things slide wasn't really her forte.

"I honestly didn't mean it, Theresa. You just caught me at a bad time. You see, I was just talking to my cat and... You know what? Never mind. Fresh beginning. Hello, Theresa, what can I do for you?"

Theresa sucked in her cheeks in a manner that made me think of the fish I had had for dinner the night before. "I came because I'm trying to be a good neighbor. Not that you make that an easy task. Nonetheless, I feel it's my duty to inform you that while looking for parking I saw your car, and it seems someone has broken into it."

"Oh, God damn it!" This was the second time someone had broken into my car. "Did they break the window?"

Theresa smiled. "Driver's side."

"Damn it!"

"Well, I just thought I should tell you. And say hi to your cat for me." Theresa left in a considerably better mood than she had arrived in.

I slammed the door and turned to see Mr. Katz looking at me questioningly. "I don't have time for this. I have a date in—" I checked my watch "—twenty minutes."

Mr. Katz swished his tail and headed back to the bedroom to see if he could do more damage to my sweater collection.

"Argh!" I grabbed my keys from the small table in the entryway. Something was missing. When I came home I always put the face to my CD player on the table next to the keys. Except when I forgot it in the car. If I tried a little harder, could I be a bigger idiot? Defeated, I went out to inspect the damage.

I had parked a little more than three blocks uphill from my apartment, somewhere around five o'clock the day before. I really needed to get an alarm system—although what were the chances I would hear it when I was parked ten miles away? Thanks to an inordinate number of SUVs blocking my line of sight, I wasn't able to spot my car until I was less than ten yards from it.

I stopped breathing for a second. It was unlike Theresa to understate things, but even from a slight distance it was clear that my Acura hadn't just been broken into, it had been vandalized. The hood and the trunk had been popped and remained open. When I got closer, I could see that the driver's side window had indeed been broken, but the biggest damage was to the interior. Not only had they dumped everything out of the glove compartment, but they had also slashed up the interior of both the front and back seats and pulled the stuffing out in several places. There were slashes all over the floor, as well. Hesitant, I looked in the trunk and found that they had also slashed the carpeting in there, along with the spare tire. My hands started trembling and I gripped the top of the trunk to steady them. Who would do this? I pressed my lips together and went to the front of the car to see what else had been destroyed or taken. I forced myself to peek under the hood. The engine was intact.

Why was that? If the object was to cause as much damage as possible, shouldn't they at least have cut a few wires or something? I peered through the broken glass to get a second look at the mess inside. My CD player was still there. Last I had checked, the main reason people broke into cars was to steal their stereos. My stereo wasn't state-of-the-art but I was pretty sure it was theft-worthy.

"I thought I was supposed to meet you at your place."

I jumped at the sound of Anatoly's voice. He was standing in the doorway of an apartment complex parallel to my car. His eyes traveled behind me to the Acura. "Looks like somebody made an enemy. You know the owner?"

"What are you doing here, Anatoly?"

"What do you mean, 'what am I doing here?' I live here."

"In that building right there?"

"The one I just walked out of. Your powers of deduction are staggering."

"And you didn't hear anything when some lunatic was ripping apart my car?"

"*Your* car?" Anatoly's eyebrows shot up. He walked closer for a better look. "I don't understand, are you a drug dealer or something?"

"Excuse me? Someone messes with my car and you want to know if *I'm* a drug dealer?"

"Look at the car, Sophie. Whoever did this was looking for something, and when they didn't find it in the glove compartment or the trunk they assumed it was valuable enough for you to hide it inside the seats."

"Well, if they were looking for drugs they got the wrong car."

Anatoly was examining the trunk now. "Well, they were looking for something."

"Oh, for God's sake! I wouldn't even know how to hide something in the upholstery of my car without ruining it. Let alone in my spare tire. What the hell could I possibly possess that I would even want to hide that well?"

"Could be a number of things. Do you have some compromising photos of the mayor and the latest Playboy bunny that you were planning on blackmailing him with? Although I think Willie Brown proved that San Franciscans aren't concerned with such things."

"Give me a break. I'm not blackmailing anyone. This is real life, not one of my books…." I looked at the car again. In what seemed like slow motion, I opened the passenger side door and touched one of the fresh cuts in the seat.

"What's wrong?" He stepped behind me and put a supportive hand on my arm.

"Nothing. Look, I don't mean to blow you off, but I think I should go report this."

"I'll go with you."

"It's really not necessary. I've had my car broken into before. You just go to the police station, file a report, and when the SFPD has a slow day they'll look into it. That will be right around the time the sun collides with the earth."

Anatoly just stared at me.

"I'm trying to be funny."

"I can see that."

"Well then, laugh and go away."

Anatoly didn't move. "Are you going to drive the car to the police station?"

"Now you're the one trying to be funny. I can't possibly drive this thing."

"Why not? The engine seems to be intact," he pointed out while checking under the hood. "And the only tire they slashed was the spare."

"The police station is only a few blocks away, I'll walk. It's not like they have to look at the car. All I have to do—"

"This isn't a normal break-in Sophie. The police should see the damage in order to know what they're dealing with."

I wrinkled my nose in disgust. The last thing I wanted to do was sit in the seat that only hours ago some creep had been merrily slashing away at.

"Here's what we'll do," Anatoly said. I rolled my eyes but chose not to interrupt. "I'll go upstairs, get my camera and take some pictures of the damage before we move it."

"Like I said before, *we* don't need to do anything."

"Here's my cell phone." He pulled his Nokia out of his jacket pocket. "Call the police and tell them we're coming over."

I pulled my hair back with enough force to damage some of the weaker strands. The guy was asking to be smacked. "I'm going to say this one last time—"

"Why don't you call them as you walk down there? I'll meet you with the car after I'm done with the pictures."

Okay, there was something appealing about that. At least I wouldn't have to get in the car. Of course the plan did have a few flaws. "That means I'd have to trust you with the keys to my car."

Anatoly grinned. "And I'll have to trust you with my cell. Considering the condition of your car, I think I'm taking the greater risk."

No arguing with that one. "Okay, here's the key. I'll meet you at the station. Do you know where it is?"

"I've passed it a few times. This will be good. Our first stop on my tour of San Francisco."

I shook my head and started downhill toward my destination. Having my car vandalized was a lot more than a minor annoyance, but my insurance would take care of it. What was really bothering me had little to do with my actual vehicle.

What was really bothering me was that for the second time in three days I was reliving a scene from one of my books.

The cop let out a low whistle as he considered the car. Anatoly, who had magically found a parking spot on the same block as the police station, was now standing aside as the officer, a big burly guy with a furry mustache going by the name of Gorman, studied the slash in the spare tire. He looked up from the damage and his eyes bore into me. "Do you have any history of drug use or dealing?"

"No!" I tried to ignore Anatoly's laughter.

"Well, they were looking for *something,*" Officer Gorman stated as he slammed the trunk closed.

"Yeah, we've established that. I don't own anything that would be worth hiding in my upholstery."

"Uh-huh," Gorman said. He looked me over, then turned back to the car. "Anyone who might be after you?"

Anatoly took a step closer to me. How much should I say? After all, most of my fears were based on nothing more than an overactive imagination, right? My fingers automatically began to fiddle with my necklace. "I can't think of anyone offhand."

"Uh-huh." Gorman eyed Anatoly. "Who are you again?"

"I'm just a friend of Sophie's."

"Uh-huh."

I bit my lip. If only the cop could say something useful. Hell, I'd settle for a completed sentence.

"Come inside, we'll finish the report."

That was probably as close as I was going to get. "Anatoly, will you wait out here for me?" I asked. "Make sure nobody else messes with it?"

"There's not much left to mess with."

"Just stay with the car, okay?"

I followed Gorman inside to his desk. This was embarrassing enough without Anatoly standing over my shoulder. Gorman gestured for me to take a chair. I remained standing. "I thought we were done with the report."

"Just a couple more questions."

I hesitated for a moment before sitting across from him. I wasn't relishing the idea of being interrogated in a police station, even if I didn't have anything to hide.

"Sure you're not hiding anything?"

Oh my God. I was being interrogated by the police department's resident psychic. Maybe I could just visualize the events of the last week and I wouldn't have to say anything at all.

"Miss Katz, did you hear me?"

Okay, so he wasn't a very good psychic. "A little over five weeks ago I got a typed note in the mail. No return address. It just said, 'You reap what you sow.'"

"'You reap what you sow'? Anything else?"

"Nope, that was it."

"Know who might have sent it?"

"No, like I said, no return address."

"Uh-huh." Gorman made a note at the bottom of his report. "Do you still have the note?"

"Well, here's the thing. I wanted to have a fire that night and I didn't really like the note, sooo…I burned it."

"You…you burned it?" Gorman shook his head. "Smart."

"Well, I didn't know I would be needing it." I scooted my chair forward. Gorman may not be Mr. Personality but maybe he could help me make sense of some things. All I had to lose was my dignity, and that was going pretty cheap these days. "I'm a writer. I write murder mysteries."

"Uh-huh."

"This last Thursday, the same day that woman Susan Lee was killed, I received five prank phone calls. The caller didn't say anything—there was just silence and a click."

"Any calls since Thursday?"

"No."

"Uh-huh." I noticed that this time Gorman didn't write anything down. He probably found my account so riveting that he knew he'd never forget it.

"So, that same night I came home from an art opening at Sussman Gallery and I found a broken glass."

"A broken glass?"

"Yes, a broken glass on my kitchen floor."

"Any idea how it broke?"

"Well…I do have a cat."

"Uh-huh."

"But the thing is, the glass was in the middle of the floor. I don't have a big kitchen, but it would be hard for Mr. Katz to knock a glass that far off the kitchen counter."

"Mr. Katz?"

"My cat."

"Uh-huh."

"Okay, so here comes the really weird part. In my second novel, *Sex, Drugs and Murder,* my protagonist, Alicia Bright, well, she sometimes gets prank phone calls and in one scene she comes home and finds…a broken glass!" I sat back in my chair and waited for Officer Gorman to react.

"Uh-huh."

Not the reaction I was looking for. "Okay, I know, glasses break all the time, right? That's why I decided not to call the police."

"Good decision."

"But now there's the car thing. In my book, Alicia Bright's roommate's car is vandalized in almost exactly the same way mine was. You see, the bad guy, Jeremy Spaulding, knows that Alicia's roommate, Kittie, has a cassette tape that could prove that his father was involved in a political scandal. Kittie's father produced X-rated films, so she had all these contacts to the pornography underworld."

"Uh-huh."

"Okay, that's probably not all that relevant. Besides, you could always read the book, right?"

Officer Gorman just stared at me. Apparently that one wasn't even worth an "uh-huh."

"The point is…" The point. What was my point again? "Oh, yes. The point is that things are happening to me that happened in my book. I am living *Sex, Drugs and Murder!*"

This time it was Officer Gorman's turn to sit back in his

chair. He put his fingers together steeple-style, furrowed his brow and was silent for what seemed like an hour. Finally, he looked up and made eye contact. I knew he had formed his theory. He leaned forward and I did the same. I could feel my heartbeats increasing in speed.

"You sure you don't do drugs?"

# CHAPTER 6

"Before she met him she had assumed that being sexy and obnoxious were mutually exclusive traits."
—*Sex, Drugs and Murder*

Feeling frustrated and embarrassed, I waited for Anatoly on the steps of his building. It figured that it took me less time to walk back to Anatoly's than it did for him to find a parking spot. After the exchange with the police, I had no intention of telling him about the similarities between the vandalism to my car and the one in *Sex, Drugs and Murder.* I was probably just being paranoid. But still, the slashing of the upholstery, even the spare tire… I rested my head in my hands. I needed Advil. Or a Bloody Mary. Maybe both. And to make everything worse I was wearing black and I had no makeup on. If I was going to be a damsel in distress I could at least be an attractive damsel—not some washed-out, big-haired bimbo.

"Are you okay?"

As usual I hadn't heard Anatoly coming. "Where'd you park?"

"Up by Grace Cathedral."

"That's eight blocks from here."

"You really need to get a garage."

I put my head back in my hands. "My head hurts. I need a drink."

"I wasn't aware that alcohol cures headaches."

"Don't mess with me, Anatoly, I'm in a bad mood. My car was trashed, the police officer I reported it to thinks I'm on crack, and I'm not wearing any lipstick!"

Anatoly looked perplexed, but he waved it off and knelt down beside me. "I won't pretend to understand the lipstick part but I do understand the rest. Leave a message with your insurance company and deal with everything else on Monday. For now, let's go get a beer...."

"I want a Bloody Mary."

"All right, a Bloody Mary..."

"And some Advil."

"Right. We'll go find a bar that serves Bloody Marys, non-prescription pain relievers and cosmetics, and we'll start over. How does that work for you?"

I smiled for the first time in over two hours and pulled myself out of my hunchback position. "Well, it would probably make more sense for me to make a quick run to my apartment for the Advil and the lipstick, but you're on the right track. There is still one problem, though."

"What's that?"

"Unless you bought a car since I last saw you, we have a conspicuous lack of transportation."

"Ah, now there you are mistaken. I don't have a car yet, but I do have a bike."

"A bike? Like...a bicycle?"

Anatoly clenched his teeth. "No, a bike like a motorcycle. I own a Harley."

I shot to my feet. "A Harley? You bought a Harley?"

"I didn't steal it."

"Wow." I looked around before spotting it across the street. "Is that it?"

"That's it. And I have two helmets. I'll go get them."

I crossed over to the bike to get a better look. I had never ridden one before, nor could I picture Anatoly on one. People who rode Harleys had long beards and wore all kinds of bizarre-looking leather stuff. Anatoly didn't even have stubble.

He came up behind me and handed me a helmet. "Ready?"

"When you buy a Harley, don't you have to join a biker club or something?"

"You mean like the Hell's Angels?"

"I guess. I don't know. I just assumed guys who drive Harleys are in some sort of club."

"I'm sorry to disappoint you but I'm not in a club. Are you going to put your helmet on?"

"Hey, these are real helmets!"

Anatoly muttered something in Russian.

"What, no little beanie caps for you?" I watched as he put on his helmet. "What if I get helmet hair?"

Anatoly put down the face visor, straddled his bike and revved it up, so I decided to be obliging and climbed on as well. The second I wrapped my arms around his chest, the incident with my car was pushed from my mind. It's hard to be aloof when your nipples are smashed up against the broad back of some guy giving you a lift on his Harley.

"Okay, we're going to stop by your apartment so you can get the things you need, and then where?" he called back to me through his helmet.

"Then we head toward North Beach." My breath caught as he revved the engine again. He maneuvered the bike away from the curb, and I felt the pressure of the wind as we accelerated. Anatoly's body leaned to the left as he turned the bike toward my apartment. It was as if he was an extension of this incredibly powerful machine. No, that was wrong. It was like the powerful machine was an extension of him.

Anatoly knew his way around enough to get to North Beach. He easily parked the Harley (a major advantage of owning a bike), and I brought him to the bar of a trendy little restaurant.

I surveyed the patrons. Was there anyone suspicious around? Anyone who showed more of an interest in us than was appropriate? Anyone who looked like they just finished ripping up an Acura? We pulled a couple of bar stools up to a table. I hesitated, feeling uncomfortable about sitting with my back to the window. This was so ridiculous. Who did I think I was? Malcolm X? I was here to have a good time and distract myself. I let my eyes quickly run over Anatoly's physique while he was busy checking out the restaurant. Distraction accomplished.

"Nice place." He gave me one of those little half smiles that made my tummy get all tingly. "You look nice too. In fact, you look like you're feeling a little better."

"That's because I'm wearing lipstick."

"That's why you look nice or that's why you're feeling better?"

"Both."

"I have nothing against lipstick, but you don't need it. A woman whose lips are as naturally full and pink as yours should know that she doesn't have to do anything artificial to make them enticing."

"What can I get you two?"

"Huh?" I could barely hear the cocktail waitress and I certainly couldn't see her. All I could see were Anatoly's dark brown eyes looking at my lips.

"What would you like to drink?"

I stared at her for a moment and tried to focus on her question. "To drink, right—what do I want to drink?" The waitress tapped her pencil against the pad. Maybe I should order a beer instead of a Bloody Mary. I wouldn't want Anatoly to think I was a hard-core drinker. Better to make *restraint* the strategy of the day. I could do it. I was strong. "I'll have a Corona."

Anatoly's forehead creased. "I thought you wanted a Bloody Mary."

"Okay, a Bloody Mary."

He laughed softly. "I'll have a Pacifico."

Oh great, now he thinks I'm a lush. Well, I couldn't take the order back now. Of course, after drinking the Bloody Mary, ordering one would seem like less of a big deal. That was the new strategy. If I couldn't make the impression I wanted, then I would just drink enough so that I didn't give a damn.

"Sooo…" I searched for something to say; I was feeling very self-conscious about my mouth. "Why did you leave New York?"

Anatoly shrugged. "It was time for a change. I'd visited San Francisco a few times before and liked it. Interesting mix of people."

"Have you been anywhere else on the West Coast?"

"Just L.A. I had a friend down there."

"*Had* a friend?"

"Yeah, he moved up north."

"Anywhere around here?"

"No, nowhere near here."

The drinks arrived. The waitress put mine down without even looking at me and then presented Anatoly with his like she was making a sacred offering. "Here's your Pacifico."

"Thanks, that will be all for now." I used a volume a notch above what was appropriate.

She went off to harass some other unsuspecting couple.

"Now, what were we talking about?" Anatoly took a swig of beer. "Ah, yes, why I moved to San Francisco."

"What?" I was watching our waitress, who was now at the bar. I was pretty sure that I could see brown roots.

"We were talking about my move."

"Right. I mean wrong. We were talking about your friend. Where'd he move to?"

"My mistake." He looked past me to the pedestrians pushing past one another on the other side of the window. "I lost contact with him a while ago. I'm not exactly sure where he is right now."

"But you know he's north."

"That's an educated guess based on what I know about him. Any more questions, or are you satisfied?"

"Touchy, touchy. Okay, let me think." I toyed with the celery stick in my drink. "All right, here's a question. Where'd ya learn to speak such good English?"

Anatoly chuckled. "I've been in this country for over twelve years now."

"Yeah, but there are a lot of people who spend their entire adult lives in a foreign country and never become fluent in their second language or grasp the use of slang as you seem to have. Hell, you even conjugate your verbs."

"I've spent a good portion of time with a lot of people who speak almost entirely in slang. Plus, in my line of work I often find it advantageous to sound less foreign." For a split second I thought I saw a glimmer of regret pass over his face, but if I had, it was gone as quickly as it came. I wondered if I had found yet another subject to which he was sensitive.

"And what exactly is your line of work?"

Anatoly took a few more gulps of his beer before answering. "I'm a contractor."

"A contractor? Like a contract killer?"

"Yeah, that's right, I'm a contract killer. Would you like a business card?"

"Naw, but I might want a list of references." I tried to scoot my stool forward without having to get up. "So I guess you're a contractor in the more legal sense, as in you fix houses and stuff."

"And stuff."

"Well, this is a good city for that line of work. There are lots of old Victorians that are falling apart as we speak. But why is it so advantageous to sound less foreign?"

Anatoly shrugged. "Construction workers seem to be more willing to take direction from men who sound like locals. I think my clients prefer it too."

Anatoly didn't exactly sound local. "Do you have any clients right now?"

"I've been doing a few odd jobs here and there and I have a few bids out, but for the most part it would be fair to qualify me as being between projects."

"You might want to consider sounding a little more Russian again."

"I'll take it under advisement. So how about you? How did you get into writing?"

"Oh, it's a pretty mundane story. My ex-husband screwed me over, I wanted to castrate him but I didn't want to go to jail, so I wrote a book about castrating him."

"Your first book is about castrating your ex?"

"Well, it's supposed to be about another woman castrating and killing a whole bunch of men, but if you read between the lines, yes. It's a book about me castrating and killing my ex-husband."

Anatoly grinned and swallowed some more beer. "So you write fantasies."

I laughed. "Well, my fantasies at least. No, actually I just write ordinary mainstream fiction. The difference being that the crimes I write about may not have happened, but they could have. I take great pains to make sure that the books I write come across as being very realistic."

"But they can't be that realistic. You're not a cop or an investigator, and as far as I know, you're not a criminal, which means you have no firsthand experience in the things you write about. It's not possible for you to know what real-life crime is all about."

"Have you read any of my books?"

"No, I don't think I have."

"Well then, you're being a bit presumptuous, aren't you? Not to mention an asshole."

Anatoly nearly spit his beer all over the table. "You're getting a lot better with your insults."

"It's nice of you to give me so many opportunities to perfect my technique."

"You can practice on me anytime. I'm available nights and weekends."

I was tempted to ask what other services he offered, but forced myself to keep my mouth shut.

He rested his forearm on the table. "Have you had any serious relationships since your marriage?"

"Not a one. What's really sad is that I'm not lucky at cards either."

Anatoly's eyes locked with mine. "Luck has a tendency to change."

For a moment I couldn't find my voice. I took a long drink of the Bloody Mary. I was nervous. The sad thing was that I couldn't figure out if I was nervous because I was beginning to really like Anatoly or because I was afraid someone was trying to kill me. That really couldn't be healthy. I searched my mind for a nice safe topic.

"So you moved from Russia to Israel to the U.S. Sounds like a lot of life-altering changes."

"I was in Israel for just under four years. Then, as soon as the American Immigration office saw fit to allow my admittance, I was on my way to the States."

"You were in the Israeli army?"

"Of course, it's mandatory service." He paused to drink. "I was in the Russian army too."

"Oh my God, you're a mercenary."

"I was a citizen of both countries."

"Okay, but two armies? I don't know. There's something odd about that."

"Most women find it exciting."

"Are these the same women who developed a crush on Steven Segal?"

Anatoly leaned back from the table and grinned. "You know, I never asked about that. I have been with women who've had a thing for Jean-Claude Van Damme. Is that the same thing?"

"Pretty much. Were you ever in a kill-or-be-killed situation?"

"No, never during my length of service was I in that particular situation. I was lucky."

I had to think about the wording on that one. "What about *outside* your length of service."

"I've never been in combat outside of Israel or Russia either."

"But you have had some close calls here?"

"What makes you say that?"

I hate it when people respond to a question with a question. It almost always implies guilt. "Anatoly, I don't mean to grill you, but I do have a few set standards when it comes to dating. They are as follows—I never date men who are con artists, murderers or spawn of the devil. I just need to know that you don't fit into any of those categories."

Anatoly's body relaxed a bit as he leaned toward me. "I'm not a con artist. I have never committed murder. I'm a little murky on the devil-spawn part, but my mother decided to stay in Israel, so hopefully that will be a nonissue."

"Well, two out of three ain't bad." I took another bite out of my celery stick. "So, what kind of close calls have you had outside of the army?"

"Does your family live here?"

"Gee, that was subtle." I wanted to press him for more clear answers, but I could see his jaw tightening. Better to shelve the question for another day when I had more energy, patience, and a car to get home with. "My mom, my sister and her husband and baby. My father died eighteen years ago."

"I'm sorry. Were you close?"

"Very. I think I take after him in a lot of ways. Of course, I'm close to my mom too, and my sister and I talk regularly, but she and I are just very different people. I've always looked for the road less traveled—she, on the other hand, married a CPA."

"Got it. How long have you lived in Russian Hill?"

"I've been in the same flat for the last nine years."

"I've never been in the same city for nine years. Are you friends with all the neighbors?"

"I hate them." Anatoly stifled a laugh. "Fortunately the guy on the first floor is always out of town and the woman below me and I have an unspoken agreement to only acknowledge one another's presence once every five years, so it works for me. In fact, she was the one to tell me about my car this morning, so with any luck, she'll be giving me the silent treatment for the rest of the decade."

"All right, I'm sure there are other benefits to staying in the same place for so long. Rent control for instance."

"Oh God, yes, If it were to go on the market today the landlord would probably raise the rent by a good thousand dollars a month. Plus the landlord lets me do anything I want, as long as it brings up the property value. Hey, maybe you could do some remodeling for me. The timing's perfect. I just finished my last book, so it wouldn't be disruptive to my work."

Anatoly rearranged his legs under the table. "My plate's pretty full right now."

"I thought you said you were between projects."

"I am, but I expect that one of my bids is going to be accepted any day now. It's a big job and I want to keep myself available for it." He polished off the rest of his Pacifico. "Do you want another drink?"

"No, I think I'm done for awhile."

"Good." Anatoly signaled to the waitress that he wanted the check. "I want to walk up to Coit Tower. It's one of the few San Francisco monuments I haven't gotten around to visiting."

"Yeah, it's beautiful in a phallic kind of way, but you have to climb up a pretty steep hill to get there."

The cocktail waitress came over with the check. I suppressed a little smile. There were definitely brown roots.

After sticking his wallet away in his back pocket, Anatoly's focus came back to me. "I think you can make the walk." His eyes ran up and down my body. "You look like you're in very good shape."

My cheeks heated up and I squirmed in my seat. My feminist side was telling me to be offended, but I couldn't quite get myself to obey that particular dictate. I was too busy picturing Anatoly naked.

"Shall we?" Anatoly asked.

"Mmm-hmm." Whatever he was asking me to do, the answer was yes.

He extended his hand to me. Was it normal to be turned on by holding a guy's hand? Then again, this guy did have those mighty fine hands. He led me out of the restaurant.

My libido came back under control during the climb to Coit Tower. The road leading there wasn't quite at a ninety-degree angle but it was about as close as you could get without making walking up it a gravitational impossibility. By the time we made it to the top I was a sweaty, puffing mess that even lipstick couldn't compensate for. Anatoly wasn't even winded, which did nothing to improve my spirits.

I sat down on the low concrete barrier that encased the bell-shaped parking lot. "Is there a reason we didn't take your bike up here?"

"We wouldn't have gotten the full experience."

"Oh yeah. I wouldn't want to miss the experience of having cardiac arrest or anything."

Anatoly laughed and shook his head. "Do me a favor, shut up and enjoy the view."

I responded by sticking my tongue out at him before turning my back on the white phallic-shaped monument to absorb the rest of my surroundings. It really was beautiful. From where I stood you could see both the Golden Gate and Bay bridges. The weather was perfect for sailing, so the water was decorated with little white triangles gliding over its surface. It wasn't officially tourist season yet but there were still a fair number of men and women scattered around the monument snapping their cameras and speaking in foreign tongues. It was so peaceful and welcoming that any nagging fears left over from the morning's episode seemed to just blow away in the breeze. No matter what awaited me at the bottom of the hill, I knew that as long as I was here I was safe. I greedily inhaled the fresh sea air.

"It's spectacular, isn't it?"

Anatoly turned his back to the Bay. "Yes, 'spectacular' is a good word for it."

My breath quickened slightly.

"Sophie, there is something I've wanted to do all day."

"What's that?"

He answered by gently caressing my cheek. He leaned forward and touched my lips with his. It was gentle, tender and extremely hot.

He backed up just enough so he could speak. "More?"

"More would be good."

Anatoly moved in again. This time the kiss was deeper. He parted my lips with his tongue as one hand held me tightly against him and the other hand moved forcefully up my back. He abandoned my mouth in favor of my neck, and I silently thanked God that I had tossed aside the turtleneck.

Anatoly released me, and it took every last morsel of self-control not to cry out in protest. "I think I'm done looking at Coit Tower," he said. "Perhaps we could go somewhere a little quieter?"

You know, safety is overrated. It was time to leave this little utopia and start living dangerously…in my apartment. I ran a teasing finger down Anatoly's arm until its path was stopped by his watch. "Wait a minute, is that right? Is it really five-fifteen?" I checked my watch for verification. "Shit. I'm supposed to be at that surprise party at six."

"Surprise party? Do you really have to go?"

I bit down on my lip. My going to the party was really important to Marcus. Of course, getting laid was really important to *me*. "It's for a sick friend of Marcus's. He's a big fan of my books and I promised Marcus that I'd show up as kind of a celebrity-guest type thing."

"How sick is he?"

My shoulders slumped. "He has AIDS." I reluctantly tucked my hands into my pockets. "Do you want to come with me?"

Anatoly sighed and shook his head. "I wasn't invited, and you really should spend your time and energy on the guest of honor. I think it's best if I don't come."

Well, it looked like I wasn't going to get to come either. "Will you at least give me a ride?"

Anatoly draped an arm over my shoulders. "Your chariot awaits."

"'I equate days to music,' she explained. 'Some play out like Pachelbel's Canon performed by the New York Symphony Orchestra. Others are more like a badly composed Beatles medley that you're forced to listen to while on hold for the dentist.'"

—*Sex, Drugs and Murder*

The party itself was fun if not particularly memorable. I signed a few books and managed to enjoy myself, although I made a point of telling Marcus what I had sacrificed to be there. He showed his appreciation by cutting me an extra-large piece of chocolate cake that he personally dosed with brandy.

When the festivities were over he gave me a ride home and idled the car in front of my apartment. He turned the music down so we could hear ourselves talk over the Material Girl. "Thanks so much for coming, Soph. It just made Steve's night."

I nodded. "He's a nice guy. He told me that when things get bad he escapes into one of my books. Considering what he's escaping I think that may be the greatest compliment of my life."

"Yeah." Marcus pulled gently on one of his locks. "That boy has gotten damn skinny. The reason we wrapped things up at nine is that he tires out so fast. He did seem to be having fun, though, didn't he?"

"Yeah, he was having fun." I covered Marcus's hand with my own. "The party was perfect. You did good."

Marcus smiled slightly and looked into the darkness.

I nudged him gently in the ribs. "Speaking of doing good, I didn't expect to see Donato there tonight."

Marcus's smile became more animated. "Mmm-hmm, Donato and I are a thang. He's fun, he's romantic, and damn girl, you should see him when he starts working those hips— and I am not talking about dancing, okay."

"I guess I'll have to take your word for it. He's kind of eccentric, isn't he?"

"Greek gods often are." I could see his eyes twinkle, despite the poor lighting. "He's meeting me at my place in an hour for a private worship session."

"Private worship session, huh? Well, far be it for me to keep you from your religious duties." I kissed him on the cheek and gathered up my purse and coat. "Do you have time to give me a deep condition and trim on Tuesday?"

"Honey, for you I'll make the time. Call the salon, they'll pencil you in."

"It's a date, then." I popped out of the car and watched as Marcus drove off.

"Hi, Sophie."

I turned to see Andy smiling down at me. "Hey, Andy, what are you doing here?"

He shuffled his feet awkwardly. "I just helped Mrs. Murphy carry some groceries home."

I noted the time. Nine-thirty, a bit late for a little old lady to be grocery shopping. Of course, for all I knew Mrs. Murphy could be some young socialite afraid of breaking a nail.

"Was that guy your boyfriend?"

"Hmm? Oh, Marcus? I wish. No, he's just a friend. I don't have a boyfriend." As soon as I said it I realized my mistake. Andy was about to ask me out, and I had just ruined what would have been a perfectly good excuse to say no.

"Well, Andy, it was good to see you. I've got to get upstairs—my cat's probably really hungry by now." Where were my keys? I felt them at the bottom of my purse. Great, now if I could just get inside quickly enough...

"Would you like to go out with me sometime?"

Shit.

"I could take you somewhere really nice. I've been saving money from my paychecks."

I looked at my keys hanging in the unopened lock. "Listen, Andy, I'm really flattered but—"

"But you don't want to go out with a retard."

"God, no! You're not a retard." Was he angry? I didn't even know he had a temper. "It's just that, well, I've got a lot going on right now and I simply don't have any time, so I've decided to hold off on dating for a while."

"So you're not dating anyone?" The cloud that had briefly darkened his features slipped away and was replaced by befuddlement. He looked like a kid who had just discovered he'd wandered too far from his parents.

"Nope." Not unless you're tall, dark and Russian, in which case I'm all over it.

Andy shifted his weight from foot to foot. "I guess I understand that."

I doubted that, but he was willing to accept it and that's all I cared about.

"Well, like I said, I've got to go feed the cat." It took concerted effort to hide my relief.

"Okay, Sophie. I'll see you soon, right?"

"Of course, Andy, I'll see you at the market." I was so good.

I felt my guard go up the minute I got into the apartment. I turned on every light and spent about a half hour meticulously checking for broken glass or anything unusual, but everything was as it should be. I stood in the middle of the living room and scowled at my published novels neatly lined up on the top bookshelf. How sad was it that I had actually lost the ability to tell the difference between fiction and reality? Dena has always said that prolonged sexual abstinence leads to early senility. I bent down to scratch Mr. Katz behind the ears.

"I'd better get Anatoly up here fast before I hurt myself diving through a looking-glass trying to find Hogwarts."

The next morning I let my fingers do the walking through all the emergency auto-window-replacement ads. The problem was that I didn't consider my need for a new driver's side window an emergency. It wasn't a new car, and I was pretty sure that the insurance company was going to consider it totaled, so why should I care if some homeless guy wanted to take a nap in it?

I closed the phone book and relaxed back into the chair. It was a typical cold, foggy San Francisco day. Perfect for lighting up a fire, taking the phone off the hook and reading a good book. I looked over at the bookcase.

There was a book on the top shelf that was slightly out of place. Funny, it hadn't been that way last night....

I mechanically rose from the chair. With every step toward that bookcase my heartbeat got a little louder. Without being able to see the title, all I could tell was that it was a novel from my series. I pulled it out. *Sex, Drugs and Murder.*

I dropped the book.

There was no uncertainty this time. And if it had been in the right place before I went to bed and if I hadn't left the apartment since then that meant someone had been in here....

"Oh my God." I could see the front door from where I stood. It was bolted and locked. I couldn't see any evidence of forced entry, but then there was always the window. Had they come in when I was asleep? When I was taking a shower? Were they still here? I tried to block out the faint street noise that filtered through my bay window in order to focus on any sounds that might be coming from inside. I thought I heard a quiet *thump*—so subtle that I couldn't swear that I had heard it at all. It could've been nothing. A figment of my overly anxious mind or a bird that had inadvertently brushed against the panes of glass in the bedroom.

Or it could've been an intruder lying in wait.

Mr. Katz purred and curled around my feet. Keeping my back against the bookcase, I bent my knees and with one arm scooped up the cat and with the other carefully picked up the book by the pages without touching the cover. I straightened to a standing position.

"Are you ready, Mr. Katz?" Mr. Katz struggled against me.

I took that as a yes and ran for the door. I fumbled with the locks, almost dropping the book and my pet. I needed to get out. I needed to get out and call the police, and this time they were going to take me seriously. I flew out the door and down a flight of stairs to the flat below, Mr. Katz hissing and clawing the whole way as I held him in a death grip. I pounded on the door of my neighbor's quarters.

"Theresa, it's me, Sophie. Let me in, it's an emergency."

Theresa threw open the door looking predictably sourfaced. Her expression became even more pinched when she saw Mr. Katz. "If you think you are going to bring that fleabitten animal into my home..."

I pushed past her. "Theresa, I'm not kidding, there really is an emergency. I need to use your phone."

"You're trespassing. If you and your rodent don't get out of my flat this instant I am going to call the police. Do you understand me?"

"Oh, for God's sake. Here, I'll save you the trouble." I dropped Mr. Katz in favor of her princess phone sitting on the antique side table.

"Nine-one-one emergency," a voice recited on the other end of the line.

"Someone's broken into my home."

"Are they still on the premises?"

"I don't know."

"Where are you, ma'am?"

"I'm at my neighbor's in the apartment below."

"What's the number of your place?"

I gave her all the necessary information. After listening to my end of the conversation, Theresa seemed somewhat less inclined to kick me out and instead pulled a kitchen chair under her doorknob. The dispatcher didn't let me off the phone until the assigned officers buzzed the apartment. I picked up my book and Mr. Katz, who, by this time, was only marginally less traumatized than myself, and fought the urge to kick the door down as I waited for Theresa to let us out. I stepped out into the foyer just in time to see Officer Gorman coming up the stairs. We looked at each other, unsure of how to react.

Gorman's partner, a short, muscular young guy, ran up the stairs after him. He looked at Gorman questioningly.

Gorman nodded to him. "The next one up." He jerked his head back in my direction. "It's open?"

"Yeah, I didn't hang around long enough to lock up."

"Stay here." He and the short guy took the stairs two at a time.

I knew that I should stay where I was, but now that the police were there to give me a false sense of security I felt my curiosity getting the better of me. I gave them a few minutes to get in and look around before cautiously climbing the stairs after them. When I stepped through my door, Mr. Katz leaped out of my arms and dashed under the coffee table, a maneuver that almost sent Officer Gorman sprawling.

I shrank into the corner. "Sorry about that, he's a little nervous."

"Uh-huh."

The young cop came out of the bedroom. "No sign of anybody here. No sign of forced entry either."

"Nope."

I slammed my fist against the wall. "I did not make this up. Somebody was here. I don't know if they came and left in the middle of the night or if they were here more recently, but I know they were here."

The young one scratched the back of his head. "What was it that alerted you?"

"There was a book out of place."

A good sixty seconds passed before either of them found his voice. Finally Gorman cleared his throat. "A book?"

I squeezed my eyes shut. This just couldn't be happening again. "Okay, I know how lame that sounds, but you have to hear me out on this. I am not a crackpot. I know someone was here and I know it was the same person who vandalized my car."

Gorman sat down on the couch and the other officer leaned against the wall wearing a rather bemused expression.

I took a shaky deep breath. I had to make them believe me. "Okay, I told you about *Sex, Drugs and Murder,* right?"

"Sex, Drugs and Murder? Is that one of those alternative lifestyle courses they teach at Berkeley?" asked the young cop. Gorman lifted his hand as if to say, Don't ask.

"Look." I held the book out in front of me by the corner of two pages. "This is the book. This is also the book that was out of place on my bookshelf. It was placed on its back so that it was sticking out. Someone wants to be sure that I know that they are reenacting my book. And I think I just might be playing the part of the murder victim."

Neither of the officers said anything.

"All right. Maybe I'm not the murder victim. Maybe I'm the protagonist, Alicia Bright, and it's my job to fig- ure out the crime. But I could be Kittie. Don't you guys get it? What the fuck am I supposed to do if I'm Kittie, the victim?"

"Drink milk?"

The young cop busted up laughing.

I bit down on my tongue. What exactly was the penalty for assaulting an officer? "You know, my life might be at stake here. Is it too much to ask that you pretend to care?"

The young cop pulled a glove out of his pocket and after putting it on took the book. "Tell you what. If it'll make you feel better, we can dust this for prints. You'll have to come down to the station and give us a set of your own prints so we can compare. If someone with a criminal history has touched this, we'll know."

Gorman looked at the other cop as if he had caught my infectious disease.

"Hey, what can it hurt? Joey's working today, he'll do it." Gorman shook his head but didn't offer any protests. The cop turned back to me. "How 'bout you? You up for it?"

Okay, they may not have been convinced that I was sane, but they were at least willing to check out my story. I put a calming hand on my stomach. "Thank you so much. Can we do that now?"

Gorman rose to his feet. "Yep." He motioned for his partner to follow him out, but before he made any progress I reached out a restraining hand.

"I've got a question."

"Uh-huh."

"Was there ever a point in your life in which you spoke in full sentences?"

"Nope."

"Didn't think so."

When I got back to the apartment, Mr. Katz was still hiding under the coffee table. I tossed my purse on a chair and prepared a bowl of kibble as a means of apology. The trip to the police station had been awful. The only prints on the book were mine. Neither Gorman nor his partner thought anything I said held any credibility, and for a few scary moments I thought I was going to be booked for making a prank call to 911. Were they right? Was I losing my mind? I looked over at the empty space on the top bookshelf.

No, someone had been there. Someone was toying with me.

I placed the bowl of cat food in front of the coffee table, and Mr. Katz cautiously inched out from underneath.

I gently stroked my cat's ruffled fur. "Maybe we should stay somewhere else for a while." But what good would staying somewhere else be? I would still have to go outside. And how long would I have to stay away from my home before it was safe? A week? A month? How would I know?

I used my index fingers to apply gentle pressure to my temples. There had to be a smart thing to do. I just had to figure out what it was.

The phone interrupted my thoughts. I put my hand on the receiver and let it ring again. I was actually leery about answering my own phone. I shook my head. I couldn't let them do this to me. I wouldn't. I picked it up on the fourth ring. "Hello?"

"I've got to get out of the house."

"Leah, this really isn't a good time." I collapsed onto the love seat. Ever since my sister had given birth to my nephew a year and a half ago, our contact had been reduced to frequent quasi-therapy sessions in which I listened patiently and pretended to empathize with her trials and tribulations as a stay-at-home mom. Normally I could rise to the occasion, but at the moment I was a bit too caught up in the trials and tribulations of being a potential homicide victim.

"I'm not kidding, Sophie. Jack is absolutely driving me nuts. I cannot spend another day following him around the house as he systematically tears the place apart. You're taking us out to lunch at Chevy's."

"I am? I hadn't realized. Am I paying?"

"Of course you're paying. It's your way of being supportive of me while I'm on the edge of a breakdown."

"How considerate of me. Where's your husband?"

"Bob had a golf game today."

"Is that his way of being supportive?"

I could practically hear Leah grimace.

"Are you going to meet me at Chevy's or not?"

I considered the alternatives. Go to lunch with my sister and her toddler son, or hang around my place and wait for someone to hack me up with an ax. It was a tough choice but the scale did seem to be tipping slightly in Leah's favor. "You'll have to pick me up—my car's out of commission."

"So now I have to drive across the city just to have lunch at Chevy's?"

I loved my sister. Really I did. "You don't have to drive anywhere, Leah, you could stay home. But if you want to have lunch with me, particularly if you want me to *treat* you, then yes, you'll have to come get me."

"Fine. We'll go to the Chevy's at the Embarcadero, then. I'll be there in forty-five minutes. Be ready, I don't want to have to wait long with Jack in the car."

"Well, I wouldn't want to inconvenience you. I'll see you in an hour."

"Forty-five minutes."

"Whatever." I hung up and went back to trying to massage my headache away.

An hour and a half later Leah buzzed the apartment. I gave Mr. Katz a goodbye pet. "I'm going out for a little while. If anyone tries to break in while I'm gone, I want you to meow really loud, okay?" Mr. Katz kneaded the rug in response.

I met my sister down at her car and slipped into the front passenger seat. "Have trouble getting out of the house?"

"You have no idea." Leah pushed her Volvo into Drive and headed toward the Embarcadero.

I twisted myself into a position so that I could see the back seat. "Hi, Jack! How are you today?"

"NO!"

"Jack's going through a 'no' phase," Leah said.

"A 'no' phase—got it." I didn't get it at all, but then again I didn't have to. All I had to do was remember to use contraceptives.

Leah pressed a button to crack open the moonroof. "Half the reason I'm late is that nitwit Cheryl."

I made a face at the mention of Leah's sister-in-law's name. She *was* a nitwit. Kind of like her brother.

"She called while I was trying to get Jack together and I simply could not get her off the phone. Can you believe she's still groaning about that whole Tolsky thing?"

"The Tolsky thing?" I pulled the sun visor down and checked my lipstick in the mirror. "Why, was she going to write a screenplay for him too?"

"No, she just thought she was going to get to meet him." Jack began to babble to himself as Leah carefully maneuvered around a cable car. "He made a reservation at the Ritz the morning before he killed himself. Cheryl had the pleasure of taking the reservation and canceling it."

I snapped the sun visor back up. "Wait a minute, you're telling me that Tolsky made a reservation at a San Francisco hotel less than twenty-four hours before he killed himself?"

"Apparently so. Can you imagine how impossible Cheryl would have been if she *had* met him? It's bad enough listening to her go on and on about the time she met Meg Ryan. I mean, she's a hotel clerk, not a Hollywood insider."

"Leah, doesn't that seem strange to you? Why would anyone make a hotel reservation shortly before committing suicide?"

"Who knows what he was thinking? The man was obviously sick. Did you see his movie *Deathly Seduction?* Ugh. Anyone who could produce and direct something so—"

Jack let out a scream at a pitch that would have damaged the hearing of a dog. Leah whipped her head back in his direction to chastise him.

"Leah, look out," I gasped.

She brought her attention back to the street just in time to miss a bicyclist, but in doing so almost slammed the car into a bus. The tires squealed against the pavement as she struggled to gain control. She hit the brakes and the car jerked to a stop as the traffic light turned red. I sat immobile, clinging to the door.

Leah cleared her throat. "Jack's going through a screaming phase too."

I'm never having kids.

For the rest of the ride Leah focused on driving and I focused on deep-breathing exercises. When we arrived at our destination Leah locked Jack into a high chair and collapsed into her own seat. "God, I'm tired. Jack had a bad night last night."

Well, he was having one hell of an afternoon. I flipped open the menu. "Have some coffee."

"That will just make me agitated."

"Then have a margarita."

"Sophie, you can't think that I would drink alcohol while watching Jack."

"Okay, *I'll* have a margarita."

"Hello, ladies, would you like to order something to drink while you decide?" asked a young man with bright red hair and a smile that was only somewhat strained.

"I'll have the mango margarita," I said.

"My son will have a glass of milk and I'll have a glass of your sangria."

"Got it." The waiter scribbled our order down and left us to study the rest of the menu.

"I thought you couldn't drink while watching Jack."

"Wine doesn't count." Jack began to fuss, and Leah handed him a napkin. "Here, honey, why don't you tear this up?" Jack started happily ripping the paper to shreds.

"So what happened to your car?"

"Oh somebody fu—" I cast a quick glance at Jack. "Somebody messed with it."

"What do you mean they 'messed with it'?"

"They slashed up the seats, rug and spare tire. Probably the work of some strung-out kids." I had no intention of telling her about the events of that morning. Leah had a tendency to overreact, and I still hadn't gotten rid of my headache.

Leah frowned and tapped her nails against the table. The waiter came with our drinks and took our order before she voiced her thoughts. "I heard about the woman who was killed in your neighborhood."

"Yeah, pretty ugly, huh?"

"I hope you're being careful, Sophie." She twisted her wedding band around on her finger. "I worry about you living all by yourself."

"I don't live by myself. I live with Mr. Katz."

"You know most women don't start talking to their cats until they're eighty."

"Yes, well, I've always been precocious."

Leah sighed and gave Jack another napkin to destroy. "I don't suppose you're dating anyone."

"Actually, I am."

Leah nearly choked on a floating piece of fruit. "You are? Why in God's name didn't you tell me?"

"I did tell you, just now."

"But I had to ask. That doesn't count."

I took a much-needed sip of my margarita. "Okay, let's pretend you didn't ask. Leah, guess what? I'm dating someone."

"Ha, ha. All right, smarty, who is he? And don't leave out any details."

I gave her a brief rundown on Anatoly, including his physical description, career background and a list of his previous residences. By the time I'd finished, the waiter was back with our food.

Leah sliced up some quesadilla for Jack before he started systematically dropping each piece on the floor. "Well, he's Jewish. That'll make Mom happy."

"I have no intention of ever introducing him to Mom. And I don't want you talking to her about this, either—got it, Leah?"

"You're going to have to tell her about him if it gets serious."

"We've been on one date. It's not serious."

"But it *could* get serious. Honestly, Sophie, you can't be so cautious. You're not a kid anymore. Statistically speaking you're more likely to get hit by a truck than get married again."

"People get hit by trucks all the time."

"This isn't a joke. Now let's see, did you say you've only been on one date with him?"

"Well, it's more like one and a half. I went to an opening at a gallery with Marcus, and Anatoly was there. The two of us hung out and shared a cab home. Does that count as a date?"

"No."

"Oh." I tasted my drink again. "What counts as a date, then?"

"He has to ask you to go out at a specific time and date and you have to say yes. He has to come pick you up, then you engage in some activity together and you leave together."

"Huh. Okay, Anatoly and I did engage in an activity together and we left together so—"

"It doesn't count." Leah chewed on her enchilada. "You haven't slept with him, have you? You know you have to hold out until at least the third date, otherwise he'll think you're easy."

"I didn't sleep with him."

"Well, thank God you have some sense."

"I didn't have a chance. By the time things started getting really steamy between the two of us I had to get going to a surprise party. But next time I see him I'm definitely going to be wearing the good underwear."

"Sophie. You can't be serious. You know, this is Dena's influence. You spend all your time hanging out with her at her sex shop and now you've turned into a slut."

"Slut! Slut, slut, slut, slut, slut!" Jack was happily banging a spoon against his tray as he proudly yelled out his new word at the top of his voice.

Leah grabbed Jack's shoulders and desperately tried to defuse the situation as the neighboring tables shot us alarmed stares. "No, no, honey. You misheard mommy. I didn't call Auntie Sophie a slut, I called her a…a…a mutt! That's it, honey, Auntie Sophie is a mutt."

I slid down in my seat and considered asking the waiter to put another shot of tequila in my margarita. Obviously, I had made the wrong choice today; I should have waited for the ax murderer. When Jack finally quieted down, I threw out the one comment that I knew would distract Leah from her current line of questioning.

"God, Leah, you must be exhausted."

Leah brightened. "I am exhausted. Honestly, I don't know how I manage. Yesterday I put off doing errands because I was afraid that if I got in the car I might fall asleep at the wheel."

"Wow, that's tough."

"Tell me about it." She tossed her processed hair over her shoulder with a well-practiced dramatic touch. "The other day it took me fifty minutes to get him down for a nap. Fifty minutes, Sophie. I was so drained from the ordeal that I couldn't even use the hour that he was asleep productively. I actually sat on the couch and watched MTV News of all things. And while watching it I realized how completely out of it I am. I used to be hip, remember?"

Leah was never hip. "Of course I remember."

"Now I don't know half the singers they were talking about. I mean, who on earth is JJ Money or DC Smooth?"

I perked up. "Oh, were they talking about the charges against DC Smooth? You know it was an article about that case that first brought Anatoly and me together. It was the front page story in the *New York Times* the day that he tried to steal the paper from me. God, I find that whole messy situation so interesting. It has book potential written all over it. I don't think he did it, do you?"

"He tried to steal your newspaper?"

"Long story. Anyway, I've been following this and the pieces just don't fit. DC claims that JJ Money called him up and challenged him. Told him to meet him in the VIP room of some nightclub to settle some old scores, right?"

"Well I..."

"DC goes and he's ready for action. He's got a switchblade and a gun, tells a whole bunch of people that he's going to set JJ Money straight." I sat up a little straighter as I narrated. "He goes to the club and waits. JJ Money's a no-show, so DC gets antsy and decides to go outside to see if he can find him. Again he tells some of his friends what he's up to."

"I really—"

"Next thing you know, DC's in some nearby alley standing over JJ Money's body. JJ Money's been shot with a gun left at the crime scene, only its not DC Smooth's gun but JJ Money's own gun. I don't care how high DC might have been, nobody's stupid enough to tell the world that he's going to go fu— Mess with someone and then shoot that same someone and *then* hang around long enough to tell the cops that he didn't do it." I hit my spoon against the table for emphasis. "And why shoot him with JJ's own gun? It just doesn't make sense."

"Sophie?"

"Yeah?"

"I don't care."

I pressed my lips into a tight little smile. I had forgotten who I was talking to. One should never interrupt Leah when she is talking about herself. It just isn't done.

Jack was now carefully pouring milk over the food that surrounded his high chair.

"Jack, stop. Did you hear me? Mommy said no. Oh for God's sake, where is the waiter with our check? Do you see what I go through?"

I spent the rest of the time at Chevy's helping Leah do damage control after Hurricane Jack, furiously waving down our waiter and listening to Leah tell me how put-upon she was and how I should marry and have kids so we could be put-upon together. The ax murderer was in for a letdown. If the lunch didn't end soon I was going to kill myself.

CHAPTER 8

"As if her own neuroses didn't complicate her life enough, now she had to deal with everyone else's."
——*Sex, Drugs and Murder*

Eventually Leah did drive me home. I jumped out of the car and watched her drive off. One of us had to have been adopted.

I went up to my apartment and let my hand rest on the brass doorknob. I stood there for a full two minutes. I wanted to smack myself for being such a wimp. This was my home. Some idiot rearranged my bookshelf and now I was afraid to go inside? Where was the Sophie that had nonchalantly walked through the slums of the city by herself at night while doing research for her novels? Where was the woman who had won a tug-of-war with a street punk who had tried to steal her purse?

I drew in a deep breath and opened the door. I laced my keys through my fingers in the way Dena had taught me. If I had to punch someone they would be seriously cut. I stepped into the entryway and was greeted by what seemed to be a calm and collected Mr. Katz.

"No visits from deranged fans this afternoon?" Mr. Katz purred expectantly. "Okay, I'll pay attention to you in a second, just let me do a quick walk-through."

I checked every room and narrow closet, keys in hand, and scrutinized every shelf dresser and countertop to see if anything was displaced. When I was sure that everything was in order, I lowered myself onto the sofa and allowed Mr. Katz to knead away at my black chinos. I stroked his fur and tried to formulate a plan of attack, but none was forthcoming. I needed help with this. I let my hand rest on the phone although I didn't have the slightest idea who it was that I was going to call. Fortunately I didn't have to figure it out because someone called me first. My fingers tightened around the receiver. I no longer feared that it would be a prank call. I just desperately hoped that whoever was on the line could offer me some viable solutions. I brought it to my ear.

"Please tell me this is my guardian angel."

"Why do you need a guardian angel?"

"Anatoly." I let my body relax against the leather cushions.

"Right on the first guess, I'm flattered. Why do you need a guardian angel?"

"It's nothing, and even if I was serious, I wouldn't ask you to fill that role. You wouldn't make a good angel. Dark angel maybe. What's up?"

"I was just calling to find out when I was going to see you again. Are you busy tonight?"

"Only if we make plans." Anatoly was an infinitely better escape mechanism than my sister and her Tasmanian Devil.

"Good answer. How about a late movie with a few drinks afterward?"

"Funny, you don't strike me as the movie type." I balanced the receiver between my ear and shoulder as I tried to remove Mr. Katz's claws from my thigh. "Do you have a particular film in mind?"

"They're playing *Suspicion* at The Roxie."

"Hitchcock?" I dropped Mr. Katz on the floor and jumped to my feet. "You like Hitchcock?"

"Is that a problem?"

"Are you kidding? I think I want to bear your children!"

There was a silence on the line.

"Anatoly, that was a joke."

"I realize that. I've just never elicited such a strong response by simply picking the right movie."

"I'm easy."

"Really?"

"Mmm-hmm, just ask my nephew."

Another silence.

"Um, that was an inside joke that didn't carry over too well, you see...you know what? Never mind. When are you picking me up?"

I could make out Anatoly's muffled laughter. "The movie starts at nine-forty, so why don't I come and pick you up at a quarter after?"

"I'll be here with bells on."

"She's easy and she wears bells. What more could a man want from a woman?"

"Goodbye, Anatoly."

I hung up and turned to Mr. Katz. "So, on a scale of one to ten, how badly do you think I came across in that conversation?"

Mr. Katz blinked his eyes.

"Good idea. If I were you I wouldn't answer either."

I spent the rest of the day and early evening hours trying to fix my kitchen window. In the end, I wound up leaving a lengthy message on my landlord's voice mail asking that he send someone out to take care of it immediately, knowing full well that in landlord-speak "immediately" often translated into three or four days.

Anatoly showed up at nine-fifteen on the button. I pulled out a hair and placed it in the crack of space above the dead bolt. It was hard to see, but if anyone came in, the hair would fall, hopefully without their noticing, and I would know there had been an intruder. Of course, they could just take the easy way and go in the partially open window by the fire escape, but I preferred to think that my stalker liked to be challenged.

I met Anatoly at the door and leaned in to give him a lingering kiss. "So I guess all that military service taught you something about punctuality."

"Or perhaps I was just eager to be in your company," he countered as he handed me a helmet.

I couldn't stop myself from rolling my eyes. "Or perhaps you're well practiced in the art of bullshit."

Anatoly laughed. "It's actually a course you have to take before becoming licensed as a contractor, B.S. with Style."

"Great," I yelled as Anatoly started the ignition. "I'll try to remember not to trust you."

"And you'll forgive me if I don't remind you of that." The conversation ended at this point as we roared toward the theater.

When we got there we made the requisite purchase at the concession stand before going to find our seats. Anatoly tried to steer me to two empty spots at the end of a row but I pushed him farther towards the center.

"Normally I prefer aisle seats just in case I have to make a quick trip to the ladies' room midfilm," I said. "But this is Hitchcock, so I'll hold it."

Anatoly placed the soda in the cup holder farthest from me before taking off his jacket. "Have you seen this before?"

"I think I've seen everything Hitchcock's made. This is the one where Joan Fontaine marries Cary Grant only to find out after the fact that she can't trust him. I know something about that from my last marriage. A case of life imitating art."

Anatoly was quiet for a moment. "If I remember correctly, Cary Grant turns out to be a good guy in the end. So in this case the fiction seems to be preferable to the reality. Unless,

of course, you're in my position. I'd much rather date a di-
vorced woman than one who is still married."

"Well, aren't we Mr. Morality?"

"Why, are you unconcerned with the marital status of
your dates?"

"No, no, I steer clear of the men with gold bands around
their ring fingers. It's not that I don't empathize with women
who are unwittingly married to lecherous bastards, but I'm
not particularly interested in donating my time, effort and
body in order to open their eyes to the truth." I popped an
overly saturated popcorn kernel in my mouth. "Do you know
that they actually changed the ending of this movie because
the studio didn't want Cary Grant playing a bad guy? The way
it was originally written he ended up killing her. It would
have been better that way. I always like it when the leading
man turns out to be the villain. No one ever expects it."

Anatoly gave me one of his disarming half smiles. "You
do have a dark side, don't you."

I didn't have time to respond. Like Leah I have a few rules
of my own, and one of them is never to talk over a Hitchcock film.

When the movie was over we walked over to the 500
Club, a neighborhood bar a block away from the theater. Well,
Anatoly walked; I floated. So far the evening had been as close
to perfect as it could get. I had a gorgeous guy on my arm,
Hitchcock on the big screen, a big tub of greasy popcorn
and now an alcoholic beverage. We seated ourselves at an intimate little table and I enjoyed a particularly strong martini
while checking out my surroundings. Our fellow patrons
ranged from those who were trying too hard, to others who
weren't trying at all. The result was an appealing atmosphere
that felt open and accepting. It occurred to me that for the
last few hours I hadn't thought about *Sex, Drugs and Murder*
or my psychotic fan. I was actually relaxed. Well, somewhat
relaxed; every ten minutes or so Anatoly would cast me a look

that caused my pulse to race up to a speed that could break the sound barrier, but other than that I was perfectly calm. And his taste in movies... God, maybe the man had relationship potential after all. I could feel him staring at me again. No doubt about it, I wanted him. But Leah was probably right; I should hold out for one more date. I met his gaze and then quickly hunched my shoulders in an attempt to hide the state of my nipples. The guy hadn't even touched me yet—how could I be reacting this way? I decided to take a stab at casual conversation.

"Nobody does suspense like Hitchcock." My pitch was a note too high to be perceived as casual. I took a steadying breath and tried again. "I swear I will spend my entire career aspiring to his creative genius."

Anatoly smiled. "I'm glad you enjoyed it." He reached forward and rested his hand on top of mine. "You look beautiful tonight."

"Really?" I lowered my voice to a husky whisper. "What does it for you? The wrinkled khakis or the helmet hair?"

"The whole package," Anatoly said before pulling me in for a kiss.

I have always believed that you can judge a man's skills as a lover by the way he kisses. If that was true, Anatoly was a sex god. It couldn't have been more than sixty degrees in that bar and I still felt the need to remove my jacket as well as a few other choice pieces of clothing. Leah could afford her rules—she was married. Last time I had sex, Jack hadn't even been conceived yet.

Anatoly released me. "Are you ready to go?"

"Yeah, I guess I'm ready to head out."

"Are you sure?" The goading tone in which he asked the question was unmistakable. "I wouldn't want to rush you."

"Anatoly, do me a favor. Stop being such a smug bastard and let's get out of here before you start pissing me off."

"Got it." He left a few bills on the bar and escorted me out.

On the ride home I rested against Anatoly's back and vi-
sualized how the rest of the evening was going to play out.
Anatoly would bring me to my building. I would ask him
up for a nightcap. A nightcap…was that too cliché? But then
again, who the hell cared if it was cliché or not? The point
was, I would get him to come up to my apartment and, in
so doing, I would be killing two birds with one stone. I
would have a man who was trained in the art of combat ac-
company me inside *and* with any luck I would finally get laid.
Hell, maybe I'd even get him to fix my window for me.

I was so absorbed in my planning that I didn't notice
when Anatoly passed my turn. When he did stop the bike, it
was in front of his place. He paused for me to dismount before parking.

I pulled off my helmet. "What are we doing here?"

Anatoly took off his helmet as well. "We're going up to
my place."

"Really? I don't remember you asking me."

"I didn't have to ask. It's obvious that you wanted to."

I felt my anticipation transform into acute annoyance.
"Uh-huh. And this is the world according to Anatoly?" Really, this was a little egotistical even for him.

"I just call them as I see them."

I smiled and placed a gentle hand against his cheek. "Great.
Then you can tell me what you call it when you see me walking away." I tossed the helmet at him and started toward my
building.

I could hear him calling after me but I had no intention
of turning around. Of all the nerve. I jammed my hands in
my pockets to better protect them from the sting of the damp
cold. Yeah, I had wanted to sleep with him and maybe that
had been obvious from the way I'd responded to his advances, but there was a certain etiquette that needed to be
observed. Maybe things weren't as black-and-white as Leah
liked to paint them, but at least he should have had the cour-

tesy to ask me what I wanted before just bringing me to his place with the expectation of getting screwed. What a schmuck. And I didn't sleep with schmucks any more than I slept with Neanderthals.

The empty streets just fueled my aggravation. If I could just forcefully push by some pedestrians or scream at a honking car I might be able to release some of my mounting frustration. But no, all my Russian Hill neighbors had to be responsible and retire early on Sunday nights, leaving me with nothing to scream at but the stars, and I couldn't even do that thanks to all the fricking fog. I finished the three-block trek downhill and turned the corner onto my street. I squeaked in surprise upon finding myself face-to-chest with Andy.

"Andy." I faltered and checked my watch. "It's 1:00 a.m. What are you doing here? Wait, don't tell me—you're bringing more groceries to Mrs. Murphy."

Andy didn't smile. "I was waiting for you."

"At 1:00 a.m.?" What the hell was going on? My previous vexation was forgotten as hundreds of little alarm bells started going off in my head. But this was Andy. The guy I had once seen crying over a dead pigeon. He wasn't any threat.

"I came after work. I wanted to give you a flower." I looked down at his clenched hand and saw what at one time must have been a daisy. All the petals had been pulled off and the center had been crushed.

I tried to laugh. "So I guess you changed your mind?" I took a step back as he moved forward.

"I saw you get on his motorcycle. He's your boyfriend."

"No, Andy, he's not, he's just a—"

"You're a liar. You kissed him! I saw! I saw! You lied to me!"

This was not okay. I glanced up at the dark windows of the apartment buildings around me. Was he shouting loud enough to wake anybody? Should I scream? But even if I did, how helpful would that be in a city full of people who had become accustomed to hearing the loud ravings of drunks and derelicts? No, it had always been my experience that keeping cool was the best way to handle volatile people. If I could remain calm I could probably calm him down too. After all, this was Andy.

"Andy, I didn't lie to you. Now it's late and I'm tired. I'm going to go home and go to bed. I think it would be a good idea if you did—"

Suddenly I couldn't breathe. This was the moment when I needed to scream, but his hands were too tight around my throat. My back was slammed against the wall of a building. *Go for the eyes.* That's what Dena always said. I reached my hands out, thumbs extended, but I only grazed his cheeks. He was so tall. I don't think I ever really realized how tall he was. I could feel myself being lifted off the ground. I kicked at him but it was useless. Little dots began to float before me, multiplying as they went. I was going to die now. Would everything just go black? How long would it take? Dear God, if I could just have one last breath of air.

And then I was on the ground, and the air I had been deprived of flooded into my lungs with such force that it caused me to hack and convulse. Things still weren't in focus. Andy was on the ground screaming—but who was on top of him?

"What's going on down there? I'm calling the police!" It was a voice from one of the windows above. My vision began to clear and I saw Anatoly. He had his knee in Andy's stomach and was using both hands to bang his head into the pavement.

I began to make sense of what was happening. "Stop!" I screamed. "Pin him, don't kill him! He doesn't know what he's doing!" I crawled to Andy's head and grabbed Anatoly by the shirt. "I'm okay! It's okay! Just pin him!"

Anatoly looked at me. The cool calculation in his eyes made me recoil. He looked down at Andy, who was now clinging on to consciousness and whimpering like an injured child. "She called me retard. I didn't mean to. It's not nice. It's not nice."

The sirens came and the police told us to lie flat against the pavement. Considering our position that was an easy feat to accomplish. For Andy, it wasn't even a choice. At first I thought the dampness against my face was the result of the mist, but as I heard the second set of sirens approaching I realized that it was tears.

In a matter of minutes another squad car arrived and then an ambulance. The police separated the three of us so we could be questioned individually. I don't think Andy was ever able to give them a coherent answer, and it wasn't long before the paramedics loaded him onto the ambulance. A uniformed cop climbed on with him and the vehicle disappeared down the street with its siren blaring. I tried to ignore the pain speaking caused me so I could answer the questions of the blond sergeant standing by my side, but for some reason I was having a hard time making sense of his words. I mumbled something about being cold, and he told me I was in shock. He draped a blanket around my shoulders and helped me into his police car. I heard him say something about taking me to the hospital for an exam and I nodded my consent. I looked out the window and locked eyes with Anatoly who was busy answering the questions of one of the other cops. We didn't break eye contact until the squad car I was in pulled away from the curb and drove off.

Two and a half hours later I was still shaking. I was sitting on the cushioned examination table in a stark hospital room. I had been questioned, a woman had taken pictures of the rapidly forming bruises on my neck and I had been checked for any lingering injuries. Andy was in another room somewhere being nursed back to health so that the waiting policemen could lock him up. I was finding the whole thing impossible to grasp. How could my turning down a date transform a sweet guy into a raving psychopath?

"How you doing?" I looked up to see the curly-haired detective who had questioned me earlier. His lean body resting against the door frame seemed to offer little protection against everything that awaited me outside the room.

"How's Andy?"

The detective gave a rueful laugh. "That's awfully generous of you." He scratched the back of his head and took a few steps forward. "Manning has a hairline fracture in his skull and a minor concussion, but he'll live. No thanks to him, you will too."

I put a protective hand over my throat.

"We weren't formally introduced before. I'm Detective Joe Lorenzo."

I tried to smile but I couldn't find the will to do it. "I don't know what set him off. I made up some excuse when he asked me out, but still…he had always been so nice to me, to everyone."

"Not to everyone—at least not to the woman he recently killed in your neighborhood."

My stomach did a little nauseous flip-flop. "Susan Lee? Are you sure?"

"We took his prints." Lorenzo lowered himself onto the doctor's stool. "They're a match to the ones that were all over the crime scene. The doctors don't want us interrogating him yet, but I was able to sneak in a few questions. He's not denying it."

"After Anatoly pulled him off of me he was mumbling something about being called a retard. I've never said anything derogatory to him. Do you suppose that was something she said?"

"Very possible. Manning has frontal lobe damage. That can occasionally result in impulse control problems and violent behavior." Lorenzo crossed his arms and cocked his head to the side. "I just got off the phone with Gorman. He told me that the damage done to your car was treated as a standard vandalism. I'm sorry about that. You understand he was just following procedure."

"You think Andy was the one who tore up my car?"

"Most likely. Infatuated people sometimes do weird stuff."

"Are you going to check the car for his prints?"

"Has it been parked on the street or in a garage?"

"The street. I haven't driven it since it was vandalized."

Lorenzo sighed and pinched the bridge of his nose. "And the window was broken, right? So it wasn't—isn't—locked?"

I let my gaze fall to the speckled linoleum floor. "It didn't seem like a necessary precaution considering the state of my car." I silently cursed myself. I should have called the emergency window-repair place.

"We might dust it in hopes of finding more evidence to support our case, but a lot of time has passed. Theoretically he could have touched your car after the vandalism. A print would be a nice bit of circumstantial evidence, but nothing more."

"What about the prank calls?"

Lorenzo shook his head to indicate he hadn't been informed of that portion of my fun-packed week.

"On Thursday I received a whole bunch of prank calls, at least four. They didn't say anything, just hung up," I explained. "After the fourth one I told the caller that I was married to a cop so he'd better cut it out. That night he called again. I got the weirdest feeling that he knew I was lying about the cop thing."

Lorenzo pulled out a miniature notebook from his pocket and jotted something down. "How many of these calls have you had since Thursday?"

I shook my head. "None. It was just that day."

Lorenzo clicked his pen and returned the notebook to his pocket. "I'll ask the D.A. to put in a request for Andy's phone records, but if your number doesn't show up it won't be worth pursuing further. There's no real need to worry about this. While it would be nice if we could prove that he vandalized your car or called your home, it won't be necessary for a conviction. We have enough now to get him on assault, and we'll probably get him on second-degree murder."

He stretched his long legs into a standing position. "The D.A.'s office will be in touch with you about your testimony, but for now you're free to go. If you want a minor sedative to help you sleep tonight, I'm sure the doctor will prescribe one for you. But you'll probably sleep a lot better now anyway knowing that we got your stalker in custody." He turned to leave.

"Not really, no."

Lorenzo turned back around. "I'm sorry?"

"I won't sleep better and you don't have my stalker."

"Got it. You feel sorry for Manning because of the brain damage." Lorenzo's lips curled into a patronizing smile. "Hey, if you don't want to call him a stalker, then don't. Call him an amorous guy with murderous impulses. The point is, we got him and you're safe."

"You don't get it at all. Andy may be my attacker, but the person who messed up my car and broke into my flat is still out there. Andy's not clever enough to have pulled all that off so smoothly."

Lorenzo's jaw was jutting out a bit now. "Listen, I know you've been through a lot tonight and you're not thinking clearly, but Gorman and his partner aren't at all sure that anyone ever did break into your place. It's also unlikely that a guy who was obsessed with you just happened to try to kill you a day after some mystery person ripped apart your car. That coincidence is just a little too hard to swallow."

"Well, maybe you're just not very good at taking pills. And, for the record. I *am* thinking clearly."

Any softness in Lorenzo's features was now gone. "Good night, Miss Katz. I'll see you at the trial."

I tried to yell after him as he strode out of the room, but I found that the effort was still too painful. I squeezed my eyes closed. None of this made sense. It was obvious that the police were willing to overlook a few inconsistencies in order to wrap everything up neatly. Unfortunately those oversights could cost me my life.

A hot cup of tea, a warm bed and a good cry is what the doctor should have prescribed. Actually, tea spiked with brandy, that's what I needed, but I had no brandy at home and all the liquor stores would be closed. I really wanted to get up and walk out of the examination room but I wasn't able to move. I had almost lost my life to someone I had trusted. So what would this anonymous stalker do to me given the chance?

I was terrified of being alone. Of course, I could call my mother or Leah, but then I would have to tell them what happened, and I definitely wasn't up for any more hysterics. There was Dena and Mary Ann, but they would be only slightly less frantic than my family and they definitely wouldn't be able to hold off on questioning me until the next morning. That went double for Marcus. So alone it was. I accessed my last resources of strength and pushed myself off the table.

When I stepped into the lobby, five microphones were thrust into my face.

"Ms. Katz, can you describe the attack?"

"How long have you known Andrew Manning?"

"Did you have any idea what he was capable of?"

"What do you think should happen to Manning now?"

This was a thousand times worse than any hysterical mother. I fought back the tears stinging my eyes. I sure as hell didn't want to be seen bawling on the morning news. What I wanted to do was tell them all to just go away, but I couldn't trust myself to talk. What a fitting ending to the most horrific night of my life.

I looked from reporter to reporter trying to find any hint that the mob would relent. It was then that I caught sight of Anatoly walking briskly toward the group. When he reached the huddle he pushed his way past the camera crews to my side, and I felt his protective hand find a resting spot beneath my shoulder blades. "Miss Katz is suffering from a severe sore throat due to the attack," Anatoly reported. "She will be able to answer questions after she's had a day or so to rest her voice."

The journalists voiced some protests, but Anatoly maneuvered me through the horde, his hand never leaving my back. I half expected the reporters to block our way, but there was something very authoritative about Anatoly's manner. You kind of got the feeling that no one wanted to mess with him.

Outside the hospital a few cabs were lined up in wait. We sat down in the first one and Anatoly gave the driver my address. "How do you feel?" he asked, addressing me for the first time since our less-than-hospitable exchange hours earlier.

"Like I need to pull the covers over my head and not come out for a week."

"Got it. Is there anything you really need to do this week?"

The flicker of amusement dulled my depression. I regarded him without making eye contact. "I assume the police talked to you?"

"Of course." He propped an arm up against the back of the seat. "There was some question of my using excessive force, but it didn't take long for it to become clear that I was just protecting you."

"Did they tell you about Susan Lee?"

"Yes."

"They say he killed her. And if you hadn't shown up he would have killed me too."

Anatoly raised an eyebrow. "I guess I'm not such an asshole after all."

"No, you're still an asshole. You're just an asshole with really good timing."

Anatoly let out a rich, full laugh. It was contagious; I began giggling along with him despite the pain. It didn't take long before the giggling turned into hysterical laughter. I put one hand on my throat in an attempt to soothe it and the other on my convulsing stomach. Anatoly, who had quieted down, gently pushed a stray curl away from my face and that was all it took. I was sobbing against his shoulder as he silently held me. My mind drifted back to a few days earlier when I had been comforting Andy in a similar manner, and that just made me cry harder.

By the time the cab arrived at my apartment I had begun to pull myself together. "Are you all right?" he stroked my hair and used a thumb to wipe away a stray tear.

"Yeah, I'm okay."

Anatoly looked incredulous.

"Well, it was a pretty stupid question now, wasn't it?" I wiped the remaining tears with the back of my hand and searched my purse for money.

Anatoly beat me to the punch and paid the fare. He got out of the cab and waited as I climbed out after him.

"I'll walk you up to your door."

"Thank you. That would be great." Without speaking we walked up to the third floor. Anatoly stood at the head of the stairs as I stuck my key in the lock. I paused as I summoned the nerve to ask for yet another favor. "I don't suppose you could step in for a minute while I get myself settled?" I asked, keeping my eyes glued to the door.

"I'd love to."

"Don't get the wrong idea, Anatoly."

"I wouldn't dream of it. I've learned my lesson about being too presumptuous."

"Good." I quickly ushered him in. Mr. Katz came out of the bedroom to cajole some cat food out of me, but after seeing Anatoly, changed his mind and quickly retreated. "He doesn't like strangers."

"Smart cat."

"I was going to make myself a cup of tea. Would you like some?"

Anatoly waved his hand in refusal. He sat down on the couch and watched from the living room as I put the kettle on. "Did you know him well?"

"I wouldn't ever have qualified him as a close friend, but I would have felt comfortable vouching for his demure disposition. I guess that means I didn't know him at all, huh?"

"Not necessarily." Anatoly rubbed his eyes and yawned. "The police said he had frontal lobe damage. People with that condition can be very unpredictable. They can come across as relatively stable, well-adjusted individuals and then something happens and they just snap. The brain's mysterious that way."

I waited for the water to boil before sitting down in a chair opposite him. "The police think he's the one who tore up my car."

"Really?" He scratched the stubble on his chin. "I suppose that's possible. What do you think?"

"Possible." I took a sip of my tea. I toyed with the idea of telling Anatoly my real theories. After all, he seemed to want to listen. Maybe he could help. I looked up at Anatoly and noted that he had eased back farther on the sofa and was resting his eyes.

"I'm sorry," I said, glancing at my wall clock that read 2:00 a.m. "You must be exhausted. If you want to go home, I totally understand."

His lids retracted enough to display the red veins surrounding his pupils. "Do you want me to stay?"

I hesitated, unsure of what he was asking.

"Don't worry. I realize the mood right now is not one of romance. If I stay I'll sleep on the couch, but after everything you've gone through tonight, I thought you might not want to be alone."

Melt. Once again Anatoly had gone through an apparent metamorphosis. That, or I was talking to the only man in the world who was able to balance being an egotistical jerk with being exceptionally insightful and considerate.

"If you're sure you don't mind. You wouldn't have to stay on the couch. I have an extra bedroom with a fold-out futon."

Anatoly nodded. "That sounds perfect."

I got up to make the bed for him. Maybe I would tell him about all the other stuff tomorrow. Right now it was time to sleep.

 **CHAPTER 9**

"No one can make you doubt yourself more than the people who claim to believe in you most."

—*Sex, Drugs and Murder*

I woke up at eleven, which wasn't nearly late enough considering I hadn't turned the lights off until 4:30 a.m. But Mr. Katz was making the possibility of further sleep an unreachable goal due to his repeated attempts to curl up on my head.

I reluctantly rolled out of bed and examined myself in the mirror. The bruises on my neck had come to resemble monstrously large hickeys. Great. Hopefully it would be cold today, because I was definitely wearing a turtleneck. For now I settled for a terry robe over my cotton pj's. When I got to the kitchen I found Anatoly in the living room jamming his feet into his socks and boots.

"Going somewhere?"

"I didn't realize you were up." Anatoly looked up from his laces. "My God, you look like you've been making out with a vampire."

"Gee, thanks for the compliment, but sorry, vampires are Dena's thing."

Anatoly looked confused.

"Forget it, never mind. Do you want some coffee?" I went into the kitchen and pulled out some whole beans from the freezer.

"I don't have time right now." He threw on his jacket before giving me his full attention. "But I'd love to take a rain check."

"Have an appointment with a potential client?"

"You got it."

I poured the beans into the grinder. "I guess that means more java for me."

"It's nice to know you do drink normal coffee and not just those whipped-cream-sugar drinks they serve at Starbucks."

"Say it with me. Caramel. Brownie. Frappuccino. Not a milk shake, not a whipped-cream-sugar drink, a Caramel Brownie Frappuccino."

"Right. I'll call you later, okay?" He brushed his lips against my forehead, then started to leave.

"Anatoly?"

He stopped. "Yeah?"

"Thanks for saving my life. That was really nice of you."

He came back and gave me a more heated kiss. "Anytime." And he was gone.

Mr. Katz walked purposefully across the living room, reclaiming his space now that our guest had left. I realized I had felt so safe with Anatoly there.

Maybe Detective Lorenzo had been right. It was a pretty big coincidence that Andy had tried to kill me one day after the whole car thing. Still, it didn't make sense. It was highly possible that Andy had seen me driving around the block looking for parking. He might have been able to recognize my car. But the sequence of events was off. The Acura had been vandalized on Friday night or Saturday morning. I had turned Andy down for a date on Saturday night. Plus, he hadn't really gotten mad at me until he had seen me with Anatoly on Sunday night. So what was the motive for messing up my car? And even if he had read my books, and I had my doubts about that, Andy didn't strike me as anywhere near detail oriented enough to pull off a copycat crime. Of course, it was true that the crime he would be copying was fictional and described detail-for-detail in print.

Then there was the glass and the book. I was sure that someone had been in my apartment. More to the point, they wanted me to know they had been here. They had taken great pains to be obvious enough to spook me, but subtle enough to give me nothing of substance to take to the police. It was genius. Andy wasn't a genius.

I poured the ground beans into the espresso machine. Assuming the stalker wasn't Andy, the person who did these things hadn't done anything violent. Whoever was responsible could just be pulling a head trip. I had no reason to believe otherwise at this point. It was certainly a better possibility than the alternative.

By the time I was done with my coffee, five reporters had called for quotes. I left my answering machine in charge of fielding questions and went to submerse myself in a hot bath. When I got out of the tub there were seven more messages. In addition to calls from reporters, I was also getting calls from every acquaintance that had access to my number. The story about Andy had been on the morning news shows and apparently the entire world, along with a few alien life-forms, had been watching. My mother had seen the report, become hysterical and called my sister. Then Leah had become hysterical and they had decided the best way to handle their mutual hysteria was to call me on a three-way conference call so I could have the pleasure of calming them down simultaneously. Then I got to listen to them berate me for not phoning them immediately. They understood why I might not want to face my friends right now, but they were family.

Then Dena called, who was as close to hysterical as Dena got. Not to mention pissed. She understood why I might not want to deal with my crazy family right now, but how could I not call her? Then came the call from Marcus who had not seen the report himself but had heard about it from Donato, and was deeply hurt to have gotten the news thirdhand. By the time I was done talking to Mary Ann I found myself questioning whether surviving the attack was really such a good thing.

By two o'clock I decided I needed to get out of the apartment. Unfortunately, that didn't work out so well either, since the first person I bumped into was Alice, who was, of course, hysterical.

I retreated back into my home, double-locked the door— an act provoked more from fear of my loved ones than of any stalker—turned the phone's ringer off and turned the volume on the answering machine to its lowest setting.

I located my cat resting by the bay window. "That's what I like about you, Mr. Katz. You know when to shut up." Mr. Katz just continued lounging, thus proving my point.

I stood in the middle of my living room and tried to figure out how to get through the day with my sanity intact. I went over to the bookcase and ran my fingers over the novels on the top shelf. My hand stopped on *Sex, Drugs and Murder*. I hadn't looked at the book since I had taken it back from the police station and I hadn't read it since its completion. I felt the raised print on the cover. Mr. Katz jumped off the windowsill. "I'm going to freak myself out now, so do you mind staying here and keeping me company?"

He got up and strolled to the bedroom.

"Thanks a lot. See if I comfort you if you're ever stalked by a Doberman." I sat down on my love seat and tucked my feet under me. It was time to refresh my memory.

By 7:00 p.m. Mr. Katz had decided to be the supportive roommate after all and was curled up on my lap. I hadn't moved from my chair except for two bathroom breaks and to prepare dinner for my insistent pet. I had fought the temptation to skim the familiar chapters in fear of missing an important detail. There was no longer any doubt in my mind that the break-ins and vandalism I had been subjected to were taken right out of my novel. I had included two murders in the book. There was the porn star who was raped and beaten to death with a golf club, and then there was the murder of Kittie, who was killed by four strikes of a hatchet, two to her back, one to the back of her head and one directly over her heart.

Had I written that? Was I that sick? Mr. Katz purred and rubbed his head against my stomach. I turned back to the description of Kittie's death.

Someone buzzed my apartment. I jumped to my feet, sending Mr. Katz crashing to the floor. "Sorry, sweetie. I'm just a little on edge. Of course, there's nothing to really worry about. I mean, murderers don't ring buzzers, right?"

Mr. Katz just glared at me, no longer in the mood to be comforting.

I tried to shake the tension out of my arms before pressing the intercom. "Who's there?"

"Your friends," Dena said. "You know, the ones you don't care enough about to call after life-altering experiences."

I pressed my forehead against the wall and buzzed them in. I had totally forgotten that tonight was movie night.

Upon entering, Mary Ann threw her arms around me, almost knocking me off balance. "I'm so glad you're okay," she gushed. "All I could think about today was what I would have done if something had happened to you. You're one of my best friends. You're family, Sophie."

"Okay, she's fine, so drop the dramatics." Dena was studying the pattern on my rug with an intensity that would suggest she hadn't seen it fifty million times before.

I went over and gave her a hug, as well.

"Don't make me cry, Sophie," she said after giving me a little squeeze. "And don't ever do anything like that again, got it?"

"Okay, I promise to never again put my neck in the hands of a homicidal mental patient."

Dena pulled back and patted my arm. "That's my girl."

"I'll go make some popcorn." I took Mary Ann's coat and hung it on a rack by the door. "What are we watching tonight?"

Mary Ann pulled a video out of her tote bag. "I got *The Object of My Affection* with Jennifer Aniston. It's a little old, but it's supposed to be great."

Dena fell onto the love seat. "God help us all."

"Be nice." I scanned the synopsis before handing it back. "This is perfect. Light, silly and brainless."

"Oh no, it's not brainless. It's supposed to be really thought-provoking."

"Thought-provoking? Are you serious?" Dena snatched the video from Mary Ann. "Look at the photos on the back. They're wearing pastel, for God's sake."

"It's controversial."

"How exactly is Jennifer Aniston controversial?"

"She's in love with a gay man. Homosexuality is controversial."

"Oh, really? And where exactly do you live again? Because in the city that I live in, homosexuality is about as controversial as kissing on the first date."

"Not everyone lives in San Francisco. Just because this movie didn't meet with resistance here doesn't mean that it didn't raise a few eyebrows in Jackson, Mississippi."

"Oooh, it raised eyebrows. And when was that—like five years ago." Dena clapped a hand over her heart. "Please. Is there any explicit gay sex in this?"

"No! They wouldn't!" She scrutinized the cover for something to confirm her protest. Jennifer in her evening gown and upswept hairdo said it all. Mary Ann sighed in relief.

"Then it's not controversial." Dena relaxed back into the pillows.

I was trying to block them out so I could count the seconds between pops. Nothing's worse than a bag of burnt Orville Redenbacher's.

"So, speaking of first-date kisses and explicit sex," Dena said, "how was your date with Anatoly?"

Mary Ann quit pouting and leaned on the counter dividing the kitchen from the living area.

I stopped the timer on the microwave. "It was pretty fun. I have mixed feelings about how it ended. We got in a little tiff and then Andy tried to kill me—that sucked. But Anatoly did save my life, so the evening wasn't a total loss."

"That's right—they said on the news that he was the one to rescue you." Dena plucked a piece of lint from her brown Lycra top. "Looks like you got yourself a regular knight in shining armor. To be honest, I'm kind of surprised that the two of you didn't end up at his place, considering how hot and heavy you were at the 500 Club."

"How did you know we were at the 500 Club?"

"Jason was there too. He said he waved at you but you were a little preoccupied making out with your Russian playmate."

That's the great thing about my coloring, no one can ever tell when I'm blushing. "We just kissed."

"Yeah, some kiss. Jason said that it looked like the two of you were ready to do it right there on the bar."

"Oh, for God's sake, so we made out in a bar. So what? Aren't you the one who was just arguing that nothing short of gay pornography could be qualified as controversial? Don't tell me you're shocked by a little public-kissing session."

"Shocked, no. Maybe a little titillated."

"Dena!" Mary Ann gasped. I peeked in her direction, her blush I could see.

"What? Sophie was being fondled by a guy, who, by her

description, would have turned on Mother Teresa, and you don't want to hear the juicy details?"

"I was not being fondled, I was being kissed. How is it that Jason seems to show up every time I'm with Anatoly, anyway? Is he following me or—" Oh, shit.

"Are you okay?" Mary Ann asked.

"Yeah, you look like you swallowed a lemon."

I tried to keep my hands steady as I poured the popcorn into a bowl. "Dena, what do you know about Jason?"

"What do I know about him? Well, I know he's a little odd...."

Mary Ann shook her head. "Understatement."

Dena ignored her. "He's also very sweet and really intelligent, and here's the most important part...he's fucking awesome in the sack. I'm telling you, that vampire can bite me anytime, anywhere."

I spoke up before Mary Ann could start another battle over morality versus sexual freedom. "Listen, Dena, do you remember the stuff I told you about the hang-ups and the broken glass in my kitchen?"

"Dena was telling me about that. That is so bizarre."

"Well, it gets more so." I filled them in on the details of what had happened to my car and the misplaced book.

By the time I finished, Dena was on her feet. "Jesus Christ, Sophie, that can't be a coincidence."

"I agree, but the police thought I was being paranoid. They think that Andy was the one who messed up my car, and they don't think anyone ever broke into my apartment."

"I don't think so." Dena shook her head with an air of impatience. "Anyone who keeps their novels in alphabetical order by author's last name and then chronological order by publishing date isn't going to inadvertently put a book in sideways. And the stuff about the car, well, that's *exactly* what happened to Kittie's car. That doesn't sound like the work of some crazed guy with brain damage."

"Gosh, you know what this reminds me of?" Mary Ann asked. "That poor Tolsky guy who died in the exact same way as the character in his movie. Oh, or that rap singer JJ Money, shot in both kneecaps and the head, just like in his single." Mary Ann stuffed another handful of popcorn in her mouth, temporarily oblivious to the shock that had blanched both my features and Dena's.

"You don't think there's a connection…" This was too out there. What in God's name had I gotten myself into?

"Could be," Dena said. "Some psycho serial killer who thinks it's funny to murder people in the same way they've described someone else being killed through their works. What did that note say? 'You reap what you sow'?"

I stood up and started pacing. "But Tolsky lived in L.A. and JJ Money in New York. The same guy couldn't have killed both of them."

"Come on, Sophie. Ever hear of air travel?" Dena tapped her three-inch heel against the floor. "Besides, it's not like they were killed on the same day. There were some three months between their deaths."

"But Tolsky wasn't murdered, remember?" I put my shaking hands in my jean-pockets. "It was a suicide. And it wasn't like he was shot at close range or jumped out a window, he slit his wrists. How many people kill someone by slitting their wrists?" Yesterday I would have said that Tolsky's death had a lot of suspicious overtones, but not now. Now, I was unwilling to admit that Tolsky's passing could be the result of anything other than a suicide. Entertaining other possibilities was way too terrifying. "Plus, if there were any signs that it had been a murder, the police would have picked up on it and caught his killer by now. It was a high-profile case."

Dena scoffed. "You know, for a mystery writer you certainly are naive about the judicial system. Lots of high-profile cases get fucked up. What ever happened to Jimmy Hoffa? What about JFK? He was pretty high profile, dontcha think? Do you really believe that he was shot with a magic bullet? I don't think so. Kennedy's killer is out there somewhere right now enjoying a Heineken."

Mary Ann nearly spilled the bowl of popcorn as she jumped up. "Oh. My, God. Are you saying that the same guy who shot JFK broke into Sophie's car?"

The room went silent for a moment. Dena dug her nails into her palm, and I studied the hole in my jeans. "Um, no Mary Ann," I managed to say. "I think we can safely rule that possibility out."

"Thank goodness for that." She lowered herself back into her seat and started back into the popcorn.

Dena quietly counted to ten.

I sat down next to Mary Ann. "I think what Dena meant is that the police aren't always right. They don't always catch the bad guys. And to that end, I've got to admit she has a point. With two crimes being committed so far apart and over such a long period of time, it's not a stretch to think that the police would have missed the connection." Shit, I had just acknowledged the possibility. "Of course there might not be a connection but…"

"But then again, there might," Dena finished. "Sophie, you really need to talk to the police about this."

"Are you kidding? Didn't you just hear me tell you that the police think I'm a nutcase? One of them came right out and asked me if I took drugs. And now you want me to go to them and tell them not only that I think someone is stalking me but that I think my stalker is the criminal mastermind who is responsible for the death of one of Hollywood's most famous producers and everybody's favorite hip-hop artist? They'll have me committed or lock me in rehab, or both, if the state feels like funding it. No, if I'm going to the cops again I need to have something more concrete than paranoid speculation. I'm gonna have to go to them with a suspect."

"Okay, so who's your suspect? I know we've ruled Oswald out."

How exactly should I phrase it? I gave Dena a sideways glance. Direct. Dena would expect me to be direct. "I hate to say this, Dena, but what about Jason?"

She looked like I had just punched her in the stomach. "The police are right. You are on drugs. Jason is completely harmless. He couldn't hurt a fucking fly."

"Oh, give me a break, Dena," I countered. "He's a self-proclaimed vampire."

"All right already, I admit it, he's a little different, but it's all a game, Sophie. He knows that. He told you that."

"Yeah, he also told me he wanted to be a real vampire. The man is waiting for Dracula to enter him into his coven."

"Okay, maybe if JJ Money had his blood drained out of him I'd consider the possibility. But that's not what happened, is it? How many vampires use Smith & Wessons?"

"But the blood was drained from Tolsky's body, wasn't it? Besides we just established that Jason is sort of a vampire-in-training. Maybe he's trying to prove himself worthy of the privilege. Isn't that part of the folklore?"

Dena hesitated. "I thought that was werewolves."

"Werewolves? Nobody wants to be a werewolf."

"I don't remember any of this stuff being in that movie with Tom Cruise," Mary Ann added before taking another handful of popcorn.

"No, the recent movies have been taken from modern interpretations of the legend," Dena said. "I'm pretty sure the whole proving-yourself-worthy crap came from the medieval stuff."

"I'll get the encyclopedia." I started to go to my office but stopped myself. "Oh, this is stupid. Who cares which supernatural creature did what in which book? The point is, your boyfriend is completely insane. You just started dating him, you don't know what he's capable of, *and* he's from Southern California."

"Having the bad taste to wear L.A. Gear and inject yourself with silicone doesn't make you more capable of murder than the rest of the population. Besides, Jason doesn't do either of those things. His worst offense is an overly amorous attachment to his cell phone."

"You're missing my point, Dena. Tolsky was from Los Angeles. As in Southern California."

"So? L.A. County is bigger than most countries! Besides, JJ Money lived and died in New York City and Jason didn't live in New York. But I can think of someone who has."

"Who?" Mary Ann's voice was muffled by all the popcorn.

Dena sat down and rested her elbows on her knees. "Oh, I don't know, perhaps a cocktail will help jog my memory. Anybody else in the mood for a…White Russian?"

"Oh, no!" I put my hand out, as if that would somehow block the accusation. "It's not Anatoly. He's one of the good guys. He saved my life. He's a perfectly stable, normal, sane guy."

"What does he do?" Mary Ann asked.

"He's a contractor."

"A contractor?" Dena pressed her palms into her forehead. "Sophie, everyone knows contractors are some of the most unethical people on the planet."

"Oh, goody." I put my arm around Mary Ann. "It's Morality 101 taught by Dena Lopiano, the woman who sells us edible undies."

"Knock it off and just think about it. A contractor might know how to break into this place."

"Anyone could break into my place, Dena. My fucking window won't close! The man is not a killer. I would know."

"The way you knew about Andy?"

"That was a little different. I never really knew Andy. My only contact with him was when he was bagging my groceries."

"Yeah, Anatoly, on the other hand, is bagging you. And we all know that men never hurt the women they sleep with, right?"

"I would know if I was dating a murderer. Do you really think I'm such a poor judge of character that I'd miss something like that?"

"Well, that's obviously what you think of me."

"No, I think you're an excellent judge of character. You like to date weirdos and you never fail to find men whose personalities fit the profile."

"That's it. I'm out of here. Mary Ann, are you coming or what?"

"But we haven't even watched the movie." Mary Ann was the only one in the room who remembered there was a movie.

"They all live happily ever after. Come on, if you want a ride home you'd better get your stuff together."

Mary Ann gave a little squeak of protest but tucked the video under her arm anyway. She took my hand firmly in hers. "I think your new boyfriend sounds nice. Not psychotic at all."

"Thank you."

"Can we go now?"

Mary Ann collected her bag and coat with exaggerated slowness in a deliberate attempt to tick Dena off. "Does he live nearby?"

"Just three blocks away."

Dena froze with one arm in her leather jacket. "Sophie, you said Anatoly went to the police station with you when you reported the car break-in. Did he meet you at the apartment?"

"No, he met me at the car. It was parked in front of his place." I shouldn't have said that. Now I had demonstrated that Anatoly had opportunity.

"Jesus, Sophie. I'm serious…"

"Just keep your boyfriend away from me and I'll be fine."

"I guess it's true what they say. Denial ain't just a river in Egypt." Dena held the door open for Mary Ann. "Just be sure to lock this after we leave and keep the phone by your bed. Oh, and if you plan on having Anatoly over, you might want to take a tip from Sharon Stone and keep an ice pick there as well."

I hurled a pillow from the couch at her and it landed quietly against the just-closed door, leaving me with a burning desire to throw something of greater substance. Something breakable would be good.

Mr. Katz cowered under the coffee table.

"Don't worry. I'll restrain myself. No more throwing." I gently coaxed the cat out into the open before picking him up and cuddling him in my arms.

It wasn't Anatoly. I would know. I would feel it. Yes, there were a lot of coincidences, but that's all they were. Lots of people moved to Russian Hill. It was a beautiful place to live. The fact that my car was vandalized while parked in front of his apartment made him even less of a suspect. Why would anyone with half a brain be that obvious? So there were a few chance encounters: Starbucks, the art opening…it was the night of the art opening that I had found the broken glass. Anatoly had arrived at the opening late, later than I had. What the hell did he do with his days, anyway? He wasn't really working, and he was so vague about his business. And then there was his friend in L.A. whom he had spoken of, the one who wasn't there anymore. I flashed back to my first encounter with Anatoly. What had he said about the Times article concerning J.J. Money's death?

The basic premise is the same, reaping what you sow and all that.

It took me a moment to realize that the pain in my chest was at least partially the result of Mr. Katz's claws digging in. I dropped him to the floor and checked the damage to my shirt. Anatoly was innocent. I was sure of it. Dena was just trying to deflect attention away from the whacko she was dating.

Mr. Katz purred and nuzzled my feet.

"Oh sure, try to sweet-talk me now. Come on, let's get ready for bed." I ushered him into the bedroom.

But not before checking the locks and taking the phone with me.

CHAPTER 10

"There was a con artist amongst her acquaintances. The challenge was going to be figuring out who that person was."

—*Sex, Drugs and Murder*

"She just wouldn't let up," I said. Marcus massaged a mango-scented creamy substance into my scalp. "I mean, she's dating a creature of the night and she accuses the guy I'm dating of being suspicious?"

"Head back."

I raised my voice so it could be heard over the stream of water working through my hair. "She's never even met Anatoly. I *have* met Jason, and let me tell you something, of the two of them Jason is definitely the more likely suspect."

"Up."

I relocated to a chair in front of a mirror. "I look like a drowned rat."

"Uh-oh, that sounds like an attempted murder charge ready to happen."

"Not funny."

"No, what's funny is you and Dena getting all worked up over nothing."

"Nothing?" I whipped around to confront him. "My life could be in danger and you call that nothing?"

"Do you want me to massacre your hair?"

"No."

"Then you'd best be turning that sassy little head of yours back around and stay still."

I pushed my lower lip out but did as I was told. After all, how would it look if I was murdered with a bad haircut?

"Honey, I'd die if anything ever happened to my favorite client." He blew me a kiss in the mirror. "But could you run the part about the misplaced book equating to a sinister death threat by me again, 'cause that's where I get lost."

"It's not just the book, it's—"

"The vandalized car, and Andy couldn't have done that, right? The man just tried to kill you, why would he want to hurt your car? Oh, oh, wait, you were talking about the glass your cat—I'm sorry—your psycho-killer-maniac man knocked over."

"There was the note too," I reminded him. "Or do you think that Mr. Katz has suddenly become literate."

"Okay, the note's kinda creepy, but honey, let's be real. Six months ago, JJ Money was shot in New York, and I do believe that homeboy they've arrested has been convicted by a jury."

"Juries have been known to be wrong."

"Uh-huh, and you never are. Now let's look at Mr. Hollywood. Slit wrists in the bathtub. No sign of struggle, no sign of forced entry, long history of alcoholism and depression, okay?"

"It wasn't suicide, Marcus."

"Mmm, well the L.A.P.D., those would be the boys in the cute uniforms who are actually *trained* to solve crimes, they have a different line. I'm your number-one fan, Soph, but writing about fictional criminals does not make you an expert on the real thing."

"What's your point, Marcus?"

"My point is that the real experts have found nothing to connect Tolsky and JJ Money's deaths, and certainly nothing to connect them to your messed-up car. So isn't it possible that you're overreacting just a smidge, sweetie? Not that I blame you. After what happened with Andy you're entitled to be more paranoid than McCarthy, but you need to be thinking about the possibility that neither of the men that you and Dena are dating, is a serial killer."

"But, Marcus, my car was vandalized in the exact same way Kittie's car was vandalized in—"

"In *Sex, Drugs and Murder*. Okay, I know the man had brain damage, but Andy did know how to read, didn't he?"

"It wasn't Andy."

Marcus sighed and swiveled the chair to the right. "Honey, you've been through hell, but now your little writer's mind has gotten carried away. Even if Andy wasn't responsible for all the weird stuff you've been going through, and I personally think that he was, a prank call, a broken glass and a vandalized car do not a murder plot make. Particularly if that car was vandalized while parked overnight on the streets of San Francisco by some chick too cheap to pay for a spot in a garage two blocks away."

"Do I give you shit about your parking tickets?"

"All the time, but I think you're missing my point."

I chewed on my lip as Marcus continued to snip away. His arguments did have a certain undeniable logic to them.

He ran his fingers through my dark brown mop. "Here's the thing, you may have had the opportunity to converse with her latest stud muffin, but Dena's the one who's been doing the pillow talk with him and she's in a better position to say what he is or is not capable of. On the other hand, Dena's never met your new plaything. All she knows is what you told her, and some of that does make him sound a little sketchy."

"He didn't do it, Marcus."

"Down, girl, I didn't say he did. Like Dena, I'm sure you know what your man would or wouldn't do, but what I'm getting at here is that Dena's biggest offense is acting like an overly concerned friend."

"So you're saying I may have been a tad hard on her."

"Gold star."

"I guess I should call her?"

"I guess you should."

I scrunched up my face. I hated admitting I was wrong. I started to bend forward so I could get my cell phone out of my purse, but Marcus pulled me back. "Make amends later, now we blow-dry. If we wait, you'll frizz."

"Oh, well, I wouldn't want to frizz."

I spent the next fifteen minutes getting my head decorated with curlers of various shades and sizes and the following forty sweating under the dryer. When I was done, Marcus held up a hand mirror in back of me so I could examine all angles. "Tell me I'm brilliant."

"You're brilliant, Marcus." I shook my head from side to side… God, I love it when it moves. "It looks beautiful, as it always does after you're through with it." Tomorrow I would spend two hours in front of the mirror in a fruitless effort to recreate the look he had just given me, but for the next two hours I would be gorgeous. "Stay with me while I call Dena?"

"Of course. What kind of friend would I be if I didn't stand by and hold your hand while you grovel?"

"You're just so sweet." I pulled my phone out and pressed five to speed dial the number to Dena's store.

"Guilty Pleasures, how can we make you smile?"

"Dena, it's me." I looked up at Marcus, who had become distracted. Donato had just walked in.

"Hi…I…I'm surprised you called."

"Yeah, well, I've been thinking about last night." I tried to grab at Marcus's shirt to hold him back, but he smacked my hand away and went to meet Donato. So much for watching me grovel.

"I've been thinking about it too. I'm..." Dena hesitated before continuing. "I'm sorry."

"You're sorry? I'm the one who was wrong! I totally attacked your boyfriend. I accused him of being a psychopath."

"And I accused Anatoly of the same thing, but you had reason to be paranoid and irrational—you're the one that was almost killed. I just got defensive because, well, because that's what I do. You know me, I can never just let things slide."

"I'm not sure anyone would have let that one slide." I tried to give Marcus a thumbs-up sign but he was all the way across the room running his hands through Donato's hair. Somehow his interest seemed more than professional.

"So we're good?"

I relaxed back into the swivel chair. "We're good."

"Great, because we have some celebrating to do."

"What are we celebrating?"

"Your not being killed, for one."

"Oh, yeah, that's a good one." I brushed a stray hair off my jeans. "Nothing too wild, though. I've had enough excitement in the last week to hold me over for the rest of the decade. Although...Marcus did just do my hair, so I should probably be seen in public before I destroy it."

"How about a little private bitch session in the park followed by dinner out?"

"You mean..."

"Yep, Bitches' Circle. I can be there by four. I'll bring the wine."

"God, we haven't been there in forever." I went over to the coatrack to grab my jacket. "Maybe afterward we could get a bite to eat at P.J.'s Oyster Bed?"

"Oysters Rockefeller for everybody. So did Marcus do that cool curly style again?"

"Mmm-hmm." I pressed a curl against my head and watched it spring back to life.

"I think if I ever grow my hair out I'm going to get a perm. Jason's standing next to me and he's nodding his head in agreement."

Oh, right, like she was going to keep Jason around long enough for him to see her hair grow out. "You have time to decide. Since you have company, I won't keep you. I'll see you at four."

"On the dot."

I hung up and interrupted the little moment that Donato and Marcus seemed to be sharing. "Hey, Donato, good to see you."

"And you. I heard about your ordeal. I am so glad to see you are safe."

Marcus took a reluctant step back from Donato to include me. "You're smiling, so I assume that means you and Dena made nice."

"We're meeting at the Bitches' Circle at four. She's bringing the drinks."

"If you're going out afterward you should change—that shirt has a coffee stain on it. And don't let her out-sexy you—you're the diva." Marcus got a mischievous glint in his eye and reached out to play with Donato's hair again. "Speaking of sexy, the salon's owner is on vacation, which means that her upstairs office is all empty right now and she does have the comfiest couch…."

"Okay, well, I'd love to stay and chat but…you two are completely not listening to me."

"Huh?"

"Bye, Marcus. Bye, Donato. Have fun defacing the boss's office." It was a good thing Marcus couldn't procreate. The world would have a population crisis of apocalyptic proportions.

I spent the rest of the day doing mundane things like grocery shopping and renting a car. My insurance had agreed to spring for a medium-size rental while they assessed the damage, but I decided to upgrade to a large cherry-red Mustang convertible. The mental image I had of myself cruising down the streets in some hot little outfit with the wind whipping through my now split-end-free hair was just too tantalizing to resist. Of course, this was San Francisco, so I'd have to throw a parka over the hot little outfit, and for the first day I'd have to wear a scarf on my head because no way in hell was I going to put my new hairstyle in jeopardy, but other than that the image would be complete.

I was driving along the harbor in the Marina district feeling happy, glamorous and cold when my cell phone started playing *"Frère Jacques."* I fumbled around in my purse for it before pressing it to my ear. *"Bonjour, c'est Sophie."*

"English is still the official national language, right?" Anatoly asked.

"What, you're the only one who can be bilingual? I may not have lived in three different countries, but I'm not completely unworldly."

"Right. When you answer the phone in French you're supposed to say 'allo,' not 'bonjour.'"

"Did you call for a reason?"

His laughter was cut up by the static on the line. "As a matter of fact, I called for two reasons. One was to find out how you're doing."

"Well, let's see. Thanks to Marcus, my usual frizz has been replaced by some lovely curls, I rented a pretty new car and at the present moment no one is trying to kill me, so I guess I'm just ducky."

"Your throat feels better?"

"I was just getting ready to belt out the score from *Les Mis.*"

"Not that I don't want to hear what I'm sure would be a very original rendition of the musical, but for the sake of expediency, let's cut to my second question—what are you doing tonight?"

What did I want to do tonight? Let's see, I could strip him down, throw him on my bed, or vice versa… Shit, what was I thinking? "I'm meeting my friend Dena at the park."

"I'm sorry, Sophie, but I can barely hear you."

I pulled back the phone and looked at the screen. It had been days since I had recharged the thing and I probably had all of three minutes before it died on me. "I said I'm going to meet my friend in the Botanical Gardens. We're going to make like Snow White and feed the squirrels among the redwoods. We're very earthy that way."

"Ah, I can hear you a little better. So what's the game plan when you're done with the tree-hugging stuff? You can't stay in the park all night."

"We're going out to dinner afterward."

"You're not putting me off, are you?"

No, I'm trying to get it on. "Anatoly, I would really like to see you, tomorrow. I just can't do it tonight."

I could make out some grumbling on the other end of the line and it took him a good thirty seconds to come back with an intelligible response. "Does seven o'clock dinner tomorrow work for you?"

"Seven o'clock is beautiful."

"Great, I'll meet you at your place. And, Sophie?"

"Mmm?"

"Don't overdo the Snow White stuff. I see you more in the role of Catwoman."

"You mean like from *Batman?*"

"That's the one."

"Huh. Catwoman was sexy."

"Yes, she was."

"Right, well, just keep in mind that I have to be much further into a relationship before I'll put on a leather catsuit for a guy."

"I'm very disappointed, to say the least. I'll see you tomorrow."

"Ciao." I hung up the phone and threw it on the adjacent passenger seat. Two seconds later it rang again. I giggled to myself, the man wanted me bad. I picked up the phone without checking the caller ID.

"Allo, c'est Sophie."

"Sophie? Is that you? What's with the French already?" Shit. "Hi, Mama."

"So it is you. It's been so long since you called that I've forgotten what you sound like."

"You called yesterday, Mama, and I called you just a week before that."

"We live right here in the same city and you have to wait seven days to call me? And how long has it been since I've seen you already? Two months? Three?"

"Three weeks, Mama."

"Three weeks! Wars have been fought and won in three weeks."

I could feel another headache coming on. "Mama, I'm driving, and it's not safe to talk and drive, so if you don't mind getting to the point...."

"You can't pull over for half a minute to talk to your mother who you haven't seen in almost a month?"

Too bad I had a headache. Otherwise I could give in to the temptation to bang my head into the steering wheel. "What can I do for you, Mama?"

"I have a bladder infection."

"Oh, I'm, um, sorry. You know, you should get some rest. Why don't you hang up the phone, get in bed and take care of yourself."

"Don't be ridiculous. I don't need sleep, I need medicine. The shul's ladies senior group is coming over to eat and kibitz and I won't have time to pick up the prescription, so I need you to. Dr. Silverman already called it in. You know the pharmacy I go to."

"Mama, I can't. I'm supposed to meet Dena in forty-five

minutes, and if I go to the pharmacy I'll be more than half an hour late. Can't Leah do it?"

"I should ask her to leave Bob and little Jack when they're both sick with the flu?"

The flu. I had to hand it to Leah, that was quick thinking. "Mama, I just can't."

"I understand, dearie. You go have fun with your friends. So I go another day without my medication. God willing the infection won't get worse. One more day won't kill me. I hope."

"Your bladder infection is not fatal, Mama."

"So you're a doctor now? My doctor, the one with the medical degree, he says it can be fatal."

"Dr. Silverman diagnosed you and then told you you might die?"

"He didn't say so exactly, but I know how to read between the lines. I can sense these things."

"Mama, I want to help, I really do but…"

"Good, use the key because I won't be able to hear you over the vacuum, and pick up some antacids while you're at it, Ethel is always bringing a new spicy recipe for everyone to taste."

"Wait, that's not what I… Mama? Mama, are you there?" I stared at the now completely battery-dead phone before throwing it down. Damn it all to hell. There was no way I was going to be able to meet Dena anywhere near on time and now I couldn't even call her to tell her. I wasn't too far from her shop. Maybe I could catch her before she left.

I turned down Chestnut Street. Guilty Pleasures was just coming into view when it happened. An SUV pulled out of a spot directly in front of the store, leaving it vacant.

I struggled to hold back the tears of joy. Getting the antibiotic to cure my mother's bladder infection was truly the right thing to do and this was the Lord's way of telling me so. I slid the Mustang into the holy space. A little cry of joy escaped my lips when I saw that there was still twenty minutes left on the meter. This is what it meant to be truly blessed.

Barbie was putting together a display of exotic oils. Today she actually looked like a Puerto Rican Barbie doll. She had styled her hair into a halo of neat thick curls that brushed the shoulders of a cotton-candy pink top that matched her lipstick. Her bottom half was adorned in a black leather micromini and thigh-high boots. Okay, her ensemble still had a few dominatrix accents, but I was pretty sure the pink canceled them out.

She looked up from her project. "I remember you. You're Dena's friend, um…"

"Sophie, right. Is Dena still here?"

"You just missed her."

Missed her? But I was blessed. All right, the Lord works in mysterious ways, I just had to figure out how he wanted me to work this. "Any chance I could use your phone to try and call her?"

"Go for it."

I walked around the counter and dialed Dena's number. As soon as I did, I heard Nokia's version of The Mexican Hat Dance coming from a drawer underneath the register. I pulled it open and glared at Dena's cell.

Barbie smiled. "She always forgets it there."

If this was God's idea of a joke, it wasn't funny. I slammed the drawer shut and rapidly tapped my fingernails on the counter. So what was plan B?

"Really needed her, huh?"

"I was supposed to meet her at Golden Gate Park at four and I'm going to be half an hour late."

"Where in the park?"

"The Botanical Gardens." I could call my mother and tell her I just couldn't do it—that would go over well. On the flipside I couldn't just stand Dena up.

"I can meet her there."

"Sorry?" I refocused on Barbie.

"I could meet her and tell her you're running late. The next salesperson should be here within the next few minutes to relieve me and I was heading over to that part of town anyway. I'm having dinner with my parents in the Inner Sunset. That's why I'm dressed so conservatively."

I eyed the boots and the mini. "Oh, that's asking a lot."

"I don't mind. It really is on my way. Besides, I was planning on asking Dena for a small raise soon, so any little thing I can do to make myself look good helps."

"You really don't mind?"

"Tell me your exact meeting place and I'll be there."

I felt a little weird about using one of Dena's salespeople as my personal messenger service, but it did seem like the only solution. She was certainly willing enough. I described the location of the Bitches' Circle to Barbie. By the time I wrapped up my directions, the next salesperson had come in, and I left to save my mother from the lethal bladder infection.

Traffic was unusually light, so the drive across town took about half the time I had planned for. I picked up the meds and dropped them off with my mother. She was so busy making the house beautiful and completely dust free that I was able to get in and out without being dragged into a lengthy discussion about my marital status.

By four-fifteen I was standing at the entrance of the Botanical Gardens. I felt a little guilty about only being fifteen minutes late. I could have saved Barbie a trip. Walking over dirt paths couldn't have been easy in those boots of hers.

I stepped to the side as a hurried tourist brushed past me. You could always identify the tourists by their insistence on wearing short-sleeved shirts while the rest of us dressed for rain and heavy mists. I turned to watch the man make his speedy retreat. There was something vaguely familiar about him. I shrugged and continued down the path at a leisurely pace. Maybe I had seen him at Walgreens or the like. I should probably be in a rush too, but it was way too pretty a place not to take a moment to stop and smell the flowers and, assuming Barbie did her thing, Dena wouldn't be expecting me for a while. I zipped up my jacket; the cold weather would mean fewer people around to bug us. This was absolutely my favorite location in the world. It was like a little piece of the country right here in the city. I had been to Central Park before. It didn't even compare. Sure, it was beautiful during the change of seasons, but like everywhere else in New York, it still had a very urban feel to it. That's why I loved San Francisco so much. It was the perfect balance between urban and suburban. There was no other city in the world that I would rather live in.

A squirrel scampered down a redwood and paused in the path in front of me. I shook my head in apology. I usually brought peanuts with me, but today I had spent my spare change on my mom's Alka-Seltzer. As I approached the Bitches' Circle I could see enough through the brush to note that someone had fallen asleep on one of the benches. Understandable considering the tranquility of the place— still I couldn't help but be a little irked. Yes, it was a public park but that was my spot. Well, it really didn't matter. After a few swigs of wine, Dena and I would get loud enough to frighten the weary traveler away.

It was then that I noticed the person was wearing a pink top. At least it *would* have been pink if it hadn't been so badly stained with blood.

I stood motionless as the sensation of numb horror rolled through my body. Without really willing myself to do so, I approached the woman.

Barbie wasn't breathing. She was barely recognizable. Little insects had already started to crawl into the large gouges made in her face, chest and stomach. I felt the bile burn my throat and I started backing up. I carelessly tripped on a root sticking out of the ground. The fall jarred me out of my shock-induced daze and suddenly I was running. I was pushing past the bushes and crushing small shrubs as I stumbled over them. There was a botanical nursery no more than fifty feet away, I could get help, they would call the police for me. When I reached it I literally threw myself against the chain-link fence.

"Open up! Please! I need help!"

But the facility was closed for the day. Everyone had left. I heard some rustling in the foliage behind me. A bird? No, it sounded too big for that. A raccoon? *Don't panic, don't panic, just breathe and think.* No one would be stupid enough to hang around the scene of their own crime. The noise had to have been made by an animal. Or maybe a tourist who decided to go off the path. It wasn't the killer. If it was a tourist, maybe he or she could help me. All I needed to do was call out.

I heard the noise again and quickly changed my mind. I ran toward the main entrances. They would be closed up in a matter of minutes and after that the only available exits would be in places much less conspicuous. Less conspicuous was not good.

I got to a more open space. Now there were a few people around. A pasty-skinned man with red dreadlocks was lounging under a tree. A Samoan woman was chatting on a pay phone. A group of teens all wearing heavy jackets and baggy jeans was huddled around the fountain. How would someone look after brutally murdering a young woman? Would they look scared? Crazed? Or would they have the presence of mind to just blend in? I looked over my shoulder just in time to see a man locking up the gates behind me. I ran to his side and grabbed his sleeve through the bars.

"Please help me. She's dead. Oh my God, oh my God…he killed her, she's dead."

The man narrowed his eyes. "You know it's a felony to drop acid in a public park."

"What? No, listen to me, there is a woman on one of your park benches that has been hacked up with an ax or something."

"Okay now, why don't you just calm down...."

"*You* fucking calm down! Oh shit, this isn't happening. I'm the one who sent her here and now she's dead. Barbie's dead."

"Oh no, whatever will happen to poor Ken."

Without even thinking about it I moved my hand from the sleeve to the collar of the city worker's shirt and yanked him against the gate. "Listen, asshole, a woman has just been killed and is lying on a park bench some sixty yards away. Either you call the police now or I will hurt you, got it?"

"I'll call the cops."

"Good idea." I released him and watched as he retreated into a trailer that I assumed was used as an office. I slid down to the ground and pulled my knees up to my chest. This couldn't be happening. Andy had been arrested. I had just come to accept that the majority of my fears had been based on nothing but an overactive imagination. And now Barbie was dead. She had styled her shoulder-length dark hair in a manner similar to the style Marcus had given me just hours ago, gone to my hang-out spot and been murdered. She wasn't supposed to have been there, I was. Dena and I.

Where was Dena?

 CHAPTER 11

"Alicia understood how a person could be driven to the act of murder. What she never could grasp was why anyone would want to inflict pain."
—*Sex, Drugs and Murder*

I slowly turned my wrist so I could see the numbers on my watch. Four thirty-eight. I used the iron bar to pull myself up and crossed over to the now abandoned payphone.

"Hey, where you going? The police will be here any second."

I ignored the park worker, who had apparently fulfilled his promise, and put two quarters into the slot. It took three attempts to dial because my fingers kept slipping. Finally, ringing. *"I can't get to the phone right now. If you're feeling friendly, leave a message."*

"Dena? Dena it's me, pick up. You're there, right? Please pick up." Silence.

I put the receiver back in its cradle. A police car pulled up and two officers went over to talk to the park worker who subsequently pointed in my direction. I stayed rooted by the phone. Where was Dena?

The cops crossed over to me. The shorter one folded his arms across his chest and smiled. "So you're the one who found the body?"

I couldn't find my voice so I just nodded.

"Well, I'm Officer Campbell and this is Officer MacLean."

"Sophie Katz."

"All right, Miss Katz, care to show us where you found this guy?"

"Girl, found this *girl*." The last thing in the world that I wanted to do was go anywhere near that area again, but clearly drawing them a map and hoping that they found her in a timely manner wasn't an option. "I'll show you."

The policemen followed at a close distance. "Sorry you had to see this," Officer MacLean said. "It's never pleasant. Usually we find homeless people in other areas of the park. They rarely come into this part."

Homeless people?

"Usually the cause of death is overdose. Occasionally, it's natural causes, but we got to take a quick look to make sure there's nothing suspicious before we turn it over to the—"

"You don't understand." I stopped and turned around. "This isn't a homeless person. I knew this woman. And she didn't overdose, somebody killed her. They killed her and now my other friend is missing and I can't find her. I can't find her anywhere."

The expression on the officers' faces had changed. Campbell's hand was now resting on his gun. "Why the hell weren't we told this when we were called?"

"Don't look at me. I practically had to physically threaten that guy to get him to call you at all."

MacLean took a few steps away and started talking into his radio. Campbell scanned the area. "Okay, let's take this from the top. You lead us to the body and tell us exactly what happened, all right?"

MacLean joined us again. "Backup's coming, let's go."

I led the way to the Bitches' Circle and told them the events of the last hour. I took some comfort in the fact that someone was finally taking me seriously, but the main thoughts running through my mind were of Dena. When we finally reached the circle, I hung back and studied the bark of a large redwood.

I heard MacLean take a sharp breath in. "Holy shit."

My eyes traveled from the bark to the wood chips on the ground. Something was glittering among them. I knelt down and discovered it was a silver lighter with the letter *B* engraved on it.

"Don't touch that!" I looked up to see Campbell glaring at me. "Larry, get her out of here. Have her wait by the main entrance. Be sure to get a full description of her friend so we can get an APB out. I'm going to radio in and make sure the team knows what's up."

MacLean came over to my side, carefully sidestepping the lighter, and led me out of the area. That was actually a major relief. I heard the sirens of more police cars and then an ambulance. When we finally got to the main entrance I collapsed on a bench. I robotically answered MacLean's questions about Dena. He said something about not going anywhere but I barely registered it. There were cops everywhere now, some with dogs in tow, others in plain clothes. They were questioning all the remaining visitors and asking for ID. The park worker who had called the police for me was now being interrogated in earnest about thirty feet away from me. He caught my eye and mouthed the word "sorry."

I looked away without acknowledging him. I could care less if he felt guilty about not initially believing me. I could care less about him. I had to focus on pulling myself together. But every time I tried to form a coherent thought, images of Barbie overwhelmed me. There was so much blood. Was it possible for one person to bleed that much? Where the hell was Dena? I couldn't panic. I had to think logically, had to work this through. The lighter…had the *B* been for Barbie?

But it had been so far from the body. Of course that didn't mean anything. Barbie could have dropped it on the way in, before the attack. Or maybe she had seen the attacker, dropped the lighter and tried to get away. Or maybe the lighter wasn't hers at all. Maybe it belonged to the murderer. Whose name started with *B?* No *B* initials in Dena's name, thank God. Who else, not Anatoly Darinsky. What had been Jason's last name…Jason, Jason…Beck.

I jumped up with the intention of running to the phone, but I was blocked by two plainclothes officers. The woman was around my height with medium brown hair pulled back into a low ponytail and the man was Latino with his hair cut in a military style buzz cut. The woman flashed a warm smile. "I'm Detective Peters and this is Detective Gonzales. We need to ask you a few questions. Why don't we sit down."

I felt like screaming. I didn't have time for this shit. I had to find Dena now. "I really have to use the phone first."

"Why is it so urgent that you use the phone?" asked Gonzales.

"I don't think *B* is for Barbie."

"Excuse me?"

"They found a lighter at the scene that had the letter *B* on it. I saw it. I don't think it stands for Barbie, I think it stands for Beck. Jason Beck. That's Dena Lopiano's boyfriend."

It took Peters all of two seconds to grasp my implication. "Do you know where this guy lives?"

"No. He works at some bar in the Lower Haight. I'm not sure which one."

I gave them a description of Jason, while Gonzales scribbled it down. "I'm on it." He gave his partner a quick nod before leaving us.

Peters sat down on the bench and gestured for me to do the same. I glanced once again at the phone. There was really no one to call, the police were already there and Dena… Dena wasn't home. I just felt like I should be actively doing something, making phone calls, turning every stone over by hand until I found my friend, my best friend.

"Miss Katz?"

I became aware again of Peters's presence. I sunk down to sit beside her without responding.

"Miss Katz, why do you think your friend's boyfriend might have done this?"

"Because he's out of his mind, that's why."

"Can you elaborate?"

"He thinks he's a vampire."

"A vampire?"

"Yeah, or at least he wants to be a vampire and is trying to be one, I'm not quite sure."

Peters put her pen down. "So this guy's a wannabe vampire."

"Something like that. Look, I'm not really clear on the specifics. All I know is, he thinks he's Dracula, and that all the other legendary characters of his kind are real, and he lives in hope of being added to the coven of some blood-sucking literary figure."

"Wait a minute, are you serious?"

"Yes."

"And your friend is dating this guy?"

"She has a taste for the offbeat."

"I guess." Peters made a note to herself. "Okay, let's talk about the events that led up to your finding the body. You told Officer MacLean that the only reason Barbie was here was to tell Dena that you were going to be late. How did that come about?"

"My mom's bladder infection."

Peters's pen hovered over her notepad.

"I'm sorry." I pushed my hair back with both hands. "I'm not being very clear. I'm just a little shaken up."

"That's understandable. Let's just go step-by-step, okay? Take your time. Now what's this about your mom's bladder infection?"

A new realization overtook me. She was taking everything I said to heart. I could tell this woman about the events of the last few weeks and there would be an investigation. They would find my stalker, figure out who killed Barbie, and everyone would be safe, again. Including Dena. I had to believe that Dena would be safe too. I angled my body so that I was facing Peters.

"Well, the events that led me here really started two weeks ago when I got this weird note in the mail…." I went through every detail of the things that had been happening to me and made a point to include the dates and names of the police officers I had reported them to. I went into more details about my suspicions concerning Jason, although I did leave out Dena's suspicions about Anatoly. I also omitted the part about JJ Money and Tolsky for fear that I would come across as a conspiracy-theorist freak. I ended my account with the discovery of Barbie's body.

"The thing is, Barbie and I had worn our hair done in a similar style today and we have the same skin color. I can't help but think that she wasn't supposed to be the target of the attack. That the real target was me. I think I was supposed to die the same death as Kittie."

There, that was it. I had told her the whole story. And throughout my account there had not been one scoff, one eye roll, one snicker, nothing. Well, maybe not nothing. I could tell by Peters's expression that she was definitely taking me seriously, but there was more to it than that. Her mouth now formed a straight, tight line and her eyes seemed to have narrowed from their original shape.

"Miss Katz, who can attest to your whereabouts for the last three hours?"

"My whereabouts? Well, like I said, I picked up my mom's prescription about forty minutes ago, then I brought it to her—wait a minute. Are you accusing me of something?"

"I'm asking you a simple question, that's all. What pharmacy did you go to?"

The panic that had begun to subside began to rise again in the pit of my stomach.

"Miss Katz? Do you remember what pharmacy?"

"What? Oh right, Golden Gate Pharmacy on Noriega. I'm sorry, but why is this relevant, what exactly do you think I did?"

Gonzales approached, smiling broadly. "Miss Katz, we found your friend."

My eyes widened. "D-Dena?"

"She had some car troubles. She came by here to see if you had left yet. I filled her in on what's going on. She's pretty upset. She's waiting for you outside the gate."

I jumped up, and Peters rose too. "I think we should question Miss Lopiano first."

Gonzales's smile disappeared. He looked at me with a new intensity, then at Peters. "Got it. Do you think Miss Katz should come down to the station with us for more questioning?"

"No, I have all the information I need from her right now. Thank you for your cooperation, Miss Katz."

"I can't see Dena?"

"I'm sure she'll contact you after she's answered a few of our questions."

The look on Peters's face told me there would be no negotiating on that point. I nodded to Gonzales and turned to leave.

"One more thing, Miss Katz."

"Yes?"

"If you're planning on leaving the city, we'd appreciate a phone call."

I had no idea how I was able to keep it together enough to drive home. Every time I got stuck behind a slow car or a red light, I had to battle the overwhelming urge to leap out of the Mustang and run home as fast as I could. That's all I wanted now. To just be barricaded inside my flat with Mr. Katz and to never come out. I was forced to park four blocks from my place. Normally that would have been a minor irritant, but today the length of the walk was way outside my comfort zone. I peered at the sky through the windshield; it was now a cool shade of blue-gray. I stepped out of the car, took a deep breath of the rapidly cooling air and booked it to my apartment.

I was at the door to my building, keys ready, when I felt a hand reach out and grab my shoulder. Without hesitation, I spun around and punched the intruder square in the jaw.

Unfortunately, the intruder was Anatoly. "What the fuck did you do that for?"

"Well, why the fuck did you sneak up on me?"

"I didn't sneak up on you. I was walking by your place on the way to my own and I saw you and stopped to say hello. And then you punched me."

"Oh yeah? Well, well…actually that was probably out of line, huh?"

Anatoly didn't answer. He just stood there and massaged his jaw.

I pursed my lips to suppress a nervous giggle. Every instinct was telling me that this man would never hurt me. Unfortunately, it didn't appear that he could say the same about me. "You have time to come up? I could use a friend right about now."

"You just punched me."

"Oh, give me a break. You could stand up to terrorists in the Middle East but you don't think you can handle yourself against little old me?"

Once reminded of past exploits, Anatoly removed his hand from his chin, although he clearly wanted to continue to cradle it.

"Come upstairs and there might be some ice in it for you."

I was amazed at how normal my voice sounded. As if my world wasn't on the brink of collapse.

Anatoly shook his head. "You are the craziest woman I have ever met." But he followed me up anyway.

When we got up to my apartment I made a point to lock the door behind us before retrieving the ice pack from the freezer.

"Are you going to tell me why you hit me?"

"You have no idea what kind of hell I've just been through. Actually, I'm kind of glad I hit you. It was like a stress reliever. I feel like I can think straight again."

"Great."

"Anatoly, I need some advice."

"Can I get the cold pack first?"

"What? Oh God, I'm sorry. Here you go." I gently placed the pack against the spot where I had hit him. "Is that okay?"

He slid his hand over mine. "Yeah, it's okay."

The image of Barbie's corpse bleeding all over the dirt temporarily blinded me. I needed to talk to Anatoly about what was going on. I needed someone else's opinion on what I should do, because I was completely out of ideas. But I also needed him to hold me. I desperately needed to lose myself, if only for a little while. I needed him to help push the images out of my head and force me to experience the moment and nothing else. I just needed him.

I pushed myself up on my tiptoes and, removing the ice pack, kissed the spot where I had decked him just minutes ago. "Better?"

"Much better."

My lips made the journey to his, and when his tongue began to toy with mine my fear was scorched by an even more intense desire.

He maneuvered his hands under my shirt and caressed my back. I felt my bra loosen and a little moan escaped me. He was backing me into the bedroom now; I could feel him pressed against me. I was pulling on his neck, trying to bring him closer, although by that point it was a physical impossibility. His teeth were grazing my neck. I don't think I have ever been so desperate for someone in all my life. I wanted to touch every part of him, I wanted him to devour me. I wanted him to fill me. We were in the doorway of the bedroom now. His breath tickled my ear.

"I read your book."

"You what?"

"Mmm, there are some things in it I'd like to try."

My heart stopped beating. Dena's warnings were blaring in my head. Anatoly was still touching me but I couldn't feel him. All I could feel was terror. I pushed myself away from him. "Get out."

"What?"

"I'm not kidding. Get out now or I swear I'll scream."

"What the…?"

I squeezed past him, ran into the kitchen and lunged for the butcher knife. "I want you out of here now."

"Sophie, I don't—"

"NOW!"

He rushed me. He grabbed my arm and slammed it against the refrigerator. The knife fell to the ground. He held my wrists above my head, his face hovering above mine, and it quickly became clear that I no longer had any control over the situation. "I don't care if you are a psychotic bitch, you are never to pull a knife on me again, got it?"

I opened my mouth to scream but no sound came out. Anatoly released my arms and gave me a final shove against the cold door before turning around and leaving.

I spent the next hour crouched on the floor staring at the door, the knife in one hand and the phone in the other. When it rang, I pressed the talk button and lifted it to my ear without uttering a greeting.

"Sophie? Sophie, is that you?"

I exhaled for the first time in what felt like a century. "Dena. Are you all right?"

"Mentally or physically?"

"I am so sorry about Barbie," I said.

"What the hell is going on, Sophie? What's happening?"

"I don't know." I looked down at the knife. "I just don't know."

"Sophie, I'm really freaking out here. Can you come over?"

"Anatoly just left."

Dena was quiet for a moment. "He just happened to show up?"

"Something like that. You might have been right about him."

"How far away did you park?"

"Four blocks."

"Okay, here's what we'll do. I'll go over there. Watch from your window. When you see me double-park, come on down, quickly."

"Got it. Oh, and…Dena?"

"Yeah?"

"Bring your Mace."

"I'm holding it right now."

Forty minutes later Dena showed up with Mary Ann in tow. I had been waiting in the lobby, so I was able to jump into the car before Dena even pulled to a complete stop. Mary Ann leaned back and squeezed my hand. I managed a meager smile.

"I didn't expect to see you here."

"I figured there's safety in numbers," Dena said.

"I'm not really comfortable about leaving Mr. Katz."

"Mr. Katz? Are you kidding me?" Dena made eye contact through the rearview mirror. "My employee was just killed with a hatchet and you're worried about your cat getting lonely?"

"I'm sorry, of course you're right. It's just…it's just I'm a little confused about what to feel or think. It's like I'm living in this horrible nightmare that I can't wake up from. I'm pretty sure that someone is trying to kill me and nobody seems to be able or willing to help me."

"We're going to help you." The definitiveness in Mary Ann's voice startled me.

Dena looked at Mary Ann and then back at the road. "Yeah, we are. We are going to find the asshole who's doing this, we'll get the proof we need, and we're going to get his ass locked up. Enough is enough. I've lost an acquaintance, I'm not going to lose a friend."

"And how exactly do you propose we do all that?" I rested the full weight of my head against the window. "The police don't believe me. They think I'm a suspect, for God's sake. If this is the guy who killed Tolsky and JJ Money, then he's gotten away with the murders of two people who are a hell of a lot more resourceful than me. So how are we supposed to stop him now?"

"Simple," Dena answered. "We beat him at his own game, or more accurately stated, we're going to beat him at your game."

"I don't get it," I said.

Mary Ann looked relieved.

"Sophie, he's acting out a part," Dena explained. "He's following the script to a tee, and you wrote the script. Now all you have to do is play the part of Alicia Bright."

"Alicia Bright never dies," Mary Ann said slowly.

"Right. And she always gets her man," Dena said. "And Sophie is a lot more qualified to play the part of her own heroine than this psycho is to play the part of her villain."

"But this isn't a work of fiction, Dena. This is real life. My life."

"This is life imitating art, and you're the artist. So, Miss Bright, it's time to go back to my pad, put our heads together and solve this mystery."

I rolled my eyes. "Go team."

"I think Dena's right," Mary Ann said. "We can figure this out. After all, we're three intelligent women, right?"

Neither Dena nor I commented.

By the time we arrived at her apartment in Noe Valley I had begun to buy into Dena's reasoning. As long as he chose to commit the crimes in my novels, there was not a single thing that he could do that I couldn't predict. I could do this. I could solve this. I didn't have to be the victim, I could be the hero for a change. I pulled off my jacket and started clearing some space on Dena's dining room table.

"Okay, Dena, you get all three of my novels out. Even though he's only been working from *Sex, Drugs and Murder*, we should be prepared in the event that he chooses to branch out. Mary Ann, you act as secretary and write down everything that's happened up to now and compile a list of suspects."

Dena gave me a high five. "Raise the roof. Alicia Bright is in the house."

CHAPTER 12

"If you want to turn your life around you're going to have to start making things happen and stop allowing things to happen to you."

—*Sex, Drugs and Murder*

At a quarter to midnight Dena, Mary Ann and I were all reviewing each other's notes. We had each taken one of my books and had recorded every crime that I had ever written. The only violent crime in *Sex, Drugs and Murder* that our killer had yet to reenact was the beating with the golf clubs, but in the other books people had been lynched, burned, drugged and decapitated, just to name a few. It kind of gave me the creeps, which was rather sad, considering I'm the one who wrote it.

"I should have written romance novels instead."

"Erotica would have been good." Dena tossed the book she had been reviewing in the middle of the table. "I wouldn't mind reenacting some of that."

"You're such a pervert," Mary Ann said.

I raised my hands for a truce. "We're sticking to the subject at hand. Let's do suspects again. Who knew when and where we were supposed to meet?"

"Jason knew," Dena admitted.

"I told Anatoly."

"Well, I wasn't invited so I didn't tell anyone," Mary Ann's lower lip protruded enough to form a guilt-inducing pout.

"That was an oversight that I would think you would be thankful for," Dena pointed out through clenched teeth.

"Okay, so other than Anatoly, Jason, Marcus, my mom, and obviously Barbie, did anyone else know?"

Dena rested her elbow on the table. "I think that's it."

"And no one knew that Barbie was going, unless of course she told someone."

"I guess we'll never know the answer to that," Mary Ann said.

"Hell, they all could have told someone," Dena said. "Your mom makes a career out of telling the world your business, and Marcus is a hairstylist, for Christ's sake."

"I'll call Marcus in the morning and find out." I jotted a little note to myself. "The only people my mother had time to tell this to are the women in her senior group, and they were all too busy tasting Edith's new spicy meatballs to bother with me."

Dena laughed. "I hope they had antacids on hand."

"I bought them the economy-size bottle." I gnawed at the end of a ballpoint pen. "Did Jason see Barbie when he was at the store this morning?"

Dena's back stiffened a little and she turned her gaze to the wall. "He left ten minutes before she got there."

I thought about that for a moment but decided I'd get back to Jason later. I shuffled the papers in front of me until I came to the "Sequence of Events" page. "All right, we know why I was late. What about you, Dena, what exactly happened to your car?"

"Nail in the tire. I must have rolled over it right when I was leaving the store. It was bent in half so it started a slow leak, but apparently every time the wheel went around it pushed the nail in a little farther. It wasn't until I had driven five miles that enough air had escaped for me to realize what the problem was."

"Pretty convenient coincidence." I tapped my pencil against the table. "I've never gotten a nail in my tire before. Plus, you weren't exactly parked next to a construction site. You were on Union which has got to be one of the most pristinely kept streets in the city."

"That is weird." Mary Ann used her hands to sweep her hair up into a playful crown of curls. "Hey! I just thought of something. What if it wasn't a coincidence at all? Maybe somebody did it on purpose."

"Naw," Dena said. "I think it was an accident. Kind of like the whole Tolsky wrist-slitting thing."

"You're never going to let that go, are you?"

"Will you two knock it off?" I slammed my hand against the table. "I can't be bothered with playing referee tonight. We need to move on to the…the details of the murder." I didn't want to do this. I didn't want to relive it, but I knew this was the only way. The prone image of Barbie filled my mind again. "It was…very…very…well, it was excessive."

"Hacking somebody up with a hatchet is pretty excessive all right." Dena crossed her arms in front of herself protectively. "But we already discussed this. He's just copying the crimes that you wrote about in your book."

"That's just it. I wrote that Kittie was killed with just four strokes of a hatchet. Two to the back, one to the chest, and one to the back of the head." I paused to suppress the urge to gag. "Barbie was hit a lot more than that."

Dena swallowed hard. "How many times did he hit her with it?"

"I don't know. A lot. Dena, if I hadn't seen what she was wearing earlier I wouldn't have known who she was."

Dena looked away. "She told me her parents were in town for a visit. She was going to meet them tonight for dinner. I wonder if they know. Do you think the police will be able to notify them?"

Mary Ann made little circular motions with her hand against Dena's back. "The detectives will find them, I'm sure. Did you know her well?"

"No, I make a point not to socialize too much with the salespeople outside of the store. But she was a lot of fun to work with, though. She had moved here from Las Vegas, left an abusive boyfriend, checked herself into rehab, gotten clean and sober, just really got her shit together. A lot of good it did her."

A new possibility rang in my mind. "How abusive was her ex?"

"I don't really know. She didn't talk about him a lot. I got the feeling he was a major prick, though, and my guess is he's the reason why she went by 'Barbie' instead of her birth name—whatever that is. She was always making comments about how Mark wouldn't let her do this or that, stupid shit like dye her hair or get her tongue pierced."

Both Mary Ann and I automatically put our fingers over our tongues. "The police will probably consider him a suspect," I said. "Does he still live in Vegas?"

"I assume so. I remember her commenting once that he was the main reason she left. He did call the store a few times. It rattled her a lot. I don't think she's the one who told him where she worked."

"Well, it's pretty unlikely that he's responsible for any of this." I made a sweeping gesture over the books and papers that now littered the table. "It doesn't really fit. Still, it couldn't hurt to check into it."

"You know, Barbie and Kittie had a lot in common." Dena tapped her ring finger against her chin. "Both of them had sketchy pasts, both were promiscuous, or at least perceived as such. Maybe she was the intended target after all."

"Possible. Maybe you could do a little research into her life and history? Do you have a way to get in contact with her friends and family?"

"I know I have a few 'in case of emergency' phone numbers, plus her parents will probably contact me to collect the few things she kept at the store. I'm sure I could manage a few delicate questions."

"Right," Mary Ann said, "because you're so good at being delicate."

"I can be delicate." A sly smile crept onto Dena's lips. "You should see what I can do with a feather."

I hesitated for a moment. "What can you do with a feather?"

"Sophie, please don't encourage her," Mary Ann said.

"Okay, okay, let's get back to the murderer. If he's being a copycat, why did he hit her so many times? And why did he hit her face?" All that blood…don't think about it. "You know, I don't think that Barbie's resembling Kittie is all that relevant after all. No one knew she was going to be there. I really think somebody who was expecting me saw the hair and the skin coloring and the whole thing was a horrible case of mistaken identity."

"All right, but if the assailant was Anatoly, he would have known instantly that it wasn't you."

"True. It might have taken Jason an extra second, though. He could have approached her from behind thinking it was me and only realized his mistake after she saw him. Then he would have had to kill her to keep her from talking. Plus, he would have been pissed off, so that would have made him extra violent."

"It's not Jason."

"Dena, I'm not trying to be a bitch here but we have to look at all the possibilities, and Jason is a possible suspect. He knew I had done something to my hair because he was

standing next to you when we were on the phone this morning, and he had opportunity to put a nail under your car."

Dena opened her mouth to disagree but then reluctantly
closed it. She had never been very good at ignoring facts.

"Do we know if either Anatoly or Jason has read your
books?" Mary Ann asked.

Dena did a double take, and I brightened in surprise.
"Good question, Mary Ann."

"Thank you."

"No, really, it was relevant, thought out…" Dena gave me
a quick shake of her head. I was overdoing it. "Right, well,
both Jason and Anatoly have made a point of telling me that
they have."

Mary Ann wrote that down in her notepad. "What about
the connection between Tolsky and JJ Money? Do we have
any more information about that? Did Jason or Anatoly have
opportunity in those murders?"

Dena and I exchanged looks. "Um, those are things we
need to look into too," I said. "Maybe tomorrow you could
go to the library and look up any articles that you can find
on the two guys."

"Articles on Anatoly and Jason?"

Dena smiled and put her arm around Mary Ann. "Thank
God, for a minute I thought aliens had come and taken over
your body."

"Huh?"

"That's my girl."

"Ignore her," I said. "The articles that I want you to look
up will be on Tolsky and JJ Money." Mary Ann scribbled
their names. "Look up DC Smooth, too—that's bound to
turn up some stuff. Keep an eye open for anything that
sounds strange that has happened in the last year. Did they
make any complaints about stalkers? Did any weird stuff
happen to them in the months before they died? Also see if
you can find pictures of the funeral, and check for Jason or

Anatoly in the background. It's a long shot, but it can't hurt to look."

"I'll call Jason and see if I can get him to admit to any trips to New York."

Mary Ann's pencil stopped. Dena was looking past me into space. I knew how difficult this was for her. I felt like going around the table and putting my arms around her, but I knew she wouldn't accept that.

"Be sure to do it on the phone," I said. "Try not to meet him in person until we're able to prove his innocence, okay?"

Dena recognized my olive branch and smiled. "What about Anatoly? Are you going to try to pry information out of him?"

"I don't think Anatoly's talking to me."

"Why not?"

"I kind of punched him in the jaw. I apologized and everything but then he started talking about my book and I pulled a knife on him. He got a little pissed off."

Dena clucked her tongue. "Men are so sensitive."

"What I *will* do is try to get an appointment with Tolsky's daughter," I said. "She doesn't think his death was a suicide and I want to know why."

"I guess we all have our assignments, then." Dena stretched her arms over her head.

Mary Ann giggled. "This is so neat. I feel like one of Charlie's Angels."

"Funny, I was thinking more along the lines of Powerpuff Girls… How's the mantra go?" Dena tilted her head to the side. "'Part sugar, part spice and part kick-ass'? I want to be in charge of the kick-ass part."

I balanced my chair back on two legs. "Dena, as far as I'm concerned, you always kick ass."

"I know."

"Okay, just remember that this is not a game. People have been killed and we have to make sure that we're not added to the list. Study the crimes from my books, review them every day. I think I'm the target, but if Barbie was purposely assigned the role of Kittie, then we're all in danger. So stay alert, stay far away from any public lynching sessions and, whatever you do, don't play any golf."

Mary Ann made another note to herself. "No public lynching…no golf, got it."

The room got very quiet. Mary Ann looked up from her writings. "That was a joke, guys."

We all busted up.

Mary Ann and I slept over at Dena's. Well, maybe *slept* is the wrong word, at least in my case. My fear had been replaced by pure adrenaline. Who needed the SFPD anyway? Dena, Mary Ann and I were going to crack the case on our own. Just like the Powder Puff Angels, or whatever. We could do it. The alternative was…well, there was no alternative that I was willing to entertain, so there it was. We would be victorious.

Mary Ann woke up at nine and we both had time to shower and down some coffee. She went off to the library to do some research before her evening shift at Neiman's, and I went home where I was greeted by a very angry Mr. Katz.

"I'm sorry. I know you don't like being alone. I was over at Dena's trying to figure out a way to stop my would-be killer."

That didn't seem to pacify Mr. Katz at all, so I tried distraction instead. "So, anything exciting happen while I was gone? Any strange sociopaths come in and rearrange our bookcase or anything? No? How about phone calls, any phone calls?"

I looked at the flashing number on my answering machine. Eleven. I had been gone for less than twenty-four hours and I had eleven messages? Nobody's that popular, or at least I'm not, which meant that there was something wrong. I looked to Mr. Katz for some kind of clue, but he seemed nonplussed about the whole thing, so I resorted to pressing the button.

The first message was from my mother. "What is this, you're discovering bodies now? Leave it to you to be attacked on Sunday and find a dead person on Tuesday. Why can't you live a nice normal life like your sister? All this violence is giving me ulcers already."

So the media had served up yesterday's incident for public consumption. Fantastic.

The next ten messages consisted of nine calls from reporters and one message from MCI, who could apparently save me a bundle on my local calling plan. It was in anticipation of days like these that God invented the delete button.

I reluctantly called my mother back and was relieved when there was no answer. I really was a horrible daughter. Leah hadn't called, which meant either that she didn't know or more likely that she did know but didn't leave a message. I looked at Mr. Katz, who was swishing his tail over an empty food bowl. "I might still be able to save myself from the familial doghouse if I go over to Leah's right now and tell her about yesterday in person. That way I could tell Mama that I stopped by her house first but she wasn't home." I shook a knowing finger at my cat. "It's all about plausible deniability."

Mr. Katz let out a loud meow, which I took to mean "I don't really give a shit what you do as long as you give me my kibble."

I obliged him and then, after taking a few minutes to contemplate the issue of Leah, grabbed my purse and car keys and went off to her home in Forest Hill to do the "right thing."

Leah answered her door two minutes after I rang the bell. She was wearing a very expensive pair of diamond studs that Bob had recently bought her, a pristine knee-length beige skirt and a white silk blouse featuring an eye-catching blue stain that bore a suspicious resemblance to smashed fruit. Her eyes narrowed when she saw me.

"Well, will you look what the cat dragged in."

"Huh, that's funny. Last I checked the polite way to greet visitors was to simply say 'hello.'"

"Don't 'hello' me. I swear I just don't get it. Are you trying to put yourself in dangerous situations? Are you *trying* to get yourself killed?"

"So, I take it you saw the news this morning."

"Yes, I saw the news! And it's on the front page of the paper, Sophie! Bob called to tell me that it's all his associates will talk about, how his sister-in-law is the new Calamity Jane. You could at least have told me personally...."

"I'm here, aren't I?"

Leah scoffed and ushered me in. "You know, Mama tried to call you, and when you weren't home she called me." She closed and locked the door behind me. "I listened to her go on for about an hour while Jack dumped yogurt on his head. I'd tell you to call her but I think she went to the senior center so she could complain about you to other people."

"Oh gee, and I was so looking forward to talking to her right now."

Leah leaned against the door and we stared at each other for a moment. Finally, she stepped forward and gave me a hug. "I'm glad you're okay," she whispered.

"Me too, I—"

We heard a crash and Leah immediately pulled away and ran to the living room, where a blue-faced Jack had poured all his toddler Lego blocks out of their container and was now dispersing them around the floor so they might better complement the sundry toy dinosaurs and crayons that were already spread about.

"Jack, honey, no...I told you, no more than three toys at a time." She put her arms out to the side to balance herself after almost tripping over a pterodactyl. "I do not have time for this. The nitwit will be here in less than five minutes and now I have to brew the tea, fix the snacks *and* clean the living room."

"You mean Cheryl? Why would you invite Cheryl to come into your home?"

"I never invite her. She just has a way of forcing herself on people. She called last night to say that she wanted to see Jack, which you know is a big lie. She probably slept with some Hollywood big shot and is looking for someone to listen to her gloat."

"So tell her to go to hell."

Leah rolled her eyes upward as if questioning why the Lord had failed to grant her sister the logic of a flea. "She's Bob's sister, it doesn't matter if they can't stand each other. It's my obligation as his wife to receive her and show her how much better our life is than hers!" She reached down and restrained Jack before he was able to decorate the walls with a red crayon.

Her eyes fell down to her shirt. "Oh my God!" She stood up and pulled the fabric away from her to give me a better view. "Blueberry! I have a blueberry stain on my Ellen Tracy!"

I sighed and sat on the edge of an ottoman. "Oh, come on, we're talking about Cheryl here. Just tell her that Cindy Crawford was seen sporting a blueberry stain at La Jolla's Cheesecake Factory. By tomorrow her entire wardrobe will have a fruit salad theme."

"It's not funny!" Leah said sharply, but I could tell by the way she turned her head away from me that she was hiding a smile. She quickly buried any hint of amusement and went back to being stressed. "I can't believe this. The minute Bob gets promoted, I'm hiring a nanny." She checked her skirt to verify that the damage was isolated to one spot. "You're going to have to watch Jack while I change."

I immediately stood up. "Oh gosh, Leah, I would but I have got to get—"

"Sit down!"

I sat reluctantly. It's funny how clichés always end up being true. I had made this visit because I had thought it was the right thing to do, and where had my good intentions led me? Straight to hell.

"Just keep him busy for three minutes, that's it. And don't let him do any further damage."

"And how do you suggest I accomplish that great feat?"

"I don't know…you're a writer, tell him a story. He has a very good attention span for stories. The pediatrician says it's a sign of giftedness."

Leah turned and raced up the stairs before I could protest. I had a hard time believing that Cheryl was going to be very jealous of Leah's life.

My eyes moved to Jack, who was holding a green crayon threateningly. I got down on my knees and wrestled the crayon from him. "A story, huh? Okay…once upon a time in a land far, far away there was a little village that lived in fear of an evil monster." I held up a *Tyrannosaurus* for Jack's inspection. He sat up a little straighter and his blue eyes widened with interest. Well, what do you know, he did like stories.

"So this monster, whose name was…" I put the *T-rex* down in front of me and tried to come up with a suitable monster name. "Smirnoff, the evil monster Smirnoff—and this mean little guy here is his sidekick, the devious Jack Daniel." Jack carefully poked at the velociraptor I had placed next to Smirnoff.

"Every Saturday night Smirnoff and Jacky D would lure the weaker willed villagers to their lair, and the next morning the people would all suffer from horrible ailments. This went on for years, and the villagers were beginning to suspect that they were doomed to a life of headaches and silly behavior until— da-ta-da-da!" I held up an impressive-looking triceratops. "Look, it's our heroine, Janice! She's come to save the day!"

"What are you teaching my son?"

I looked up to see Leah in the doorway looking horrified.

"I was, um, teaching him the about the evils of addiction. Aren't you the one that always says kids need to learn about that stuff young?"

Leah snatched the triceratops from my hand just as the doorbell rang. "Behave yourself!" She put the dinosaur on the end table as if it were a valuable centerpiece and went off to "receive" Cheryl.

I leaned over to Jack. "Some people don't need Janice," I whispered. "Some people would benefit more from the assistance of our other hero, Mr. Bong."

"Sophie! I haven't seen you in eons."

I pulled myself to my feet and tried to smile at the bottle blonde in the too-tight mini. "Hi, Cheryl, how are you?"

"Great! Oh, and look at little Jack."

Jack glanced up at the sound of his name and then promptly went back to testing the "nontoxic" label on the crayons by sticking two in his mouth.

Cheryl wrinkled her nose in distaste as I carefully removed the now slimy crayons from his lips. "Leah, you should really clean his face and get him some decent clothes," she commented, while idly adjusting the clasp of a trendy but obviously cheaply made necklace, "he'd be so much cuter that way."

Leah was standing behind Cheryl making psycho-like stabbing gestures at her back.

"Guess what?" Cheryl made eye contact with me as she waited for some kind of prompting.

I tried really hard not to roll my eyes. "What, Cheryl?"

"Less than an hour ago I stopped by the Ritz to pick up my check and you'll never guess who was there? Leonardo DiCaprio! Of course those of us who know him just call him Leo."

"Well, that's…" I shrugged, giving up on the idea of feigning interest.

Cheryl didn't seem to notice. "So tell me," she continued, "are you still going to be writing a screenplay for Tolsky productions?"

"Thanks to Tolsky's untimely death, that project's been put on indefinite hold."

"Oh." Cheryl's voice went flat. "Leah, did you say you made snacks?" She turned her back on me and faced Leah, who now had her hands innocently laced behind her back.

"Of course, Cheryl. I just picked up the most incredible Brie—"

"Ugh, do you have any idea how much fat is in that?" Cheryl looked down at Leah's figure and smiled. "Of course not, you've never been one of those superficial people who worries about watching their weight. Gosh, it must be so nice to be able to just let yourself go."

I stepped back to better avoid being electrocuted from the sparks I knew would be imminently flying from Leah's head, but to her credit (and my shock) she kept her tone steady. "Well, I suppose I do spend less time on my appearance than I used to, but that's what happens once you've settled into a committed relationship with a man... Oh, I'm sorry!" Leah put a hand on her cheek in a halfhearted attempt to fake embarrassment. "You've never had a meaningful relationship. How thoughtless of me to have brought attention to it!"

I was impressed. Leah had actually learned how to insult people without messing up her good-wife-and-mother image. If I had been in her shoes I would have said something much less elegant, like, "Get the fuck out of my house." Although as far as I was concerned, my way would have produced better results.

Jack, who had been toddling around the room, removed Janice from her display position and started smashing her against a defenseless Smirnoff. I stepped in front of him so that he was partially hidden behind my legs. "So, Cheryl, I understand that Tolsky made reservations at the Ritz the night before he died."

Cheryl started at the sound of my voice and turned around in surprise. Apparently, after I had given her the bad news about my screenplay she had promptly forgotten my presence. "Yes, that's right, I never got to meet him," she said dismissively before turning around again to trade more insults with Leah.

"But he'd stayed at your hotel before," I pressed. "I remember him mentioning that he was staying at the Ritz when I met with him."

Cheryl regarded me with renewed interest. "I'd forgotten that you lunched with him. Was there anyone else with him? You know he and Tarantino were very close."

"I've never met Tarantino." Cheryl's eyes glazed over again, so I tried to come up with some phony celebrity sighting that would keep her attention long enough for me to sneak in a few more questions. "Leah, you did tell her what we did after the meeting, right? You know, about how you, Alex Tolsky, George Lucas and I all got together for five-o'clock cocktails?"

Leah's smile could have outshone the sun. "You know, I may have forgotten to mention that. You really should meet George, Cheryl, he's such a nice man…of course he doesn't fraternize too much with hotel clerks." This time her insult was somewhat undermined by Jack, whom she had to rush to before he knocked over a table lamp.

Cheryl looked like she was on the verge of setting Leah's hair on fire, but at least she was paying attention.

"So," I continued, "Tol—Alex was staying at the Ritz during that visit, right?"

"Yes, he always stays with us when he comes up to San Francisco, but I've never been at my post during the times that he came and went…. Have you and George Lucas stayed in touch?"

"Oh yeah, we're drinking buddies. Did Tolsky come up often?"

"As far as I know—and I know everything that goes on at that hotel—he's only been there three times, twice in the three months before his death."

That was a lot of visits in a short period of time, especially when you considered that he had planned on coming up again. That would have made three times in less than four months. There was something to that. "Was he planning on filming a movie up here or something?" I asked.

"Probably, everyone loves filming in San Francisco. You know Keanu Reeves was up here filming recently. He is such a cutie. He made a point of making conversation with me when he checked in and out— I think he had a little thing for me. Leah, you have no idea what it's like for me to be constantly put in the position of fielding the advances of so many attractive, rich men."

"I can't imagine," Leah cooed. "I read in *People* that a lot of the Hollywood stars have given up on the practice of hiring prostitutes and now simply have their flings with average women. I didn't believe it when I read it but it sounds like there's some truth to it after all… Jack put down the fire poker!"

This was like watching heavyweight boxing, except a lot more gory. I heard my cell phone ringing in the foyer and gratefully excused myself.

I checked the number quickly before answering. "Hey, Dena."

"Are you sitting?"

"Yeah, I'm sitting," I lied. "What's going on?"

"I talked to Barbie's parents. They told me that the police have made an arrest."

"What? Wait, hold on for a minute while I find a better place to talk." Cheryl and Leah had made it to the kitchen and Jack was close behind them. Either Leah hadn't noticed that he had gotten his hands on a permanent ink marker or she was hoping that Cheryl's miniskirt was her son's next target.

"Leah, I've got to go. If you talk to Mama before me, tell her I'm fine and I'll stop by soon."

"But you can't leave. Somebody's got to eat the Brie!"

"I'll try it next time around."

Cheryl smiled brightly at me. "Well, I'm glad we got a chance to catch up. Call me next time you and George get together. The three of us could have drinks at The Terrace."

"Yeah, that'll happen. Leah…" I ended my sentence with a little wave and ran out to the sidewalk before I pulled the phone back to my ear.

"I'm back, Dena. Now what do you mean they made an arrest? Who the hell did they arrest?"

"Barbie's ex."

"No way. But I thought he was in Vegas."

"Not for the past week. He's been in San Francisco following Barbie around. Her parents gave me the inside scoop. Jack the Ripper was a pussycat next to this freak."

"No, no, this doesn't make sense, he couldn't be the killer."

"Maybe not, but he was at the crime scene either during or right after Barbie was offed."

"How do they know that?"

"The lighter was his. The man was going ninety-five on 280. They found traces of her blood on his clothes."

My eyes traveled to my rental car parked in front of Leah's garage. "Dena, this doesn't make sense," I repeated.

"Yeah, no kidding. But I gotta tell you, with his history it's no fucking wonder that the cops think he's guilty." I leaned against the hood and waited for her to fill me in. "As a teenager he was convicted once for sexual assault and once for rape. As an adult he's done time for beating the shit out of his ex-wife and dealing coke. But the thing is, he's in three-strike country now. He could get life for shoplifting at Wal-Mart, and since they already have evidence that he's violated the restraining order Barbie had against him…."

"Got it. I want to talk to him."

"I do too," Dena said. "Actually, I want to rip him a new asshole. Do you think the cops will let me do that if I ask really nicely?"

I sighed and tapped my fingers against the windshield. "I think I should do this on my own."

"How come you get to have all the fun?"

"Because you're just going to antagonize him."

"And you're going to bring him a batch of homemade cookies?"

"I'm going to ask him questions, and if you're standing over my shoulder telling him what a prick he is, he may not be in the mood to answer."

I heard a faint scraping noise on the line, probably Dena's teeth gnashing together. "I think you're wrong on this one. I think we should do a good cop, bad cop deal. You be the good cop and—"

"Do you really think that would work?"

More gnashing. "No. But I really want to be the bad cop."

"Some other time. Hey, once we've cleared Jason, why don't you do some role-playing with him? God knows you have all the costumes and the props."

"Already done it. It's not the same as the real thing, although I did develop this rather unique interrogation technique...."

"More information than I need right now." I made a mental note to myself to drill Dena about the details later. Interrogation techniques and feathers—just had to know. "Where's he being held?"

"At the Bryant Street location. And, Sophie?"

"Yeah."

"Don't forget to ask the police about the new asshole thing, for future reference."

While driving to see Mark Baccon behind bars, I tried to wrap my mind around the latest turn of events. Of course it was possible that Barbie's ex-boyfriend suddenly decided to chop her up with a hatchet, the same weapon used in *Sex, Drugs and Murder,* just days after someone vandalized my car in a manner consistent with the same book. But somehow it seemed that the chances of that happening were right up there with Ed McMahon personally delivering me a check from Publishers Clearing House.

When I got to the jail I spent a few minutes prying information out of the deputy sheriffs. Mark was being held on charges of reckless endangerment, violating a restraining order and drug possession. He had yet to be charged with Barbie's murder. No doubt the D.A. was taking his time, making sure he had an ironclad case. After all, what was the rush? The guy wasn't going anywhere. One of the deputies escorted me to the visiting room. Several men seated behind a thick pane of glass seemed to be competing for the title of king of the trailer trash.

"Here he is."

I sat opposite a thin man with a scarred face. Where did I know him from? Maybe I'd met someone who looked like him? Simultaneously, we picked up the phone on our respective sides. His eyes moved very slowly from my waist to my chest. He never quite made it to my face. Funny, he hadn't touched me, yet I suddenly felt the need to go through a decontamination process. "You're the 'ho from the store."

"Excuse me?"

"You came out of that pussy shop and told me to go in and check it out."

The pussy...oh wait, I knew who this guy was. He was the one outside Guilty Pleasures the day I met Jason.

He was also the tourist who'd rushed past me as I was entering the Botanical Gardens.

CHAPTER 13

"Lots of people try to be sleazy but a few individuals have it down to an art form."
                                        —*Sex, Drugs and Murder*

I involuntarily recoiled.

He scratched his chin—probably lice.

"So what's your deal?" he said. "You don't look like no public defender."

"That's because I'm not."

"Then who the fuck are you?"

"Sophie Katz, I am—I was—an acquaintance of Barbie's."

"Oh fuck, I don't need this shit." He smacked the counter with the base of his palm. "First off, her name's Bonita, she just pulled this Barbie shit out of her ass. Second off, I didn't kill the bitch, all right?"

"I...I don't think you did."

Mark finally moved his gaze north of my boobs. "What's that?"

"I don't think you killed her."

Four distinct horizontal lines formed on his forehead as

he scrutinized me. After a long pause he shrugged and took a deep sniff. "If you know I didn't do it, why don't you tell the fuckin' pigs that? Did you do it?"

"No."

"Then what the fuck are you doin' here?"

"Like I said, I think you're innocent...of this, which means that whoever did do this is still out there. That makes me a little nervous, so I was hoping you could help me figure out who the guilty party really is so the police could lock up the right guy."

"You want me to help you out?"

"Oh good, you can hear."

"What the fuck do you want me to do? I'm locked up."

"Mmm, yes, I did note that. All I want you to do is answer a few questions."

He took another long sniff. "Why the fuck should I do that?"

"I don't know, maybe you don't want to be charged with a murder you didn't commit?"

"What the fuck difference does it make? This is California, bitch. They got me on my third felony as an adult. It don't matter if I get convicted of murder or violating that fuckin' restraining order—either way I got life, so why should I fuckin' care?"

"You should care because it *is* California, a state where capital punishment is alive and well. No pun intended."

Mark didn't seem amused, so I continued. "Did you see Bar—Bonita's body?"

Mark looked away. "Yeah, I saw it."

"She was hacked up—her body, her face completely mutilated. It was about as violent and gruesome as a murder can get. Do you really think that with your background the judge is going to show any leniency whatsoever?"

Mark didn't say anything.

"Good, then you won't mind taking a few moments out of your busy schedule to answer some questions."

"Fuck."

"You really like that word, don't you?"

"I like the word all right." Mark's gravelly laugh sounded out of place in the hellhole we were in, but then again, if anyone could find amusement in hell it was probably appropriate that it be the Antichrist. "Saying it ain't as good as doing it, though. Too bad they don't allow conjugal visits no more, huh? Maybe if you ask real friendly like, the guards will let you blow me through the bars. You colored bitches are always good at sucking cock. You swallow, honey?"

How trashed must Barbie have been to have hooked up with this maggot? Unfortunately, I didn't have the luxury of indulging my nausea; this was a business trip. "How was it you happened to find Barbie?" The hell with him. She changed her name to Barbie and that's what I was going to call her.

"Uh-uh, fuck this shit. You're trying to get me to admit that I broke my restraining order."

"Oh, give it up already. You called her work how many times in the last week? You don't think her co-workers are going to testify to that? Everybody knows you violated your restraining order, and I personally don't give a shit. Now let's try this again, how did you find Barbie?"

I could tell by the constipated look on his face that Mark's little hamster wheel was spinning. "I was…in the area where she works and…I noticed her get in her car and pull out."

Oh, please.

"I wanted to…to talk with her."

"About?"

"The bitch fuckin' left me for no reason, and when she split she stole five hundred bucks of my fuckin' money. Nobody steals from me. I sure as hell wasn't gonna let her get away with that shit." Mark stopped and straightened himself up, apparently remembering that he was supposed to be striving for delicacy. "Not that I was planning nothin', I just wanted to talk to her now that she'd had time to chill out. So I...I drove in the same direction she was goin'."

Thank God I wasn't a defense attorney. If this guy was ever allowed to testify, the jury would probably vote to have him electrocuted right there on the stand. "Okay, so you ended up at Golden Gate Park. Why didn't you get out of your car and talk to her right away? Why did you even let her go into the Botanical Gardens?"

"I couldn't find any fuckin' parking! That's the part that the pigs don't buy. I fuckin' hate this city. It takes four hours to park your motherfuckin' car. Is there something funny?"

I could barely stay in my chair. The inmates and visitors next to us were giving me strange looks but I couldn't stop laughing. I managed to quiet myself down enough to resume the conversation. "Let me be sure I'm getting this. You were going to assault your ex-girlfriend, but you didn't because you couldn't find a good parking space?"

"I wasn't gonna assault her, I was gonna try to talk some sense into the bitch. You know, if I had been able to find a spot sooner I might have been able to save her life."

"Wow, what a knight in shining armor you are." I tapped my toe against the hard floor. "So, you eventually found parking and you followed her into the garden. How did you locate her? The place where she was killed was a little off the beaten path."

"I started walkin' around. When I couldn't find her right away I started callin' her cell phone. She always had the loudest fuckin' phone and she always had it set to 'Jingle Bells.' When I got near the redwoods I heard it and I...I found her."

"She was already dead?"

"Yeah, she was dead. She was chopped up like a piece of fuckin' meat. I don't get it, man. I could see some guy getting pissed and slapping her shit around, or maybe she'd been leading him on and he wanted to bend her over and show her what a 'ho is good for, but to hack her up like that, that's really sick."

"Here comes that bile again."

"What?

"Nothing." I rubbed my hands against my jeans in a fruit-less attempt to rid myself of his vileness. "Okay, so you found her hacked up. How did the blood get on your clothes?"

"By being a fuckin' idiot, that's how. She was lying on her stomach and for some stupid reason I turned her over to see...fuck, I don't know what I wanted to see. It was pretty fuckin' obvious she was dead. Fuckin' stupid thing to do."

"Why didn't you notify the police of what you saw?"

"What the fuck you been smoking? What was I gonna say? That while violating my restraining order I found my ex, who happened to have been whacked just a few minutes ear-lier?"

"Right, so when you left, did you see anybody suspicious around?"

"Suspicious? Fuck, I don't know. I wasn't lookin'. I had to stay focused on how I was going to get my ass back to Vegas before the cops came looking for me."

"Uh-huh, so it was a pretty quick mourning process, then?"

"What?"

"Never mind. Okay, so you didn't see anyone who seemed out of place, or dressed kind of...funny."

"Funny how?"

"Well, like someone wearing clothing that could hide a hatchet, like a trench coat or say...um...a cape?"

"A cape?"

"Yeah, you know a cape, like a vampire's or something."

"What, are you shittin' me?"

"Okay, how about a tall guy with dark hair and big hands?"

"Hey, I told you, I don't know who I fuckin' saw, I wasn't paying attention. The only person I remember seeing was... was you."

I stole a quick look at the nearby deputy. "You saw me just as I was getting there and you were leaving."

"I don't fuckin' know that."

"Excuse me?"

"How do I know you were just getting there? Fuck, you coulda been just getting back after droppin' off a bloody ax in your trunk."

"I'm here trying to prove you're innocent and you're trying to pin the crime on *me?*"

"Hey, baby, it's all good. I like 'em twisted. It just means I gotta remember to tie you up before I fill that drippin' pussy of yours. You do have some cream in those panties, don't you, sweetheart? I can always tell when a bitch's wet for me. I'm talented that way."

The inmate in the neighboring chair chuckled. He winked and stuck his tongue out at me suggestively. My jaw had gotten so tight that it actually ached. I took in a sharp breath and managed a fake smile. "The next time you get laid, there won't be any pussy involved." Mark lost a little of his color. I leaned in conspiratorially. "I think the term is fudge packing, and you being the skinny little thing that you are, I have a feeling you'll be the one playing tight end." I pushed my purse strap up on my shoulder preparing to leave. "I don't have any more questions."

I got back to my car and rested my forehead against the steering wheel. If I hadn't been so intent on finding the true killer, I really wouldn't have had a problem with Mark taking the rap for a crime he didn't commit. And, who knows, maybe he actually was guilty. Hell, he could even be my stalker. But not likely. Mark wasn't the obsessed-fan type; maggots rarely read books. *Hustler,* maybe.

I propped my chin up enough so I could stare out the window. There was nothing more I was going to find out about the details of Barbie's death. Mark was the only other person who had seen the body directly after the murder and he didn't know anything useful. I had to work this from another angle. It was time to talk with Shannon Tolsky.

When I got home I thumbed through my address book until I found a number for Tolsky Productions. After Tolsky's death, the project of turning my book into a movie had been put on hold. I hadn't pushed the issue because at the time I was busy writing my latest novel, and when that was done some psycho decided to dismantle my life. If it isn't one thing, it's another. Shannon was in publicity, which had nothing to do with me. Still, I had a contract with the company for which she worked. That should give me a little leverage. I picked up the phone and started dialing. It took me over a half hour just to be put through to the correct office. Finally I got a woman who identified herself as Miss Tolsky's receptionist.

"Hi, I'm Sophie Katz. I've been commissioned to adapt one of my books into a screenplay for Tolsky Productions. I was wondering if Miss Tolsky has any openings within the next few days to meet with me."

"Miss Tolsky doesn't usually deal with films until they're produced and ready to market."

"I realize that, but I'm hoping she'll make an exception for me. I spoke to her father a few weeks before he…well, about two months ago now, and there were some things that we discussed that I was hoping she could clarify for me."

"Hold, please."

Okay, maybe a contract wasn't quite enough leverage to pull this one off.

"Miss Tolsky says she can see you tomorrow at three. Does that work for you?"

Maybe I was worthy of Cheryl's envy after all.

The waiting room looked like a cross between a music video and a spread out of *Home Beautiful*. Everything was perfect, right down to the waxed leaves of the ornamental fig tree. I crossed my legs at the ankles and tucked them under my chair in hopes of drawing attention away from my scuffed shoes. I had spent a ridiculous amount of money on the last-minute airfare, and the only morning flight that had been available took off at 6:00 a.m. My return flight was scheduled to leave LAX at 8:00 p.m. So instead of packing a change of clothes and some toiletries for a fourteen-hour vacation, I had opted to bring just a purse and deal with being rumpled and baggy-eyed, since that seemed to be my look of late anyway. What I had forgotten was that people in L.A. don't rumple. Okay, maybe there was a little rumpling going on in South Central, but not in the Valley. Plus, they don't have bad-hair days, they sure as hell don't wear scuffed shoes (unless that's the style, in which case they'll shell out an extra four hundred dollars for a pair of pre-scuffed Manolo Blahniks), and, thanks to collagen injections, the only bags these people had were made by Kate Spade.

The receptionist cautiously put the phone down, mindful of her manicure, and framed her mouth into a placid smile. "Miss Katz, Miss Tolsky will see you now."

This was my moment. The thing was, I had no idea what to do with it. The woman I was about to see, justifiably assumed that I had come to discuss some business matter, while in truth I was here to drill her about the details of her father's death. For the last twenty-four hours I had been trying to come up with a way of stating my purpose without getting kicked out on my tush, but so far I was drawing a blank. The receptionist arched an eyebrow expectantly. I gritted my teeth in a way that I hoped resembled a smile and opened the office door.

A woman with platinum-blond hair and skin a shade of orange that could only be purchased at one of the best tanning salons, stepped out from behind her Pottery Barn desk. I assumed she worked at Tolsky Productions, but there was little evidence of it. The only items that graced the desk's surface were a Sony flat-screen computer, a Mont Blanc pen set to complement her monogrammed stationery, and a silver 1940s-style telephone. No paper clips, no stapler, no anything that could be considered useful without being pretty.

"Miss Katz, it is so good to finally meet you in person." She extended her hand. "I'm Shannon Tolsky. I'm a huge fan of your work."

"Thank you, and please call me Sophie." I looked down at our clasped hands, thinking how she must moisturize hers twelve times a day as smooth as they were. "I really appreciate you seeing me so quickly. I know you don't usually meet with writers...."

"This project was near and dear to my father's heart. He talked about it incessantly. It really is criminal the way it's been put on hold, but maybe I could help you with that. You see, while I truly love publicity, I think that your adapted screenplay and the subsequent movie could use my talents in the areas of development and production. I know that with my help, your book could be transformed into the next summer blockbuster."

"Oh God, that's great, that's really...really wonderful. The thing is, I didn't come to talk about the screenplay."

Her surprise registered only with a few quick blinks of her eyes. "I see. Well then, why exactly are you here?"

"I wanted to ask you about your father."

Shannon's posture assumed a more militaristic position. "If you're planning on writing a book on him..."

"No! No, nothing like that. You see...I read that you believe his death was the result of a murder. Do you still think that's true?"

"Yes." She eased into her leather office chair without offering me a seat.

"Well, so do I, and I think that the person that killed him has murdered before—and since—and plans on doing it again. In fact, I think I might know his next potential victim, so I was kind of hoping you could help me nail this guy."

Shannon steepled her fingers in front of her chin. "You know who killed my father?"

"Oh, um…no. But I do have a few suspects in mind."

"You do?" She took inventory of everything from my inappropriately sullied shoes to my frizzy mop. She gently swiveled back and forth. "Anything you need me to do to prove that my father's death was not a suicide, I'll do."

What, no security guards to escort me out? This was a little too easy. "Do you mind if I sit?" Shannon nodded toward a chair. "All I need you to do is answer a few questions."

"Go ahead."

"All right, why don't we start with why you think your father was killed. I've read articles about it—there were no signs of struggle, he even wrote a note."

"The note was vague at best. Nowhere in it did he say, 'I'm going to kill myself.' It didn't even say goodbye, just a whole bunch of 'I can't live without you' nonsense directed at my mother." She reached into her desk drawer and pulled out a stress ball designed to look like the planet Earth. "He was pathetic, but he wasn't suicidal."

Well, that was catchy. Maybe they could have that one engraved on his tombstone. "Were you and your father close?"

"Closer than I would have liked. I did have to live with the man for eighteen years."

"So…you didn't get along."

"Very perceptive." She used her left hand to smooth her perfectly straight hair. "He was an alcoholic, manic depressive. There wasn't a lot to like."

"You know manic depressives have a high suicide rate."

"He managed to function perfectly well for forty-five years without so much as nicking himself while shaving. He didn't all of a sudden decide to plunge the whole blade into his wrist. Anyway, I thought you were trying to prove that my father *didn't* kill himself."

"I am. I just need to understand why *you* think he didn't."
I looked down at my palm and used an index finger to trace
my life line. "I read that your mother doesn't share your
doubts."

"But she doesn't have any incentive to, now does she?"
My eyes moved back up to Shannon. "I'm not sure I follow."

"My parents' relationship had been over for years. The only
thing they had in common was a house and a marriage license, and even that was imminently changing. She moved
out just a few days before he…before they found him. When
he died, she got everything. Everything! That's a lot more
than she would have gotten in a divorce, even in California.
And do you know what I got?"

"Something less than everything?"

"Nine hundred thousand dollars. That's it. A measly nine
hundred thousand dollars." She began to knead away at Earth.
"That's not even enough to buy a decent house. So now she's
living it up with money she never raised a finger to earn, and
I'm stuck living paycheck to paycheck until someone decides
to kill her too."

"You don't make much here?"

"Oh, please, I barely make six figures." She had pressed the
little stress ball into her desktop so that it had come to resemble a sort of Earth pancake. "The only way I'm going to
get ahead is by marrying some sugar daddy. That's what I've
been reduced to. Unless, of course, I can prove that my darling father was killed."

"You can financially benefit from his death if it was
murder?"

"He had a five-million-dollar life-insurance policy that
would have been mine."

"Uh-huh, so, if you discovered that someone slit open
your father's arteries against his will…that would make you
happy?"

"Are you here to help me or judge me?"

Funny, she looked and sounded much more socially adept than Mark Baccon, but there were some definite similarities. Something about that whole "I'm in it for myself and who the hell cares if anyone else is killed or mutilated along the way?" attitude of theirs. I sighed and tried to keep the disgust out of my voice. "It sounds like your mom made out real well. Any chance she did it?"

"The police did look into that, but she had an airtight alibi. She was at a charity ball. She didn't leave until well after midnight and then she got a ride to her friend's house where she'd been staying."

"Maybe someone did it for her—a boyfriend maybe?"

"I can only encourage you to look into it, but I seriously doubt my mother was having an affair. Who would want her? She's an anorexic shriveled old matron with no personality worth mentioning. My father, on the other hand, was involved with someone. That's what spurred my mother to move out. To be honest, I'm surprised she left."

"You expected your mom to hang out in an unhappy marriage after she found out that your dad was cheating on her?"

"You misunderstood me before. They were both perfectly happy with the marriage. It was just their personal relationship that was awful."

"Okay, you want to explain that one to me?"

"My mother liked being Mrs. Tolsky. She liked the prestige, the party invitations, the money, basically the perks of the job. My father liked having a wife. Not just any wife but the mother of his child. Do you know how many men in this town are still married to the mother of their adult children?"

"Can't say that I do."

"You can count them on your fingers. So, as you can see, my parents were part of a very elite group."

"Oh, I heard this story. He was in the Russian circus, and she, just a teenager herself, helped him defect…."

"If I have to hear that story one more time, I'll scream."

I pressed my lips back together. I didn't particularly want to hear Shannon scream. Although a bit of crying after I slapped that spoiled face of hers might be okay.

Shannon freed Earth from her clutches and studied it as it gradually resumed its shape. "Fairy tales only exist in movies. There is no greater evidence of that than my parents' marriage. There was no intimacy, no passion—it's really a wonder that I was conceived at all. Nonetheless, marriages of convenience are usually stronger than ones of romance because they are based on logic. My mother is a very logical person, so why in the world would she risk her carefully cultivated lifestyle just because her husband discreetly went elsewhere for a little companionship?"

"He was discreet?"

Shannon shrugged. "I still don't know who he was seeing."

"So how can you be so sure he was having an affair?"

"I found out from my mother. I didn't question it at the time, I didn't really care. Since his death, some of his friends and co-workers admitted to me that they suspected something. Lots of private cell-phone calls and the like, but no one I've ever talked to will confess to actually seeing him with someone. The more I think about it, the more amazed I am that my mother found out at all."

"Do you think your mother will talk to me?"

"No."

"Even if you asked for me?"

"My mother and I are not on speaking terms."

For God's sake, Hamlet's family was closer knit than this. "Shannon, do you have anything that would point to murder other than, well, other than wishful thinking?"

"They did an autopsy at my insistence and he had a blood alcohol level of .24 and he had taken several of my mother's Valium."

"That doesn't sound all that strange. You just said he was an alcoholic."

"But he didn't take pills."

"Yes, but if he was going to kill himself anyway— I mean, if I were going to slash open my wrists, I would want to be as out of it as possible."

"You don't understand. My father *hated* pills. He was tormented by the fact that my mother took Valium. When he broke his foot eight years ago he refused to take painkillers. Do you have any idea how many nerve endings are in the foot?"

"A lot?"

"Of course, he did drink himself into a stupor on a fairly regular basis. The man wouldn't touch an Advil, but he had no qualms about downing half-a-dozen vodka tonics."

"Well, everybody has to have a vice." I shifted position in my chair. "I've got to say, Shannon, the more I talk to you the more I question my conclusion that this was a murder. According to you he was an alcoholic with a mental illness who had just been abandoned by his wife of thirty years."

"Did you ever see *Silent Killer?*"

"Yes, but…"

"Scott Reynolds's wife drugs him, gets him into the bath before he loses consciousness, then slits his wrists and leaves him there to die. Sound familiar?"

"Okay, but if I remember rightly, she uses a pretty heavy-duty drug to knock him out."

"Excuse me, but what do you think hard alcohol mixed with eight Valium will do to you? Yet he managed to cut two perfectly straight lines going up the vein of each wrist. Rather impressive for a man who shouldn't have been able to stand up."

I slid my foot back and forth across the hardwood. Shannon might be obnoxious but she was clearly not stupid. "What do the police say about that?"

"All they care about is making their own lives easy. Suicide with a note. Open-and-closed case, no actual work involved."

"You don't have a copy of that note, do you?"

"Oh, no. Mommy dearest wouldn't allow that, too personal." Shannon rolled her eyes as if her mother's desire to keep her husband's last words to her private was completely ridiculous.

"But you did read the note."

"A day after his death I fulfilled my family obligations and paid a visit to the grieving widow. The note was on the nightstand. I read it while she was in the bathroom. You should have seen the hysterics she staged after she found me with it. The woman should go into acting—she'd have a gold statue for every room in her house."

"Right—well, do you have anything else that might help me?"

"No. Oh, wait, yes. There's a chance that his mistress lives up in San Francisco."

"His girlfriend lives in…" My mind immediately went to Tolsky's frequent visits to the San Francisco Ritz. "Wait, didn't I just ask you if you knew anything about his supposed lover?"

"No, you asked me if he had been discreet. I just chose to volunteer this. If you're going to play detective, you'd better learn how to ask the right questions. Isn't that what Alicia Bright would do?"

If Mark Baccon ever got out, I was definitely going to set her up on a blind date. I leaned forward and gave her my most insincere smile. "Okay, then, is there anything else you'd like to volunteer? It is your five million on the line, after all."

"Can't think of a thing."

"Do you, by chance, have your mother's number?"

"She won't talk to you."

"Why don't you give it to me anyway?"

Shannon released a rather dramatic sigh before pulling out a piece of notepaper to write down two of Margaret Tolsky's phone numbers. "Here's her home and her cell phone. I hope you like voice mail. My mother thinks it's chic to be unavailable. However, I believe the Chanel boutique is getting a new shipment today— I'll write down the address and directions, maybe you'll get lucky and catch her there. Do you know what she looks like?"

"I've seen her picture before."

Shannon nodded and walked around the desk to hand me the information. "I'm afraid we're going to have to wrap this up. I have a meeting in a few minutes. We're trying to decide how to publicize *Dark as Night*. Not that it's really necessary— DC Smooth's current living situation will give the film enough publicity to keep it in the public eye for the next ten years."

Someone must have sucked the oxygen out of the room, because all of a sudden I was finding it difficult to breathe. "DC Smooth? DC Smooth had a part in a recent Tolsky production?"

"Yes, it's not a huge role but it's memorable. The movie's already controversial, and now with DC serving a fifty-year sentence for murder, well it'll be on the cover of every magazine around, from *Time* to *Teen People*."

"So he...he did...wait." Shannon was looking at me like I was completely insane and I couldn't really blame her. Questions were spinning around in my head like a tornado and I couldn't grasp any one of them long enough to voice it articulately.

"I'm sorry but I really must ask you—"

"Are you in contact with him?" I blurted out.

"With who?"

"DC Smooth—is there any communication between Tolsky Productions and DC Smooth?"

"Well, yes. There is some communication with him. It's obviously a lot more limited now that he's been convicted, but he likes to be updated on developments."

"Can you put me in touch with him?"

"Are you a fan? He's not talking to fans."

"No, I mean yes, but that's not why I want to reach him." I took a step closer to her, eager to explain my interest. "I think there may be a connection between your father's death and JJ Money's."

"Really?" Shannon fingered her tennis bracelet as she considered the possibility. "That's a bit of a stretch, don't you think? Well, never mind, if you think researching it may prove that my father's death wasn't a suicide, then it's worth the effort. I'll see what I can do about setting up a phone appointment for you with DC. Can I reach you at your home number?"

I stood up. "That would be great. I left it with your receptionist when I made the appointment. Do you need it again?"

"No, no that will be fine." She escorted me to the door. "Just be sure whatever you dig up is tangible enough to sway the insurance company."

"It'll be my top priority."

"Right, well then, off you go."

"One more thing, you don't by any chance know Jason Beck or Mark Baccon, do you?"

"Never heard of them."

"How about Anatoly Darinsky, do you know him?"

Shannon wrinkled her upturned nose. "Unfortunately, yes."

 CHAPTER 14

"The hot ones are always gay, married, or murderers."
—*Sex, Drugs and Murder*

My hand fell from the doorknob. "You…you know Anatoly?"

"I believe that is what I just said."

"H-how?"

"My father knew him when they were children in Russia. Supposedly my father was some kind of mentor to him."

"Were they in contact while living in the States?"

"Not much. Anatoly lived in New York, but when my father went back East they would meet, and Anatoly paid a visit every other year or so. The man tries to come across as intelligent and competent, but in truth he's a complete imbecile. My father told me they met when he rescued Anatoly from some kids who were giving him a beating. My father always had to champion the underdog, and Anatoly, being a Jew and all…oops, no offense."

I knew by the way that Shannon had pronounced the word "Jew" that I should be completely offended, however the only emotion I could manage was horror. When I didn't respond right away Shannon made a show of looking at her watch. "I am sorry, but I really must get to that meeting."

"Right, I'll...I'll be hearing from you later then? About talking with DC Smooth?"

"I said I'll be in touch."

I nodded and walked numbly from her office. It felt like it took me an hour to get from there to my rental car. All my instincts had been wrong. I had shared a cab with him, spent the day with him, kissed him, hell, I had almost made love to him...just a few hours after he had chopped Barbie up with a hatchet.

I squeezed the keys into my palm until they made an indentation. How could I have been so stupid? I had been dating a serial killer. Not Dena, me. This went way beyond the standard "I went out with him twelve times before I found out he had a wife" faux pas. How could I have been so completely deceived? Dena knew and she hadn't even met him. My horror started to melt into something else—total rage. Fuck him. He thought he had me fooled? Well guess what, I was five steps ahead of him. I jammed the key into the ignition and took off in search of a Starbucks. I was going to find the evidence I needed, hand it over to the police, and beat the living shit out of him before they had a chance to haul his sorry ass to his private cell on death row.

I parked the car and called Shannon's mother on my cell as I got in line to order my Frappuccino. As predicted I got her voice mail. I cleared my throat before the beep. "Hi, my name is Sophie Katz, I'm a...an acquaintance of your daughter's and I was a business associate of your husband's. Shannon gave me your number. I was hoping that we could talk for just a few minutes. There are just a few things I need to ask you." I left all my phone numbers and hung up. Hopefully my evasiveness would pique her curiosity enough to call back. Next, I speed-dialed Dena.

"Guilty Pleasures, how can we make you smile?"

"Dena, it's me."

"Sophie. How's Hell? Or do you prefer to call it L.A.?"

"Funny, it doesn't look like Hell, in fact it looks a lot like a Starbucks."

"They have Starbucks in Hell, they only serve decaf."

I winced. "I think Dante's *Inferno* would be preferable. But I didn't call to discuss my addiction, I wanted you to know that Jason's off the hook."

"Yeah, I heard. I *told* you it wasn't him."

"What do you mean you heard? Wait a minute." I brought the phone away from my ear just long enough to place an order. "Okay, I'm back, explain yourself."

"First off, he was at a job orientation when Barbie was killed, and he has a solid alibi for the evening Tolsky was killed, I've verified all of it. Oh, and as far as I can tell he's never been to New York. Secondly I talked to Barbie's parents again. All of Mark's shit is hitting the fan. You know I saw that bastard in front of the store a few weeks ago but I didn't know who he was. I wish Barbie had seen him, then maybe…" Dena coughed in a failed attempt to disguise the tremor that had colored her last words. "So here's the deal—Mark was a chief player in a major Vegas drug ring," she continued, her voice back to its original strength. "All the celebrity addicts purchased their happy juice from this guy. Maybe not directly every time, but his hand was always in the pie in one way or another."

"Uh-huh, so how is this relevant?"

"How is this relevant? Sophie, it was *him*. JJ Money was a known addict. He went to Vegas all the time, and I'm sure Tolsky made a few trips, or if not, you better believe some of his buddies did. He had a major in with both guys. He's your stalker and he's gonna get fried for it. How's that for justice?"

I collected my drink from the counter and took a long sip of whipped cream. "So you think Mark is our psycho because he might have dealt drugs to JJ Money and Tolsky, pre-suming, of course, that Tolsky has ever even been to Vegas, which is a pretty big presumption considering it's based on absolutely *nothing.*"

"Oh, excuse me, amateur sleuth extraordinaire. Do you have a better suspect?"

"Yeah, as a matter of fact I do." I closed my eyes. I wasn't ready to verbalize it. That would make it too real.

"Sophie, you there?"

"Anatoly. Anatoly and Tolsky were friends. I know it for a fact."

"Oh, shit, Sophie."

I moved the brownie bits around in my cup. I couldn't think of anything to say.

"Are you going to tell the police?"

"Tell them what, exactly?"

"Right, we've been over this. So how are we going to collect evidence?"

"I got two leads from Tolsky's daughter that I think are worth following up on. The first involves researching one of Tolsky's extracurricular activities. He was having an affair with a woman who most likely lives in San Francisco."

The line was quiet for a moment or two. Finally I heard what I assumed was Dena sucking air in through her teeth. "So…you think Anatoly might be a…woman?"

The corners of my mouth began to shake, threatening the frown I had been wearing since I had spoken with Shannon. "No! I think that there's a chance that Anatoly knows the woman Tolsky's been dating, and maybe she knows me and that's how he decided to make me his next target, or maybe the two of them are working together. That's what we have to find out. But Anatoly's a man—that fact doesn't require further investigation."

"And you know this because you checked, right?"

"Dena."

"Because I've seen some pretty convincing transvestites, Sophie. And some of the hard-core lesbians can give a whole new definition to 'butch.' I remember this one person came into the shop and, I swear…she was a member of that group Dykes on Bikes and… Oh, fuck, didn't you say Anatoly drove a Harley? Do you think—"

"No, Dena, he's not a dyke on a bike." The woman at the next table gave me a funny look; I turned my chair away from her and continued in a hushed tone. "He's a male. He was born a male, he grew up as a male and he is now just one big male."

"How big? Are we talking cucumber or zucchini?"

"Dena, I really need you to focus here, okay? We are not talking about sex. We are talking about murder."

"Well, actually, we're talking about *Sex, Drugs* and *Murder.* You are the one who came up with the title."

"Dena."

"Okay, okay, I'm sorry. I just thought it might help to lighten things up a bit. So we have to figure out what Frisco chick was giving it up for Tolsky. What else?"

"DC Smooth is featured in an upcoming Tolsky production."

"Oh, yeah, I think I read something about that. They filmed one of his scenes between court appearances."

"Really? God, that is so weird. I mean, who are these people that they can be tried for murder one minute and then be putting makeup on to prep for their film debut the next? That is just not normal…."

"Sophie?

"Yeah?"

"Focus."

"Cute." I rested my elbows on the faux pine table. "Okay, Shannon said that she would try to set up a telephone interview with DC for me."

"My, my, aren't we the little criminal social climber. Who's next, Manson?"

"Hey, at this rate you never know. Anyway, those are the only two bits of information that Shannon gave me that might possibly lead me to some sort of tangible evidence. If it doesn't work, if I turn up nothing…"

"It'll work. We know who the killer is, we know his strategy, it's just a matter of time till we nail him."

"Time is the one thing we haven't—"

"We're going to get him, Sophie."

I slurped up the last remnants of my Frappuccino. I believed her. What choice did I have? "I have four hours before my flight leaves—what should I do?"

"Why don't you try to contact Tolsky's wife? Maybe she knows who the other woman is."

"Tried that. She's presently missing in action."

"Then try to relax and do some L.A. stuff. Go get yourself a drive-through Botox injection or something. Nothing will cheer a girl up like getting her face paralyzed."

I laughed out loud, causing a few of my fellow caffeine addicts to turn and look. "I love you, Dena. No matter how down I am you always find a way to get me up."

"You have no idea how many men have told me the exact same thing."

I giggled and leaned back in my chair. A sophisticated but anorexicly thin older woman walked through the door and got in line. She had tastefully dyed white-blond hair that she had shaped into a stylish shoulder-length cut, and her skin was unnaturally youthful. She looked incredibly familiar.

"Sophie, are you still there?"

"Yeah, I'm here. It's just that this woman walked in and I know I've seen her before but I can't place her."

"Not all that surprising considering your location. She's probably some struggling actress who landed a bit part on one episode of *Melrose Place.*"

"No, she's not really giving off a starlet kind of vibe…." I watched the woman pat her perfect hair…and then it hit me. "Dena, I know her because I've seen her picture in the paper. It's Mrs. Tolsky!"

"Wait. Sophie, are you sure? L.A.'s a big place and it would be a pretty big coincidence if Mrs. Tolsky walked into the same café that you're in just when you were hoping to talk to her."

"I know it's a miracle, but I swear to God that's her!" I slapped my hand against the table as Mrs. Tolsky approached the register. "That is why I love Starbucks. It doesn't matter how much money you have or what social world you're from, chances are you will still eventually end up at a Starbucks in order to revel in the taste sensation provided by the Frappuccino. It is the great equalizer of our time."

"I'm serious, Sophie, you need to find yourself a twelve-step program."

"Yeah, whatever, Dena. I gotta go."

I hung up the phone and walked up to the bar where Mrs. Tolsky was now awaiting her drink.

"Mrs. Tolsky?"

The woman looked me up and down. "Do I know you?"

"No…no, but I just left a message on your cell phone…."

Mrs. Tolsky angled her body away from me. "I'm sorry but I don't have time for this right now. I have to pick up my drink and go."

"Oh, this won't take long. I just think that maybe if we took few minutes to talk we could help each other make sense of what happened to your husband. I…I know how difficult it is to lose a loved one and it must be awful to think that someone you cared for took his own life, but I think that your daughter may be right about it not being a suicide."

A barista announced the arrival of a nonfat sugar-free vanilla latte, and Mrs. Tolsky snatched it up. She held it in front of her as if it could serve as some kind of barrier between me and her. "I believe your voice message indicated that you spoke to my daughter. Is that correct?"

"Yes, and…"

"Did she seem like a person whose opinion you could trust?"

I hesitated. There was nothing about Shannon that I trusted, but then again, I didn't trust walking skeletons who ordered nonfat sugar-free lattes either.

Mrs. Tolsky took my silence as a reply. "There you have it. Now, if you'll excuse me I must get to my appointment." She turned her back on me and stormed out of the café.

I ran out to the parking lot in hot pursuit. "Mrs. Tolsky, wait, just give me two minutes."

"We have nothing to discuss," she replied as she slipped into her Mercedes. "Please refrain from making a nuisance of yourself."

"Okay, just one minute, then!" I raised my voice as she slammed the door and started the engine. "I'll even buy you a Frappuccino! It's low-fat and everything!"

But Mrs. Tolsky just put the car into gear and drove away. "Gosh," I whispered to myself, "I can't imagine which of her parents Shannon takes after."

The rest of my stay in L.A. turned out to be completely unproductive. I tried Mrs. Tolsky's cell a few more times, to no avail. I drove by the Tolskys' residence in hopes that I might see her or her car in the driveway. I didn't quite anticipate that the driveway would be the length of Route 66. Louis XIV would have been green with envy.

By the time I got back to San Francisco the only thing I wanted to investigate was my bed. I was a little nervous about the idea of spending the night alone in my apartment when a former member of the Russian and Israeli armies might be trying to kill me, but at least I knew who he was now. And he knew I knew; the knife thing hadn't been real subtle. So he would have to proceed more carefully going forward. Maybe

I'd get lucky and he'd abandon his project and move on to someone else. Stephen King, perhaps. He was pretty violent.

I took a cab from the airport. No long searches for the elusive parking spot tonight. Now I could just step out right in front of my door, crawl upstairs and...I squinted my eyes to make out who was sitting on the front steps as the cab approached. It was a woman. As we got closer I could see Mary Ann's curly brown hair. What the hell was she thinking, sitting out there alone like that? I quickly paid the driver and got out to meet her. "Mary Ann, this is not safe—"

She jumped to her feet and grabbed both my hands. "I did the research on JJ Money. Want to hear?"

No, I wanted to sleep. I looked up at the windows to my place and then back to Mary Ann. She was beginning to cut off the circulation in my fingers. "Okay, come up and tell me."

I led her in, threw some food at Mr. Katz and collapsed on the love seat. Meanwhile Mary Ann was doing some kind of agitated little dance in the middle of my living room. Whatever she had discovered must have been big. I sat up a little straighter.

"So, don't keep me in suspense."

"Three weeks before JJ Money was killed, his car was vandalized in an upscale parking garage."

"They have upscale parking garages in New York?"

"Somebody painted something that looked like a gang insignia on his driver's side door. Have you ever seen the video for *On Top?*"

"Only the video they keep showing on the news. You know, where they show the guy bleeding in the alley the way JJ Money later was bleeding himself after he was shot."

"But earlier in the video someone paints a gang insignia on a car, right on the driver's side door."

The veins in my hand bulged as I tightened my grip on the armrest. Mary Ann had her hands clasped in front of her and was simply beaming as she waited for me to respond. I opened my mouth, then closed it, trying to figure out what words would fully capture the feeling I was experiencing. "Well…shit." I kind of thought those words summed it up rather nicely, but Mary Ann wasn't mollified.

"Did you hear me? I said…"

"I heard you. I guess there isn't any doubt anymore. The murders are connected. This guy has a pattern—mess with the victim's car and then…well, then kill them."

"Did anything happen to Tolsky's car?" I couldn't help but be irked by the enthusiasm in her voice.

"I don't know, but I'm sure as hell going to find out."

"I'm sure it was vandalized. I'm just sure of it. JJ Money's and Tolsky's murders are linked to what is happening to you and I am the one who figured it out." She looked like she was going to burst into a set of cartwheels.

"Congratulations, Mary Ann, that's great. Too bad I had to become the target of an intended homicide in order to prove your genius, huh?"

Mary Ann's shoulders dropped from their elevated position. "I'm sorry, that probably sounded insensitive."

"A tad."

"It's just that I think I might have a gift for detective work, and that made me feel kind of good about myself, like I was…like I was smart."

I sighed and reached my hand out to her in apology. "I'm sorry, really. I'm just exhausted, that's all. You have been indispensable in all this. I never would have made the connection between me, Tolsky and JJ Money without you."

Mary Ann was beaming again. "Thank you." She hopped onto the cushion next to me. "This is so neat. It's like I've discovered this secret talent, kind of like when I first got into makeup. I mean, I can look at someone and immediately know if they're a spring or a summer or—"

"So, did you find out anything that would link Anatoly to JJ Money?"

"No, nothing to link Anatoly or Jason other than the fact that JJ Money did live in New York and you said Anatoly did too."

"That was never in question."

"Yes, well, I confirmed it." She leaned over to pet Mr. Katz, who was gently kneading her nylons. "Oh, but I did find something to connect him with Mark Baccon."

I slowly pushed myself to the edge of the love seat. "What?"

"I said—"

"I know what you said—what did you find?" Could I have been wrong? Was it possible that the police had arrested the right guy and I wasn't the world's worst judge of character?

"I found something to connect Barbie's ex with—"

"Listen to what I am asking." I stood up so I could better resist the urge to shake her. "What did you find that connects JJ Money to Mark Baccon?"

"Oh. I was looking at some pictures of JJ Money that had been in the magazines and there was one taken at some club or party in Las Vegas, and in the far background I was able to make out Mark Baccon. I wouldn't have noticed if I hadn't just looked at a picture of him in this morning's newspaper. He looks so mean. Do you think they try to find pictures of criminals that make them look mean or do they always look like that? I've always wondered—"

"Mary Ann, do you realize what this means?"

She sunk her teeth into her lower lip the way she always does when she discovers herself to be completely lost.

"Mary Ann, Mark could be our bad guy after all."

"But you said the police were wrong about everything."

"No, I said the police sometimes make mistakes, but that doesn't mean they're not right a lot too. Maybe this is one of those 'right' times." Please, God, please let it be a "right" time.

Mary Ann freed her lip. She pulled Mr. Katz onto her lap and methodically scratched him behind the ears. "It would be nice if neither you nor Dena had been going out with a killer."

"Yeah, that would be nice." I glanced down at Mr. Katz, who was now in a purring frenzy. I scratched him there all the time and he never reacted that way for me. "You know what would be even nicer? Knowing that the man who was after me is locked up behind bars and ain't ever getting out."

"Unless he breaks out. Oh my gosh, Sophie, what if he already has?"

"It's pretty hard to break out of jail, Mary Ann, plus it would have been on the news."

"Are you sure? Remember when we watched that movie *Copycat?* Harry Connick Junior escaped and was out long enough to kill two armed guards and he almost got Sigourney Weaver and I don't think that was on the news, otherwise Sigourney Weaver would have seen it coming. Oh, and in *Bandits* Bruce Willis just jumps into a cement truck or something and drives out of the prison. He didn't even plan ahead for it."

"Mary Ann?"

"Yes?"

"Those were movies."

Mary Ann started at my rise in volume, thus upsetting Mr. Katz's little massage session.

"I'm sorry…again." My hand went up to my temples. "Really, like I said, I'm just very, very tired and on edge. I'm trying to cope with all this but…but…God, it's just so much."

Mary Ann removed my unfaithful pet from her skirt and encircled me in her ballerina arms. "It's okay, Sophie. It's all going to be over soon. We're going to figure this out and everything will be okay again. In the meantime, just remember it could always be worse."

"Someone may be trying to kill me and I don't know who. How can it be worse?"

"Well…there could be *a lot* of people trying to kill you."

I disengaged myself so that I could obtain enough distance to gawk at her. Her teeth went down on her lip again.

"Not helpful?" she asked meekly.

"I think I'm going to bed now."

CHAPTER 15

"One man's tragedy is another man's apocalypse."
—*Sex, Drugs and Murder*

I woke up the next morning groggy but less ornery than the night before. Despite my insults, Mary Ann had volunteered to spend the night. I did feel safer with her there. After all, if the killer broke in, Mary Ann could try to engage him in conversation, and then the two of us could quietly make our escape while the intruder was trying to pick himself up off the floor.

I threw on a robe, crept past the guest room where Mary Ann still slept, and went down to the lobby to collect the morning's paper. When I unrolled it a few minutes later on my dining table I was greeted by a six-by-eight color photograph of Mark Bacon. This was going to get a lot of publicity. Despite what people thought about big cities, people didn't often get hacked up in public parks. Homeless people died in the streets, gang members shot each other, an occasional wronged spouse opted for a gun rather than a divorce attorney...but going after someone with a hatchet, now that was thinking outside of the box.

The phone rang and I nearly went screaming for the door. Mr. Katz looked at me in bewilderment as I placed a shaky hand over my heart. This would be a good time to start smoking pot. I listened to my voice rattle off the greeting before the beep. "Soph, honey, you home?"

I snatched up the phone. "Marcus, if you are calling to be-rate me for not personally calling you after finding Barbie—"

"I'm calling to admit that I'm a stupid little shit. I wouldn't blame you if you dumped me and replaced me with some rising star at Vidal...although that would be a mistake because I know your hair like no one else ever will. But I'm a little shit, nonetheless."

"Why are you a shit?'

"You came to me for advice and guidance and I told you to lighten up, let your guard down, and then look what happened. God, honey, I could have gotten you killed."

I sighed and pulled a box of sweetened puffed rice cereal from the cupboard. "First off, I didn't come to you for advice. I came to you for a deep condition and trim, you just gave the advice as a little unwanted bonus."

"Go ahead, rip me apart, I can take it."

"Marcus, there's nothing to take." Mr. Katz hopped up on the counter so he could glare at me at eye level. I put the cereal down and went for the kibble. "I would have eventually come to the same conclusion you did. Maybe it would have taken a few extra hours, but in the end I would have called Dena, apologized and made a date to meet her at the park. Nothing would have been different, except you'd feel less guilty and I'd need a haircut."

"Still..."

"No stills. It wasn't your fault." I put the bowl down and managed to remove my hand before Mr. Katz inadvertently ate it. "You do believe me now, though, right?"

"You can definitely count me among the believers."

"Mmm, too bad the police aren't."

"Ugh, the police. They just always have to have their evidence."

"Well, I'm trying to get some of that."

"Are you playing sleuth?"

"Pretty much. I'm playing Alicia Bright." A few grains of the handful of cereal I had attempted to shove in my mouth fell to the floor. Thank God I didn't have video-conferencing.

"Oh, how fun. Can I play? I can be, I can be…does Alicia Bright have a sexy gay sidekick?"

"Nope. But I am the author. I could add you in."

"Oh, definitely add me. Look, despite what you said, I really do feel awful about Tuesday. Can I take you out for lunch today as an apology? We could work on your mystery."

"What the hell. Maybe you can help me make sense of everything because I'm sure as heck not doing a very good job of it on my own."

"One-thirty, then? Lulu's? I haven't been to Lulu's in ages."

"Lulu's it is. I'll meet you there."

I hung up the phone just as Mary Ann glided into the kitchen. She looked impossibly sexy in the oversize T-shirt I had lent her and her hair had this tousled "come hither" thing going for it. I, on the other hand was modeling long johns, fuzzy socks and a hairdo that was somewhat reminiscent of a mushroom cloud. I managed to swallow enough of my jealousy to give her a halfhearted smile. "Did you sleep well?"

"Gosh, no. I tossed and turned all night thinking about everything. Can't you tell?"

Life was so unfair. "Mark Baccon's in the paper today." I lead her over to the dining table and tapped the front page.

Mary Ann leaned over it and examined the photo. "Wow, he looks like a total criminal."

"He is a criminal."

"Well, yeah. I don't know if you could look like that and expect to find a nice job. You know, this is why I think people should be more open-minded to the idea of men

wearing makeup. If he just had a little under-eye con-
cealer, maybe some foundation to lessen the appearance of
that scar…"

"I'm meeting Marcus today. I'm going to bring him a little more into the loop. Maybe he'll think of something we
haven't."

"Like what?"

"Well, I don't know, I haven't thought of it yet."

Mary Ann nodded solemnly. "I wish I could stay, but my
shift starts at one."

"Too bad, we really could have used your brain power."

Mary Ann smiled and excused herself so she could go
make herself "presentable." I took the time to stuff more rice
puffs in my mouth.

By ten-thirty Mary Ann had taken off and I was left alone
to contemplate my life, whatever was left of it. I dialed the
numbers for Margaret Tolsky and left messages. This time I
said that I could prove that some of the things that came out
in the press after Alex Tolsky's death were incorrect and I
wanted to be sure she knew the truth so her lawyers could
go for a libel suit. That *had* to pique her curiosity. She may
be an elitist but she was also human.

I was slipping on my coat with the intention of grabbing
some coffee before I met Marcus when the phone rang.
Bingo. I grabbed the receiver. "Hello? Mrs. Tolsky?"

"*Miss* Tolsky," Shannon corrected. "DC Smooth will be
calling your house today at twelve o'clock Pacific time."

"Wait, you—" I checked my watch. "But that's in less than
an hour. When did you make the appointment?"

"Yesterday, before I left the office."

"So why are you just telling me about it now?"

"I've been busy."

"You've been busy?" The words squeaked out at a couple
of octaves above my normal pitch. "I'm trying to prove that
your father didn't commit suicide, I thought you wanted that."

"I do, but I also have a life to live. Besides, this idea that DC has any connection to my father's death is just inane. He lives across the country, and he was in the middle of a murder trial when my father was killed. As far as I can see, you're wasting everyone's time."

I stared at the phone. If I threw it across the room it might break, and then I'd miss the call from DC Smooth. I'd have to find something less important to smash. "If you think I'm wasting your time, why are you helping me at all?"

"I don't think you're doing any major harm. Plus, you're one of two people who believe me when I say that my father didn't commit suicide, and if you're going to try to convince more people of that, then I will try to be as cooperative as possible."

"Cooperative would have been calling me at the time you made the appointment."

"Do you *not* want the appointment now?"

"No, don't be—" I stopped myself before I said something that would piss her off as much as she had pissed me off. "I want the appointment. I'll be here at noon."

"Good. You'll let me know if you discover anything useful?"

"Oh, yeah, at least within the first forty-eight hours. I do have a life to live, after all."

"Goodbye, Sophie—"

"Wait." I held the receiver in both hands as if that would keep her from hanging up. "I need to ask you something."

"What?"

"In the months before he died did anything happen to your father's car? Was it vandalized, stolen, broken into? Anything he might have mentioned would be helpful."

"Nothing happened to his car that I'm aware of. Unless you count his paranoia over his rearview mirror."

"Meaning?"

"We had a business lunch about a month before he died. We got in a disagreement, as usual, and I left halfway through.

Fifteen minutes later he called me, irate, accusing me of read-justing his rearview mirror. He was drunk, of course."

Now why did that sound familiar? I glanced over at my video collection under the TV set.

"Oh my God, Shannon, that's it. In *Silent Killer* the first person she killed was in his car. She was hiding in the back seat. The first thing the victim noticed was that the rearview mirror was askew."

"Did you not just hear me tell you he was drunk? He probably bumped into the mirror when he was crawling into his car."

I threw my hands up in hopeless defeat. I reminded my-self that I had no real interest in convincing Shannon of any-thing. "One more question. Who's the other person who believes you?"

"Anatoly," Shannon replied. "He's as certain as I am that it wasn't a suicide. If he wasn't such an idiot he could help me prove that. Instead I'm left depending on you, as pathetic as that is. Now I really must go."

"Wait, wait, what did Anatoly say… Hello? Shannon, are you there? Hello?" I slammed down the receiver. "She hung up on me. That cross-burning little tramp just hung up on me." I wanted to call Shannon back and ask her about Anatoly, but I was afraid that I would just alienate her completely, and the truth was, I might still need her help. Best to call her after a drink. Or a partial lobotomy.

I turned on the television hoping to find something that would distract me while I waited for DC Smooth to call. As it turns out that wasn't necessary because the buzzer dis-tracted me instead. Had Mary Ann forgotten something? I hesitated before pressing the intercom. "Who's there?"

"Detective Lorenzo. I hope this isn't a bad time, but I need to ask you a few questions."

Well, he was about the last person I had expected. I buzzed him up in lieu of a verbal response and greeted him at the door. He nodded as he entered the flat. His smile lacked the necessary warmth to make it appear friendly. I glanced at my watch. I really didn't want him to be around when DC called.

"Going somewhere?" he asked before making himself comfortable at the dining table.

"I'm expecting a call from a friend. What did you want to ask me?"

"I assume you've seen the news about Baccon."

I sat opposite him and pushed the newspaper in his direction. "Kind of hard to miss."

Lorenzo looked at the picture with apparent disinterest. "It was a pleasure to arrest him. He's a real pervert. But then, you know that, don't you?"

I didn't like the way this was going. "I visited him in jail after his arrest, if that's what you mean."

"That is what I mean. Why did you do that?" Lorenzo spotted Mr. Katz and made a little motion with his fingers. Mr. Katz took a step closer and allowed himself to be stroked.

Maybe I should have named him Judas.

"I went to see him because I wanted the opportunity to decide for myself if he was guilty or innocent."

"And what did you conclude?" he asked.

"He's guilty of being a prick, but I'm not convinced he killed Barbie."

"Interesting." Lorenzo stopped petting my cat and took out a notebook and pen. "Do you think he's responsible for any of the things that happened to you?"

"I doubt it. He has no motive."

"True." He scribbled something down. This was getting boring. I glanced over at the TV, which I had left on. Montel Williams was asking why his guest wanted to marry a cross-dressing prostitute. "I was able to get the phone records for the day you claimed to have gotten all the prank calls," Lorenzo continued. "There was one call from Ooh-

La-La Salon, one from a telemarketer and several from pay phones in the Russian Hill area."

So the caller had been nearby—that wasn't good. "Marcus called from the salon. As for the pay-phone calls, I didn't hear any background noise. Maybe something was placed over the receiver."

"If you're right about Manning and Baccon, the prank caller could have been a woman."

I crossed my arms and tilted my chair back onto two legs. "I know you're suggesting something, but I'll be damned if I have any idea what it is."

"One of the phone calls was made from a pay phone outside a nearby Starbucks."

A gasp escaped my lips. "Anatoly was there that day. He had opportunity."

"Oh?" Lorenzo laid his pen down beside the notepad. "I wasn't aware of that. In fact, the only person I'm sure was there was you. You made an impression on the cashier."

I almost fell backward in my chair. "You're not suggesting that I made the calls myself."

Lorenzo picked his pen back up. "You had opportunity."

"And who do you think picked up the phone to answer the call? Casper, the friendly ghost?"

"I see you have an answering machine. Is that new?"

I shook my head so hard that I experienced a moment of dizziness. Not a good thing, since I was already feeling sick to my stomach. "So you think that I set this whole thing up to make it look like I was being stalked?"

"Your words. Not mine."

"Yeah, well, they're your thoughts. And there's a problem with your theory. The last call I received was a little after 6:40 p.m. Less than ten seconds passed between the time I got that phone call and the time that Marcus Bettencourt came over to pick me up. Feel free to ask Marcus what time he showed up. Even an Olympic sprinter couldn't run from a pay phone to this apartment in ten seconds."

"But the last call came from your cell phone."

Everything froze as I allowed the words to sink in. I had been in the shower, and after that I had had the hairdryer on. And when Marcus had come to pick me up I hadn't been able to find my cell phone. But it had been in plain view when I got home. I had originally assumed that had been an oversight on my part. But that wasn't it at all. Had the killer been in my bedroom? Or maybe the closet? My eyes met Lorenzo's. He wouldn't believe me. I knew that. And the more nervous I appeared now, the more convinced of my guilt he would become. I had to remain calm and be extremely rational. Most of all, I had to get him out of there.

"Detective Lorenzo, things have obviously changed a lot since the D.A. got those phone records for you. An arrest has been made in Barbie's murder case, which is the only crime I have reported that has been investigated. With the exception of the statement I gave after Andy attacked me, and I think we can all agree that his crimes are completely unconnected to what happened to Barbie. Mark Baccon has been charged with that crime and is awaiting trial, which means that some, if not all, of the other detectives think he's the guilty party, and the D.A.'s office obviously thinks it can convict. That means that you are doing this interview based on suspicions no one else in your department shares. And *that* means there is no real reason for me to subject myself to this." Unless the police thought I was working with Mark.... But I didn't want to verbalize that just in case he hadn't thought of it. I rolled my shoulders back and tried to look confident. "Now, if you'll excuse me, I'm expecting a phone call."

Lorenzo stood up and walked to the door. "From anyone I know?"

"Yeah, Mr. None-of-Your-Damn-Business."

Lorenzo laughed, in spite of himself. "It's always good talking to you." He went to the door and stepped over the threshold. "By the way, we dusted your car for prints. The only fingerprints inside the car were Mr. Darinsky's, who I understand drove the car to and from the station, and yours. In fact, some of yours were right around the slashes in the upholstery."

"Obviously, I touched it after I found it torn up."

Lorenzo flashed me with another one of his insincere grins. "Obviously." He calmly turned around and walked down the stairs.

My bravado left with him. The fear I had been repressing washed over me like a bucket of ice water. My arms and legs were numb and my lungs felt like they were lodged in my throat. There was no sanctuary. I could no longer go to sleep without fearing for my life. The same went for showering or even washing my face. How many times had the killer been in my home? And how many times had he been here with me?

The phone rang and I nearly bolted out of the apartment before I remembered the scheduled interview with DC Smooth. I quickly closed and locked the door and crossed the room to pick up. I felt a rush of relief when the operator asked if I was willing to accept the charges for a collect call. Who would have thought that a call from a federal penitentiary could be so comforting?

"Yo, is this Sophie Katz?"

"Yeah," I breathed. "DC Smooth?"

"That's me. So what's this about? They're tellin' me you're some kind of private investigator. Who hired you?"

I stared out the window and weighed my options. I could lie. He might be more cooperative that way. But I was tired and stressed and I was bound to make an idiot out of myself. "Um, no. I'm a novelist. But I don't want to talk to you about a book or anything. I just think that you're innocent, I've always thought that you were innocent—"

"Yo, hold up. That's cool of you to be throwing me your support and all, but I'm not talkin' to fans. I don't have an unlimited calling plan here, you know what I'm sayin'? I gotta save my minutes for my family."

"No, wait, I didn't explain myself well." I started pacing the room. I couldn't blow this. "I'm not just calling to give you support. I think that the person who killed JJ Money is still out there. I think he's the same guy who killed Tolsky, and I think he just killed someone else I knew. I want your help so I can stop him."

"That's fucked up, man. I didn't do shit and I'm doin' fifty and the motherfucker who shot JJ Money is out there icing people left and right? He's white, right? They wouldn't let a brother get away with that shit."

"I don't really know if he's white or not, but I think so. Did you ever meet a guy named Anatoly Darinsky?"

"I don't think so. What's the man look like?"

"Tall, about six foot two, dark hair, brown eyes, Russian accent."

"Naw, I don't think I know him. Is he the killer?"

"I don't know. What about Mark Baccon?"

Silence.

"Look, I know this call's probably being recorded. All I'm asking is if you know him."

"I met him once or twice in Vegas. I don't do business with the man. I think he hooked up JJ a few times, but that's just me speculatin' here. I don't know nothin' for sure 'cept the man's bad news. People have their reasons for hangin' with him, but if he didn't have connections he'd have been ratted out and locked up a long time ago."

I sat back down. "What kind of connections does he have?"

"You know, it's like I was sayin', he knew JJ, maybe a few other pop stars and movie people and shit. I'm not saying nothin' for sure, though. That's just shit I heard through the grapevine, you feel me? That's all I know."

"He's in jail now. He's accused of killing his ex-girlfriend."

"Yeah? Well, he probably did it. Like I said, bad news. You think he shot JJ Money?"

"Maybe."

"Fuck, that man has a history that makes mine look like a motherfuckin' Disney movie. If there's a chance he killed JJ, why the fuck aren't the police checking it out? It's because I'm a brother. The cops look at me and they see black. A black man who beat the system and made it big and now they're trying to knock me down. This is bullshit."

"You may be right," I said. "I don't know." I looked out the window at the gray sky. "But I'm going to find out if he did it, or if not him, who did. I'm going to find evidence— I have to—and when I do, they'll have to let you go. Racism aside, this is still a democracy. They can't lock people up for no reason."

"You're a white girl, huh?"

"Half of me is really offended by that."

"Look, you think you can get me out, go for it. You know I got a kid comin'?"

"Yeah, I think I read something about that."

"My woman's eight months pregnant. She's havin' a boy. I want to be there for my kid, you know? I don't want my son takin' shit because his daddy's on the prison block. I've done some stupid shit but I didn't do this, you hear what I'm sayin'?"

"Did you vandalize JJ Money's car?"

"No, man, I never fuckin' touched that man's ride. After he was shot, they questioned me about that vandalism shit, but I was recordin' that day so they couldn't pin it on me. If the cops weren't so set on fryin' my ass they'd be lookin' for the guy who did that. He's probably your murderer."

I nibbled on my thumbnail. I didn't think DC was guilty, but the police did have some reason to think that he was, and it wasn't just because he was black. "I know you answered some of these questions in court but could you tell me how it was that you ended up standing over JJ Money, with the murder weapon a stone's throw away?"

"Hey, I've done some stupid shit in my time. JJ Money and I was never friends. The man was always doggin' me, and I've said some stuff too, but the shit I said was true. So JJ called me that night all hopped up on some dope and he's threatenin' me. The motherfucker was even sayin' shit about my family and my lady. That shit don't fly with me. I told him he should say that smack to my face, then I hear him talkin' to some guy in the background because you know that nigger never knew his own mind. Then he gets back on the phone and tells me to meet him at Nell's."

"But he never made it to Nell's."

"No, man, and that was weird. JJ Money was a pussy, but he knew how the game was played. You don't challenge a brother and not show. Not in our world. That's the kind of shit you don't live down."

If, while in a drunken stupor, I had called some guy with a violent criminal history to tell him off and that guy then asked to meet me, I'd be a no-show too. But that was me. "So you went looking for him."

"Oh, yeah, and I found him all right. Fucker was bleedin' all over the place. I should've just taken off, that would have looked suspicious too. There was no winning, you know? I was gonna call the police, but somebody else heard the gunshots and had already made the call. So there I was. The nigger had been shot with his own motherfuckin' weapon and they still pinned it on me. I had a piece. If I wanted to kill the man, why didn't I use that? How the fuck do they think I got my hands on his gun? The whole thing was a setup and I walked into it."

Mr. Katz hopped up next to me. I moved my feet from under me so as to make a flat surface for him on my lap. "You had your gun with you that night. How come?"

"You never know when you're gonna have to defend yourself. When you do gangsta rap some fucker's always trying to get a piece of you. Shit, JJ Money and I weren't gonna shoot each other. We're rap stars, the police are always gunnin' for us. We don't need to be makin' things easy for them."

I knew DC Smooth was telling me the truth, but he had told me absolutely nothing that I could use to prove it. Yes, he confirmed that JJ Money knew Mark, but I basically already knew that. I mentally reviewed what had been said so far. What was it? There had to be something....

"Yo, you still there?"

"The guy talking in the background to JJ Money, any idea who it was?"

"Naw, my defense attorney drilled me on that too. Fuck if I know, I could barely hear the man. It was a white guy, though, not a brother."

"What makes you say that?"

"I don't know, I wasn't payin' good attention at the time, but I remember thinkin' that he just sounded different, not like the people JJ Money normally ran with."

I swallowed and let my eyes travel up to the ceiling. "Maybe he had an accent?"

"Yeah, he might of. If he did it was minor. Not like those full-on Puerto Rican dudes."

He wasn't sure. There was still a chance that it wasn't Anatoly. But that chance was pretty slim.

"Hey, my time's almost up. You got any more questions?"

"No, no, you gave me the information I needed. Thank you."

"All right, well, let me know what's up. I want to hold my kid. I just want to hold him, you know what I'm sayin'?"

"Yeah, I know. I'll do my best." I hung up the phone and looked at Mr. Katz. "Oh God. This shit is fucked up."

 **CHAPTER 16**

"Knowledge only equates to power if you can figure out what to do with it."
—*Sex, Drugs and Murder*

I couldn't help but be impressed when Donato chauffeured Marcus up to the front door of LuLu's in a new Porsche 911. Apparently crap sells. Or maybe people just wanted to give Donato money. That wasn't such a stretch; I wanted to give him money. But then, I wanted to stuff the money into a G-string.

Donato draped his arm over the door. "Sophie, how are you?"

"Hanging in there. Nice car."

"Yes, it is very freeing. I feel it helps me to release my creativity."

Now, why hadn't I thought of that? I could probably be twice the writer I am if I just bought myself a Porsche.

Marcus leaned over and gave Donato a little peck on the cheek before getting out of the car to present me with a bouquet of calla lilies. "It's a little 'I'm glad you're not dead' present."

"Do they make Hallmarks for that?"

"Probably. They make cards for families of suicide victims, why not ones for potential homicide victims? It could go something like this—'Roses are red, violets are blue, I'm really happy that you're not sleeping with the fishes.'"

I grimaced.

"Too soon?"

"I must go," Donato said, unfastening his seat belt long enough to take off his jacket, thus immediately getting our attention. "Marcus, I'll meet you tonight at the Black Cat."

"Nine o'clock, sweetie."

Donato smiled and gave me a casual wave before riding off in a blaze of glory.

"A 911, huh? Are you sure he's not bi?"

"I got you a bouquet, stay away from my man."

I fingered the arrangement. "Hmm, I get calla lilics, and you get laid. That's fair."

"Don't forget, I'm buying lunch too."

"It's gonna take one hell of a crème caramel to make up for missing out on that."

"Maybe I'll throw in a cookie."

Marcus escorted me in, and over lunch I filled him in on all my latest discoveries. At the beginning of the meal Marcus was ordering various courses with his characteristic enthusiasm and zest; by the end, the waiter was clearing away full plates that he had barely even noticed. He placed both hands flat on the table as if that would help ground him. "You do see how the killer was led to you."

"Well, the guy seems to go for people in the entertainment industry who depict violence in their work. I'm on the outskirts of the entertainment industry but my work is…"

"JJ Money had a role in a Tolsky production," Marcus interjected. "They must have had some contact during the time the killer was planning the first murder that led him to Tolsky. Tolsky met with you to talk about the screenplay you were going to write less than a month before he died—that led the killer to you."

I chewed thoughtfully on a gingersnap. "God, you're totally right. That was so perceptive of you."

"Not really, it was pretty obvious."

"Work with me. I'm trying not to feel like an idiot."

"Not an idiot honey, just a little frazzled." He rattled the ice in his drink. "I agree that you can't rule out that Baccon guy, but I still think it's probably that bastard Anatoly. He was in New York when JJ Money was killed and he had direct access to Tolsky. I mean *hello*. Can we spell *suspicious?*"

I slid down in my chair. "I know, but I just keep hoping that there's another explanation." I used my spoon to make an artistic creation with the remainder of my dessert. "What about the woman Tolsky was seeing in San Francisco? How do you think she fits into it?"

"She may not. Hell, we don't even know if the girl exists." Marcus placed his ankle over the opposite knee. "When you met with Tolsky, did he say anything useful?"

"Useful, hmm, you mean like, 'I'm being stalked by a murderous maniac named Joe and I'm having an extramarital affair with his sister, who happens to live in San Francisco'?"

"That would be useful."

"He didn't say that."

Marcus examined the exposed beams on the restaurant's ceiling. "Did he talk about anything other than work stuff?"

"No, not really." I chewed on the nail of my pinkie. "Wait, he did say he really liked San Francisco?"

"That would not be useful."

"He said he liked the European feeling of the city, the little theaters and the galleries—The galleries!" I dropped my sugarcoated spoon. "Marcus, he said he liked the galleries."

"And we should care about that because…"

"Because Anatoly said he knew the owner of the Sussman Gallery. He said they used to room together in New York."

"That boy's name just keeps popping up."

"Don't you see, Marcus?" I gripped the table to keep myself from jumping out of my seat. "It's not just that we may have established another connection between Anatoly and Tolsky, but we now know of someone *else* who knows Anatoly. Someone we can talk to."

Marcus cocked his head to the side. "It's something."

"Yes, it is, and something is infinitely better than the nothing I've been working with." I grabbed the credit card that Marcus had left on the table and waved it in the air for our waiter to see. "I don't know what your plans are today, but it's time for me to become an art collector."

I was walking so fast that even Marcus with his long legs had to make an effort to keep up. "Honey, the gallery isn't going anywhere, there's no need for us to get ourselves all sweaty and mussed."

"We're on the verge of something big. I can feel it."

We burst into the gallery, prompting the relieved smiles of the two other patrons who could now escape the attention of the commissioned sales staff.

A pudgy male associate with a high forehead and a low ponytail waddled over to us with a welcoming grin. "Hello. How are you both today?"

"We're fine," I said. I made it a point to make eye contact. That was important, because if I didn't, I might have to focus on his nicely cut Italian red blazer that he had paired with a fuchsia silk shirt. "Actually, maybe you could help us."

"That is why I'm here. Allow me to introduce myself, I'm Randolph. Perhaps there is a specific artist you are looking for?"

Marcus and I exchanged looks. He might be Randolph now, but there was little doubt that at birth he had been a Ralph. "No, we're actually looking for the owner. Oh, I'm sorry, this is my friend Marcus and my name is Sophie Katz. I'm a novelist. Perhaps you've read some of my books? They're usually located on the book racks for the *New York Times* bestsellers." Anyone who called himself Randolph would have to be impressed to be cooperative.

"Oh, of course, of course I have." Liar. "How marvelous to make your acquaintance. You are in luck. Usually, it's difficult to catch Mr. Sussman here. However, this afternoon he's been in the office all day. I'll go check to see if he's available. In the meantime, please feel free to look around. We have some new pieces that are absolutely divine."

Marcus stood with his hands on his hips and stared after Ralph as he went off to find Sussman. "Divine? Even when I'm in full camp mode I do not use the word 'divine.'"

I shrugged. "Can't blame a guy for trying. Maybe you could take him under your wing and teach him how to be a subtle queen."

"Uh-uh, it's a talent you have to be born with." He glanced around the room. "Oh, look. There's one of Donato's paintings."

I searched my mind for something positive to say. "Wow, it looks like he used a paintbrush this time. That's good."

"The man is beautiful, he's rich, he gives a blow job that Heidi Fleisch couldn't compete with, so who cares if his paintings look like the work of an angry kindergartener? Somebody's buying."

"As long as you can keep a sense of humor about it."

"It's easy to keep your sense of humor when you're being driven around in a Porsche."

Ralph returned with a tall skinny man with blond hair that was cut in a manner that would have looked rakish on a teenager but just silly on a guy who had quite obviously cleared forty. He extended his hand to me, then to Marcus. "Gary Sussman. How can I be of assistance?"

"Mr. Sussman, I'm so glad to meet you. As Ral—Randolph probably already told you, my name is Sophie Katz and

I'm a novelist. I'm writing a book in which one of my characters owns a gallery. Anatoly Darinsky suggested that you might be able to give me some insight into the art world so I can give my story a sense of authenticity."

Sussman brightened. "Absolutely. I'd be more then happy to answer your questions. And please, call me Gary."

"All right, Gary. Call me Sophie, and this is Marcus."

"I just came along for the art," Marcus said. "Randolph, show me something that will move me. I just so want to be moved."

"I know exactly what you mean." Ralph joined his hands in front of him with a clap. "There are some very stirring pieces by an artist by the name of Rizzetti. May I show you?"

"That would just be divine."

Marcus followed a floating Ralph while I let Gary lead me into his office. I surveyed the space. "Wow, what a great room." I sat down on something that resembled a chair, but then again it might have been a modern Chinese torture device.

"The artist Marian Dominick did it for me. I consider the room itself a piece of art."

"For good reason. It's as stunning as the art you show here." I was having a hard time reconciling what I knew about Anatoly and his apparent friendship with this man. My interactions with Anatoly on the night of Donato's opening had made it abundantly clear to me that Anatoly was intolerant of people who were overly "enlightened," while Gary was so excessively enlightened he was practically glowing.

Gary leaned forward in his chair. "I hope you don't mind my saying this, but you have a very exotic look. What, exactly, is your nationality?"

There was something about this man that just made a person want to mess with him. "My mother is Egyptian and my father is Israeli. They met at a party celebrating the Camp David accords."

He was silent for a beat, clearly unsure if he should believe me. Then a smile crept onto his face. "That is the most fantastic thing I've ever heard."

I wasn't sure if by "fantastic" he meant the story was wonderful or a pile of bull, but I decided not to press it.

"So Anatoly suggested you talk to me?" Gary asked.

"Yeah, he kind of mentioned it in passing. We don't know each other that well. We're more acquaintances than friends." The lie seemed more palatable than the truth, which was that I'd be sleeping with him if he wasn't trying to kill me.

"I'm not sure anyone knows Anatoly that well. I used to live with him, and I still have no idea who he is."

"Oh? I got the impression that you were close."

"From Anatoly?" Gary's eyebrows elevated a notch. "That's interesting. We lived together briefly in New York while I was getting my doctorate at NYU, but at the time all we had in common was the need to split the rent on a cheap Manhattan apartment. I'm speaking in relative terms, of course. In actuality the words *cheap* and *Manhattan* are mutually exclusive." He chuckled at his little joke.

I tried to.

"Was he a contractor in New York?"

"A contractor? Is he a contractor now?"

I paused, trying to come up with a good response. "Maybe. I might have misheard him." There, that was brilliant.

"Odd, he never so much as changed a lightbulb while we were roommates. How things change."

"What did he do in New York?"

Gary wrinkled his brow. "You know, I'm not sure. As I said, we were never close. In the few months we lived together I don't think we ever had a single conversation that lasted for more than five sentences. He had a tendency to keep to himself."

"But, you must have checked his references when he moved in?"

"He was living in the apartment before me. I was the boarder, so to speak."

I dug my fingers into the leather of my purse. This guy had to be more helpful than this. "So maybe he was a contractor in New York and you just didn't know it?"

"No, no, I don't think he was a contractor. Insurance. I think he was in insurance."

"Anatoly was an insurance salesman? Anatoly Darinsky?"

Gary laughed. "That doesn't seem to fit, either, does it? As you can tell I'm very fuzzy on the whole thing but I do remember something about insurance."

"Considering the nature of your relationship, or rather the lack thereof, I'm surprised he got back in contact with you."

"Oh, that started off as a coincidence. The first time I saw him after we went our separate ways was about seven months ago when Alex Tolsky brought him in."

"He…he came in with Tolsky?"

"Yes, Anatoly was visiting the area, as was Alex. It was just a few months before he died, poor man."

"Yes, that was…that was horrible." I tried to keep my voice smooth. I already knew that Anatoly and Tolsky were friends, so why was it that every time that fact was confirmed I got chills?

"He was such a lovely man," Gary continued. "They've crucified him in the papers, you know. All that talk about mental illness and alcoholism. In truth, the man was one of the most charming people I've ever met, not to mention brilliant. He had an incredible eye for art and was always interested in new talent. But then, I forgot, you knew him too, didn't you?"

"How…wait, how did you know that?" The only ones who knew that were some of the people who worked at Tolsky Productions and a handful of my friends, and none of those people would have interpreted my meeting with him once as my knowing him.

"Anatoly told me."

My right hand went to my stomach. "Anatoly. When did he tell you that?"

"About a month and a half ago, perhaps two months. I don't remember the exact date. He had just moved here and wanted to stop in and say hello, although the only thing he appeared to be interested in discussing was Alex. I think the two of them were very close. His suicide must have been a major blow to him."

"And then Anatoly started talking about me?"

"Yes, we were talking about Alex and he mentioned that you had been writing a screenplay for him. He asked if Alex had ever brought you in. His description of you was very flattering and, as it turns out, very accurate. You must forgive me, but at the time I had never heard of you. Regrettably, I don't read a lot of fiction—too busy reading trade magazines and trying to keep up with the fast-paced world of modern art—which brings us back to the reason you came. How can I help you come to a better understanding of the art world?"

The art world? Who the fuck cared about the art world? I had known Anatoly for less than three weeks and yet he had been talking to Gary about me over six weeks ago? How long had Anatoly been stalking me? A month? Two, three? Gary was looking at me expectantly. I searched my mind for something to ask. "Okay, let's see…um…how can you tell the difference between great art and the work of some moron who likes to smear paint on a canvas like some mentally deficient preschooler?"

Gary's mouth formed the shape of a perfect O.

"Not a good question?"

Less than sixty seconds later, Gary was showing me out of his office. I walked up to Marcus, who was listening to Ralph explain to him the significance of a photograph depicting a woman peeing.

"It's a statement about our whole society."

"Well, of course it is. Everyone I know pees—"

"Marcus, we have to go."

Ralph took a step closer to Marcus. "I was just showing him the works of—"

"We have to go *now.*"

Marcus looked from me to Ralph and made the obvious choice. "Sorry, Randy, she's the boss. But I promise to let you show me the poo-poo pictures next time."

If I had been walking fast before, I was breaking a whole new record this time. Marcus was trotting along next to me, shooting me looks of increasing alarm. "Sophie, Sophie, slow down. What happened in there, honey? What's wrong?"

"Everything's wrong!" I stopped in the middle of the sidewalk forcing the stream of pedestrians to maneuver around me. "Anatoly was Gary's roommate in New York."

"Okay, but we knew that."

"He told him at the time that he was in insurance."

"Anatoly?"

"Exactly, it's bullshit. But I bet you anything he's not a contractor, either, which means we don't know what the hell he does." Marcus inched back to avoid being struck by my hands, which were wildly waving in the air. "As far as we know his name may not even be Anatoly."

"Yeah, but he's been using it for the last decade or so, so…"

"That's not all." Marcus tugged at the corners of his jacket and waited for me to drop the other shoe. "He's been in there with Tolsky, and he came in after he died too. He came in there and started asking Gary questions about me."

"When was that?"

"Oh, about a month before we actually met. He described me to him, Marcus. Do you know what that means?"

If it was possible for a black man to turn pale, Marcus had done it. He stuffed his hands in his pockets with uncharacteristic awkwardness. "Are you going to the police?"

"Marcus! Have you been listening to me at all for the last few days? I have nothing to bring to the police. All I have is coincidence after goddamn coincidence."

"But they're not coincidences, they're…"

"Yeah, no kidding." I pressed the base of my palms into my forehead. "He's planned this so perfectly. He's allowed me to learn everything and nothing all at the same time. The guy's more devious than Stalin." I looked up at Marcus. "He's going to kill me. He's going to kill me, and nobody can help me."

"I can help you."

"No, no, you can't. You can't, Dena can't, Mary Ann sure as hell can't. There is nothing anyone can do."

"Oh, shut up, already." He grabbed my arm and pulled me closer. "Of course there are things we can do, we just have to figure out what they are."

"Oh, great, that's encouraging."

"Do you really think I'm going to let some straight boy kill off my best client? We haven't even had the chance to do that streaky color thing we were talking about. You can't die before the streaky color thing."

"Well then, maybe we should book the appointment today. Or better yet, you could hook up with my embalmer."

"Enough." Marcus made the motion of a conductor silencing his orchestra. "I have a perm to do in a half hour."

"A perm. Right. Wouldn't want you to be late for someone's perm."

"I am going to call Donato and cancel our plans tonight. You and I are having dinner."

"You're taking me out to eat twice in one day? Wow, it's amazing the things people will do for you when they expect your imminent death."

"You are not going to imminently die." Little smile lines flattered the corners of his eyes. "So we'll go dutch."

"I can't believe this."

"We will also devise a plan to stop Anatoly. He's not the only devious man alive, you know." He put his hand on his hip and snapped his fingers over his head. "Let me tell you, sweetheart, I've built a whole reputation on my deviant behavior."

"Marcus, I really don't think there's anything—"

"Ah, ah, ah, ah." He put a gentle finger on my lips. "We'll meet at P.J.'s Oyster Bed at eight-thirty. Now, let's get back to your car. Your flowers need water, and you have to give me a ride to the salon."

"Right. The perm."

 **CHAPTER 17**

"Actions speak louder than words, particularly when those actions are really stupid."
—*Sex, Drugs and Murder*

After dropping Marcus off, I drove around the city for a few hours. I considered driving right out of town. Anatoly wouldn't be expecting that. I could just go somewhere like…like where? And what was to keep him from finding me anywhere I went? He had proven himself to be highly mobile, and it wasn't like I was getting offers of hospitality from the Witness Protection Program. And what about my friends? And my family? My mother and sister were nuts, but I still loved them. I had to stay.

I was by the edge of the bay now. Dusty pink clouds hovered behind a glistening Golden Gate Bridge. I would never leave San Francisco. This was where my life was. This was where…where my cat was. Shit, I had forgotten to feed Mr. Katz. I looked again at the retreating sun. It would be dark by the time I got back to my apartment. But Mr. Katz was my baby, I couldn't just not feed him because I was scared.

Well, maybe I could.

Fuck.

I turned the car around. That cat had better be thanking his lucky stars that he had an owner who would risk her very life in order to open a can of Purina. That had to make me the best pet owner alive. That, or just really, really stupid.

I parked three blocks away and ran to my apartment, nearly knocking over a mother with a stroller and a Chinese lady with a cane. Nothing like being yelled at in two languages. I raced up the stairs and opened the door to find Mr. Katz, who looked like he was the one planning a murder.

"I'm sorry. I'm sorry, I'm sorry, I'm sorry," I said on my way to the kitchen. Mr. Katz just scowled at me and then, when I put out his food, gobbled it up.

I checked the answering machine. Two messages. The first was Leah. "Sophie, pick up, it's me. Sophie? Fine. Fine. Don't pick up. Sophie, I need you. Bob's just being horrible and I think…just call me, okay?"

Bob was being horrible? Bob was always horrible—she had never seemed bothered by it before. I almost called her back without listening to the second message, but the machine was too fast for me.

"Hi, it's me." Anatoly's Russian voice filled the room.

I stood completely still as I listened to the rest of the recording. "I was hoping we could talk. I'll be out most of the evening, but you can call me on my cellular."

I forgot about Leah. I looked at the door and assured myself that it was double locked. But there was still the window. If he climbed in through my window and killed me, I was going to sue my landlord.

He was out there somewhere, waiting for me to call and tell him I was home. Or was he? Maybe not. Maybe he was in my apartment right now. I grabbed the phone in one hand and found a knife for the other. I slowly made my way through the apartment. No one seemed to be there, not in

the shower or under the bed. Of course, there were the closets to consider. That presented a dilemma, because to open
a closet I had to either put down my only means of communication with the outside world or drop my weapon. I opted
to put down the phone, since the outside world had been of
so little help lately. Nobody in the closets. That was good.
But what if he was across the street and looking into my
apartment right now? I quickly turned off all the lights.
What next? I should peek through the bay window and try
to spot him.

I slammed my shin into the coffee table and almost killed
my cat, but I did eventually make it to my destination. There
were a few people walking around, but no Anatoly that I
could see. I sat down Indian-style on the Pergo floor. If he
had been telling me the truth about the Israeli and Russian
armies then he was well trained in the art of combat. He
would bide his time, study his target, preferably without its
knowing, formulate an efficient plan, and only then would
he attack. If he had been watching me, he would have been
clued into my awareness the minute I turned off the lights
without leaving. He wouldn't be hanging out on the street
waiting for me to see him.

But I wasn't the only person that lived in this building.
Someone else could have seen him. What was it he had asked
me about on our first date? He had wanted to know if I spoke
to my neighbors. I stumbled to the door and rushed downstairs to Theresa's apartment. She answered on the third knock.

"You may not use my phone."

"I don't want to use your phone, I just want to ask you a
few quick questions."

"No." She started to close the door, but I put my hand out
to stop her.

"I'll be quick. I just want to know if you've seen a tall guy
with dark hair around here lately. If he spoke you might have
noticed an accent."

"Your new boyfriend? Yes, I've seen him." She started to close the door again, but this time I put both hands out.

"When?"

"Take your hands off my door."

"Just answer the questions and I'll go away."

"For how long?"

"Oh, for God's sake, Theresa." I transferred more of my weight into the struggle. "I don't know—for at least a month, how 'bout that? You answer my questions and I won't so much as look at your door for a month."

"Until recently I was able to avoid speaking to you for months at a time."

I was going to kill her, just put my hands around her neck and kill her. But I could wait until she answered the questions. "Fine, I won't speak to you for one year. If the building catches fire, I promise I won't so much as knock on your door to warn you."

"I saw the two of you getting on his motorcycle when I was looking for parking, and then I saw him leaving your apartment Wednesday morning."

Wednesday morning? I had been at Dena's Wednesday morning. "You saw him leaving my apartment?"

"I'll answer your questions, but I refuse to repeat myself."

I closed my eyes. It might be easier to get through this if I didn't have to look at her. "Did you actually see him coming out the door of my apartment?"

"No, I bumped into him on the stairs when I was coming back from my morning run."

"When was this?"

"Wednesday morning."

"What *time?*"

"I don't know." She tapped her finger against the thin line that constituted her lips. "I usually start my run around five-fifteen, so it would have been a little after six. Are we through now?"

"Yes, yes, we're through." Theresa closed the door and this time I put my hand on it for balance. "I am definitely through."

I arrived at P.J.'s at ten after eight. Marcus wasn't there yet, but for some reason Dena and Jason were. Dena waved me over to the table, and I obediently approached.

"Where the hell have you been?" she asked. "I haven't heard from you in ages."

"We talked yesterday." I tried not to stare, but she was wearing an off-the-shoulder top that was displaying two rather large marks on her neck. Maybe Jason *was* a vampire.

"A day is an eternity when someone is out there trying to kill you."

"You're right, I'll try to... You know what, I'm sorry, but shouldn't you be wearing a turtleneck or something?"

Dena ran a hand over her neck. "What, because of the love bites? Why would I want to hide them? They speak to the effectiveness of the products that I sell. In this case Erotic Peach flavored oil. I have some more little bruises on my inner thighs but they're more difficult to show off."

"That's where you wore the Piña Colada," Jason said. "I think I liked the Erotic Peach the best, though."

"Better than the Piña Colada? Huh. The last guy... customer—my last guy customer said that he liked Piña Colada best."

Jason straightened in his chair. "He tasted it in the store?"

"I'm here to meet Marcus." What the hell, I owed Dena a favor, and changing the subject was easy in this case.

"Really?" Dena said. "Shit, it's been months since I've seen Marcus. You guys should join us."

"Oh, I wouldn't want to interrupt."

"Give me a break. Would I invite you to sit down if you were interrupting?"

I looked over at Jason, who was making a noble attempt to shake off his irritation over Dena's erotic-oil–tasting customers. "Jason, you sure that would be okay?" I noted that this was the first time I had seen him wearing normal clothes. Jeans and a white T-shirt. It must be a special occasion.

"Yes, join us." He managed a smile. "I've been wanting to talk to you anyway."

I lowered myself into an empty seat. "Okay, you've got me curious now."

"I understand that you suspected me of murdering Barbie and stalking you."

I sat there slack-jawed until I was able to pull it together enough to narrow my eyes at Dena, who was sinking into her chair.

"Hey, there's no need to be embarrassed. You don't know me, and you obviously had to consider all your possibilities. To be honest, I'm flattered."

"You're flattered?" Again I looked over at Dena, who was now barely visible over the tabletop.

"Yeah, it shows that I have an air of mystery about me, that people see me as someone who is on the edge, daring and just a little dangerous, you know?"

Well, that was almost right. I was sure most people must think of Jason as being on the brink of going *over* the edge. "Dena tells me you were at a job orientation when Barbie was killed."

Now it seemed to be Jason's turn to get smaller. "Yeah, I was… And I was at my sister's wedding when JJ Money was killed. I've never been to New York, but I plan on going— the vampire scene there is supposed to—"

"What's the new job?"

Dena became very absorbed in her beverage while Jason became fascinated with the design of the flatware.

"Okay, come on. How embarrassing can it be? Your girl-friend sells Gummi penises."

"Yeah, I, um, I got a sales job."

"All right, that's a start. Where's the sales job?"

Silence.

"Jason, where's the sales job?"

"Gap."

"Gap?"

"He's not selling out." Dena spit an ice cube back into her drink. "It's only temporary."

"So he's temporarily selling out."

"I really needed dental insurance," he whispered.

"Dental insurance?" I crossed my arms in front of me and thought about that. "Do vampires visit the dentist?"

"Dena!" I turned to see Marcus standing behind me. "I didn't expect to see you here."

"Marcus, *darling!*" She offered her cheek for his kiss. "This is Jason."

"Hi, Jason." Marcus leaned down and studied Dena's neck. "Jason, did you do this?"

"She was wearing Erotic Peach oil."

"Erotic Peach, huh? I always preferred the Piña Colada."

"Oh, you must be the guy customer." Jason exhaled a sigh of relief, and Dena discreetly signaled for Marcus not to question it.

"Jason has a thing for necks," I said. "He's a vampire. He also works at Gap."

"Really?" Marcus gave Jason an approving nod. "How fabulous that they're equal-opportunity employers. So, did you invite Dena and Jason so we could all put our heads together and figure out how to get the goods on psycho boy?"

"Is that why you two are meeting?" asked Dena. "To get the goods on Anatoly? Damn it, Sophie, why didn't you call and tell me?"

I cast a sideways glance in Jason's direction.

"I've checked every one of his alibis." She ticked off her points of research on her fingers. "I have proof of the date of his sister's wedding, that he was there, and, unfortunately, he really was at the orientation at Gap."

It wasn't that I still suspected Jason, I just wasn't sure I wanted to share my life with a super freak. He leaned over and patted my hand. "Nothing will leave this table. I swear on the *Vampire Chronicles.*"

How incredibly reassuring. But time was of the essence, so what the hell. I took a deep breath and went over everything, from my conversation with DC Smooth to my exchange with Theresa.

"So there you have it. Anatoly is planning on killing me, the police are convinced that Mark Baccon is the guilty party, I have nothing to convince them otherwise, and I have completely run out of options. We might as well call this what it is, a little impromptu farewell dinner party. Marcus, I want you to have my CD collection, and Dena, you can have Mr. Katz."

Dena took a sip of her wine. "Mary Ann can have the cat."

"Well, gee, thanks for your sympathy and support."

"You know I don't do well with defeatism." Dena tapped her heel under the table. "We need some more background on Anatoly. You thought he was a contractor, that gallery guy thought he was an insurance salesman. What does Shannon Tolsky think he is?"

"I don't know." I lowered my head. "I didn't think to ask."

"Uh-huh. How many murder mysteries have you written?"

Marcus shook his head. "Okay, it'd be nice to hear what Miss Hollywood has to say about all this, but we're not going to get any evidence that way."

"I agree," Jason said. "This person has already broken into her place once that we know of. She can't be fucking around doing interviews right now."

Marcus slammed his hand on the table. "That's it!"

We all looked at him expectantly.

"Don't you people get it? We have to break into *his* place. That's where the evidence is. That's the only place it would be."

Everyone was speechless for a moment until I found my voice. "Um, no."

"Why not?"

"Because, it's a felony, for one," Dena said. "And two, we are dealing with a homicidal maniac. Don't you think he might get a little pissed if he finds us in his apartment? It might be safer for Sophie to steal money from the mob and try to make a new life for herself in Brooklyn."

Jason swirled the wine around in his glass. "I don't think anything Sophie does could put her in more danger than she's already in."

"But I'm a writer, not a burglar. I wouldn't even know how to break into his place if I wanted to, and I definitely do not want to."

"You don't have to, I'll do it," Marcus offered.

Dena grunted. "Great, have your hairstylist break in. No reason to be concerned about that."

"Don't underestimate me. I broke into a few places when I was a teenager trying to be a delinquent so I could distract myself from my Barbra Streisand obsession." He toyed with one of his locks. "Didn't get caught once."

I shook my head. "This won't work."

"It could," Jason said, "we just need to plan it well."

Dena put her glass back on the table with enough force to cause the wine to slosh over the sides. "Jason, you need to shut up. This is not one of your vampire games. This is Sophie's life. We need to be logical."

"I am being logical. We'll need two people to break into Anatoly's place."

Marcus shook his head. "One would be more discreet."

"But two could search the place in half the time, and time might be a big factor. We'll also need someone to keep Anatoly occupied for a while."

Marcus smiled appreciatively. "Good point. Dena, you always pick the smart ones. A little weird, but always very smart."

Dena scoffed. "Nothing about this is smart. Tell me, Jason, which one of us do you think should be given the honor of keeping the serial killer occupied?"

Both Marcus and Jason looked at me.

Dena practically leaped out of her chair. "What the fuck are you people thinking? Maybe you two haven't been listening so I'm going to repeat a few key facts here and I'm going to use real simple words so you both can absorb this. Anatoly is trying to kill Sophie. Anatoly is a big strong guy. Sophie is not. We are not going to set little Sophie up on a date with her big burly would-be assailant. That's it. End of story."

"We'll have a guard," Jason offered. "I'll do it. I'll be her undercover bodyguard. She can meet him in a public place and I'll be there the whole time."

"N. O. No!"

"Dena, maybe they're right."

Dena looked like she was about to stab me with her fork, but I continued before she had a chance to attack. "I can't live like this anymore. Every moment of every day I'm wondering if it's my last. This could totally blow up in my face. In fact, there's a good chance of it. But maybe that's a gamble I have to take. You don't have to help me." I looked around the table. "None of you has to help me. I guess, if need be, I can break in myself. People a lot less educated than I am do it every day, so how hard can it be, right?" Nobody laughed. I rearranged the remaining food on my plate. "I have to do something. And this, well, this is definitely something."

Marcus smiled and reached over to stroke my hair. "It was my idea, honey. Of course I'll help."

"And I already said I'd be your guard," said Jason.

Dena inhaled through her gritted teeth. "This is a very bad idea." She studied me for a long time. I met her gaze and waited for her refusal. Finally, she looked away and slumped back into her chair. "Oh, what the fuck. If we're going to go to prison we should all go together. It'll be more fun that way."

I threw my arms around her neck. "I love you, I do." I turned to Marcus and gave him a hug too. "I have no idea what I've done to deserve you two. And Jason..." I released Marcus and smiled at Jason. "I don't even know what to say about you. I tried to convince your girlfriend that you were psychotic, and now you're putting everything on the line to help me."

"Hey, don't mention it. How can I ever expect to be chosen for immortality if I don't exhibit the willingness to take risks?"

I didn't really know what to do with that so I just kept smiling.

"All right, enough of the sentimental bullshit." Dena picked up the wine bottle and divided its remnants amongst our glasses. "Let's get a game plan together. We have a felony to commit."

 CHAPTER 18

"It's amazing how brave a person can be when her life depends on it."

—*Sex, Drugs and Murder*

I accepted Dena's offer to spend the night at her place, but only after I badgered her into agreeing to take in Mr. Katz as well. For some reason, Mr. Katz wasn't grateful for my protectiveness and expressed his annoyance by peeing in Dena's linen closet, thus ensuring Mary Ann's inheritance. The three of us somehow managed to set our differences aside long enough to huddle up on the couch and put the first part of the plan into effect. Dena handed me the phone, and I dialed Anatoly's number.

"Hello?"

I wanted to speak. I really did. But speaking required breathing, and as soon as I heard his voice my throat constricted, making either activity an impossibility.

"Hello? Is anyone there?"

Dena slapped me on the back so hard I almost fell off the couch. "Hello, hi, Anatoly, it's me."

"Sophie. You got my message."

"Yeah, yeah I got it." I shifted as Dena pressed her ear up against the other side of the receiver. "I'm glad you called. Um, I was hoping…I was hoping we could meet somewhere and talk."

"I'd like that."

That was it. No, "why would I want to meet with someone who just recently threatened me with a butcher knife?" just "I'd like that." Dena shook her head. If either of us had any doubts about his guilt, they had just flown out the window.

"Do you want to meet now?"

"What? No!" I grabbed Dena's arm. "Anatoly, it's late and I've had a long day, but…but maybe tomorrow?"

"Tomorrow night's fine. What time?"

Dena and I simultaneously exhaled. "Well, I have dinner plans with family tomorrow, but we could meet afterward, like at ten-thirty at Baja Cantina?"

"It's just after ten-thirty now and you said it was too late."

"I said it's been a long day. Besides, if there's ever a time that I can count on needing a drink it's after dinner with my family. So, what do you say?"

"Ten-thirty's fine. Shall I pick you up?"

"No, I'm not sure if I'll be stopping home after dinner. It's better to meet there."

"Your call. I'll see you at Baja Cantina tomorrow at ten-thirty."

"Can't wait. Bye." I hung up and looked at Dena. "All righty, then. I'm going to die."

She slipped her arm over my shoulders and gave me a hearty shake. "Hey, what's to worry about? You have the dream team on your side. A hairstylist, the city's leading expert on sex toys and a chino-wearing vampire. We're all set."

If I had drunk an entire pot of coffee I couldn't have been more jittery. I wasn't able to sleep, so I attempted to be productive. I didn't have Shannon's home number but I tried Margaret Tolsky instead. I called her home at midnight, and at one and two in the morning, to no avail. I tried reading a book but I couldn't focus. Finally, I raided Dena's medicine cabinet and found the Nyquil.

Eight hours later I woke up to Mary Ann standing over me. "What's going on?"

"Mary Ann…"

"Don't tell her anything." Dena rushed in and hovered over Mary Ann. "What are you doing here anyway? Don't you have some socialites to make over or something?"

Mary Ann didn't even look at Dena. "I know something's going on. It's 11:00 a.m. Dena was supposed to open this morning and she had a salesperson come in instead. She never calls in unless she's sick with the plague."

I propped myself up on my elbow. "I don't think you can be sick with the plague…"

"She's not sick at all! She won't tell me what's going on, so you need to. Did something else happen?"

Dena stepped between us, so that Mary Ann was forced to acknowledge her. "Nothing else happened. Sophie, understandably, didn't feel comfortable being alone in her apartment, so she came here. I offered to stay with her today because I thought she could use a friend. That's it, end of story. You can go home now."

Mary Ann sat on the corner of the day bed. "Well, if Sophie needs one friend I'm sure she could use two. Right, Sophie?"

I looked quickly from Dena to Mary Ann. "Actually, Dena and I haven't had a lot of one-on-one time lately so…"

"Lucy, I'm home!" Marcus's voice sang from the entryway. "Where is everybody?" He peeked in the room. "Mary Ann! Long time no kibitz. Are you joining our lovely little band of future felons? Might be a bagel in it for you." He held out a brown bag from Noah's.

"God fucking damn it, Marcus." Dena curled her hands up into two fists. "Do you even know how to spell *discretion?*"

Marcus glanced again at Mary Ann and winced. *"D-I-S-K-R-E-T-I-O-N?"*

"How about you're an *I-D-I-O-T?*"

"I don't get it. How are you a band of would-be felons? I...oh, oh, oh!" Mary Ann jumped up. "You're planning something. You're planning something *illegal.*"

Marcus smiled. "I'd forgotten how quick you were."

"Marcus, shut up," Dena snapped. "Mary Ann, it's not what you think. We're just...we're just going to bake a batch of pot brownies, that's all. We've all been a little stressed lately and we thought we'd take an afternoon off and smoke our troubles away. I didn't call you because I knew you wouldn't approve."

Mary Ann narrowed her eyes. "But pot's legal in California."

"No, it's not," Dena countered. "Not really."

"Well, it kind of is." Marcus rubbed his hand over a carefully cultivated stubble. "At least, I think it is for some people...you know I keep getting confused—"

"Hello." I waved my hand in the air to get everyone's attention. "She's not buying it." I looked at Mary Ann. "Are you?"

"No," Mary Ann said definitively.

"I know you want to protect her." I pulled my hair away from my face, which probably wasn't such a good idea since it would just make it easier for Dena if she decided to scratch out my eyes. "I really think we need to tell her at this point. Mary Ann can keep a secret, and it's not like we're asking her to help out."

"Tell me what?"

Dena turned around and walked out of the room, leaving my eyes intact. Marcus followed wordlessly, head lowered and bagels held high as an offering. "Sit down—" I patted the spot Mary Ann had just vacated "—and I'll tell you about the little game of Russian roulette we have planned for this evening."

Mary Ann absorbed all the information I gave her with only a few questions, none of them exceedingly stupid. When I was done she sat there quietly, stroking my cat who had planted himself on her lap. Finally she peered up at me and smiled.

"I want to help."

"No!" Dena screamed from the kitchen. I had forgotten about her batlike hearing ability.

Mary Ann went out to confront Dena, and I tiptoed after her. "You need me."

"The hell we do," Dena replied.

Mary Ann picked up a cinnamon-raisin bagel and started applying the shmear. "You need a lookout person."

"No, we don't. Sophie's going to be the decoy and Jason's the bodyguard. If they're unable to detain Anatoly, one of them will call us on my cell phone. No lookout person needed."

"What about the other people in the building?"

"What about them?" Marcus asked between bagel bites.

"Well, it would be bad if one of them saw you coming out of Anatoly's apartment, wouldn't it? I mean, wouldn't it be helpful if someone was parked across the street, someone who could tell you the coast is clear or help you make a quick escape, if necessary?"

Dena looked up at the ceiling. "You have to choose now to start making sense?"

I crossed the room and pushed Marcus out of the way so I could embrace the automatic coffeemaker. "You know, if she wants to help, why not let her? If something goes wrong, she'll be in the best position to make the necessary calls for help and she'll be able to get away easily."

"She's a makeup artist, for Christ's sake."

"And you're a sex shop owner. And you're both adults capable of making your own decisions."

Dena shook her head. "This is bad. This is very, very bad." But she didn't make any more protests.

I inhaled my coffee. "Did you stake the place out?"

"Mmm-hmm," replied Marcus. "It was just like *Dragnet*. There's a window on the side of his building that he kept open even after he went out this morning. I think I can use the molding to climb up to it, then I'll just buzz Dena in."

"I can't believe we're doing this." Dena was still glaring at Mary Ann.

"Oh, come on, Dena, sweetie. It'll be fun." Marcus grasped both her hands and held her at arms' distance. "We can put on some tight little black outfits and pretend we're the new Bonnie and Clyde."

Dena fought a smile. "You look nothing like Warren Beatty."

"You got that right, girlfriend. Warren would kill for my cheekbones."

At ten o'clock I was sitting in my apartment chewing off my fingernails with Dena and Marcus at my side. Jason was already at the Baja Cantina, and Mary Ann was in her car in her hard-won parking spot across from Anatoly's building. I had positioned myself adjacent to the phone so that I could pick up the second she called. I had spent the day pacing, doing jumping jacks and calling Shannon and Margaret Tolsky, each of whom had been perpetually inaccessible. But now none of us seemed to be able to do anything but wait. When Jason had checked in earlier I had noted that he was the only one who seemed more excited than terrified—but then, Jason lived in a different reality from the rest of us—

When the phone rang, we all jumped.

"Who is it?" Dena asked.

"I don't know, I haven't answered it yet."

"When the fuck are you going to stop living in the middle ages and get caller ID?" Dena chided.

"Sophie, honey," Marcus interrupted, "pick up the phone."

"Hel—hello?"

"Sophie, why haven't you called me back? And don't tell me you didn't get my message because I know you did."

"Leah." I looked over at Dena, who put her head in her hands. "You know, this isn't really a good time."

"Oh, really—well, when would be a good time for me to tell you that Bob is cheating on me?"

"Bob is cheating on you?"

Marcus sat up and clapped his hands. "Oh, oh, oh, family dirt. Love it."

I motioned for Marcus to shut up. "Leah…" The phone beeped. "Leah, I have another call coming in. I've got to get that." I clicked over before she had time to protest.

"Sophie, it's me. Anatoly's getting on his motorcycle right now. He's starting the engine…. Okay, he's gone."

"And so are we. Call Jason and tell him we're on our way." I clicked back over to Leah.

"I can't believe you just did that. I tell you that my husband is having an affair—"

"Leah, I'm sorry, I really am, and I want to talk to you about this, but now's not a good time."

"What!"

"Just don't file for divorce in the next twelve hours or so and I'll call tomorrow. Promise."

"Sophie—"

I hung up. "Anatoly just left, and my sister hates me."

"She'll get over it," Dena said. We all got to our feet and quickly collected our cell phones.

I watched as Dena and Marcus pulled on their leather gloves. "Please be careful, you guys."

"I'll protect Marcus. You just keep your own ass safe."

We said our farewells, and I jogged over to my car. Dena and Marcus made their way to Anatoly's.

It took ten minutes to get to Fillmore Street and fifteen minutes for a space to open up on the same block that Jason had parked on. I entered the bar and looked around.

Jason was at the bar and gave me a practically impercepti-
ble nod.

Anatoly was at a table.

I took in one last gulp of air, which I knew I wouldn't be
exhaling for a few hours. Anatoly made eye contact. I smiled,
did a little Miss America wave and walked to his side. "I see
you already ordered me a drink." I pulled myself onto the
stool next to him.

"I remembered that you liked Bloody Marys." He gently
pushed the drink over to me. His eyes slowly went over my
figure in a way that sent chills up my spine, and not chills of
fear either. This was bad. I was not in the habit of being at-
tracted to psycho serial killers. I did not want to be a can-
didate for the *Jerry Springer Show.*

"Well, I'm glad you did. We need to talk, and for this talk
it's helpful to have a drink."

"Oh?"

"Yeah." I ran a flirtatious finger around the rim of my glass.
"I owe you an apology, you know, for the other day."

"You must be referring to the day that you seduced me, lured
me to the bedroom and then threatened me with a butcher
knife. Am I to take it that my foreplay needs some work?"

I smiled. "No, no, your foreplay, at least from my limited
observation, is just fine. The problem lay with me."

"Go on."

"Okay." I lifted my glass, then put it down without tasting its contents. "Earlier that afternoon an acquaintance of
mine was murdered."

"Barbie Vega. I read about it in the paper. You're the one
who found the body, right?"

"Yes…I—I found her." I picked up my drink again and this
time brought it to my lips. I felt the spices burn my tongue, but
that was all I allowed myself. Sobriety was important tonight.

"You didn't mention that when I saw you."

"No." I bit into my lip. "I didn't want to think about it."

"That would be a tough one to forget."

"Yeah, it is."

Anatoly put his forearms on the table. "So, why did you pull the knife on me?"

Here was where I was going to have to be my most convincing. "I pulled a knife on you because I thought that you might be the one who killed Barbie."

Anatoly sat motionless. I tried to read his expression, but it was impossible.

"Don't get me wrong, I know that's ridiculous now," I said. "Mark Baccon killed Barbie. But at the time I was disoriented and distraught. As you may remember, when I first met up with you I punched you in the jaw."

"I remember."

"Well, I just got this crazy idea that you were Barbie's killer and you were there to kill me." I leaned forward and placed my hand an inch away from where his rested, an act I hoped would convey a renewed trust. "It was based on no facts whatsoever, just my own bizarre hysteria."

Anatoly took a long sip of his beer.

"I'm sorry." My eyes unwillingly traveled over to Jason before I quickly returned them to the table. "As you can see I have no good excuse, but do you think you could forgive me anyway?"

Anatoly stared at me for what felt like an eternity. Then a smile crept onto his mouth. "Of course I can forgive you. If I had a dime for every time a woman threatened me with a kitchen knife—"

"You'd be rich by now?"

"I don't know about rich, but at least I'd have ten cents."

I giggled and took a small sip of my drink. "Well, I try to be original." Anatoly's hand covered my knee under the table. I tried not to recoil. Fortunately my cell rang, which gave me the excuse to shift my weight away from him while I answered it.

"Hey, it's me, we're in," Dena said.

"Hi, you."

"The window was open a crack just like Marcus predicted, so getting in was a cinch."

"Uh-huh, great, anything else?" Dena calling me to describe the break-in was not only unnecessary, it was reckless.

"No, that's not it. We found something."

I glanced quickly up at Anatoly. "Oh, really? What?"

"Pictures, Sophie. Photos of you. Along with pretty much every book review and newspaper clipping that has ever mentioned your name. But, Sophie, it's the pictures. There are photos of you having coffee, talking to Marcus, talking with me and Mary Ann, having lunch with your sister and nephew. The guy's obsessed."

My heart fell to the bottom of my stomach. My friends and family. What if he had tried something when I was with Jack?

"Sophie? Sophie, are you still there?"

"Yeah. Look, it sounds like you're on the right track. So why don't you just keep doing what you're doing and we'll talk later."

"Got it. Be careful, Sophie."

"That was my sister." I put the phone back into my purse. "She thinks her husband is cheating on her and she's going through kind of a crisis right now." Funny how you could lie and tell the truth at the same time.

"Must be tough," he said as he tried to get the attention of our cocktail waitress.

"They have a kid."

"Like I said, must be tough. She should hire a private investigator to make sure she's right before she does anything."

"That's a little dramatic, don't you think?"

Anatoly shrugged. "People do it all the time."

"Well, I don't think that's her style. I don't expect her to call again, but I'm going to keep my cell phone on just in case I have to talk her down from a window ledge or something."

"Do you really think she'd kill herself over this?"

"No, no, I was just making a bad joke."

Anatoly lifted his eyebrows. "Considering recent events, I would think you would be afraid of jinxing yourself."

Had he just threatened my sister? The waitress came over and Anatoly ordered another beer. He eyed my drink. "Is there something wrong with your Bloody Mary?"

"No." I took another small sip. "I just didn't eat much today, so I'm taking it slow."

"I thought you just came from dinner at your parents."

"I did. I just didn't like the food." Could I be more inept?

"You look beautiful tonight." Anatoly reached over and put a gentle hand under my chin, lifting it ever so slightly. "Perhaps I'll skip my drink as well, and we can go somewhere more private."

"No!"

Anatoly started.

I swallowed and tried to make my voice smoother. "I mean, you just ordered your drink and I do plan on drinking this eventually. Can't let a good Bloody Mary go to waste, that's sacrilegious."

The cocktail waitress placed the beer in front of Anatoly, and he drank half of it in one swig. "I would hate for you to be sacrilegious." He then lifted my drink and held it in front of me. *"L'chaim."* He pressed the glass against my lips and slowly tipped it forward. If the acoustics in the room were better he would have been able to hear my heart pounding.

My cell phone rang again, and Anatoly put the glass down while I snatched the phone out of my purse. "Hello?"

"Sophie, it's Marcus. Get out of there. Get as far away from him as humanly possible."

"Why?"

"I found the hatchet. It was duct-taped to the underside of his bed. Sophie, it still has bloodstains on it."

I looked up at Anatoly. He was smiling at me and wiping off the drops of the red liquid that had spilled onto his fingers.

CHAPTER 19

"Alicia knew that if she wanted to live she would have to face the man who coveted her death."
                              —*Sex, Drugs and Murder*

"Sophie? Did you hear me?" Marcus asked. "You need to get your ass out of there."

"I heard you." I smoothed a wrinkled cocktail napkin. "You know I'm always here for you, Leah. Just give me a few minutes and I'll head on over."

"Where shall we meet—the police station?"

"No, no, why don't you meet me out by the car. That way I won't have to worry about waking Jack."

"You want Dena and me to wait in Mary Ann's car until you have a chance to talk more freely?"

"Exactly."

"Should I take the hatchet?"

"No." I rolled my eyes for Anatoly's benefit. "Don't do anything. Just wait for me."

"Okay, but hurry, Sophie. It's a bad idea to hang out at the scene of a crime, and it's an even worse idea to hang out with a murderer."

"Right, well, see you in a bit."

"You are an extraordinarily dedicated sister," Anatoly said.

"What?" My voice sounded small to me. Everything seemed small accept Anatoly, who had become enormous.

"Are you really going to rush out and comfort her right now?"

I was seeing him for the first time. He was human. "I have to go to her. She's my sister, and her life…" He had killed JJ Money and allowed an innocent man to go to prison for it, he had killed his mentor, he had killed a woman with a hatchet, and then come back to my apartment to seduce me and had not even been shaken or rattled. "Her life's a mess right now…" He had been calm and charming. "She needs me." Perfectly charming.

He scrutinized me over his beer. "Are you all right? You look pale." He gently lifted my hand. "You're shaking."

"I just—I just didn't expect this. I thought that she and Bob were really going to make it. That theirs was the real thing. But it wasn't. It was an illusion, a lie, and now…now everything's falling apart."

He squeezed my hand.

"Things, and people, aren't always as they seem. It's a hard lesson to learn, but one that is taught over and over again."

I pulled my hand away. "I have to make a stop in the ladies' room."

"All right. I'll settle the tab." He was acting concerned, but there was a note of suspicion in his voice, as well. I had to pull it together before I gave everything away.

I tucked my phone back into my purse. "I'll be right back." I brushed past Jason just as he was hanging up his cell phone. There was a thin layer of sweat covering his features. So it had finally become real to him. I knew that before this he hadn't truly believed that Anatoly was a cold-blooded killer any more than he believed he was going to become a vampire. He clung to the fantasy the way most children clung to the idea of the Easter Bunny. They would swear to its existence, but if they ever met a real six-foot, smiling, egg-throwing rabbit they would run for their lives. I suspected that's what Jason wanted to do right now.

There were a few women already in the bathroom fixing their makeup. I stood behind them and stared at my reflection. I wasn't supposed to be there. None of this was supposed to be happening. I should be having drinks with Dena, working on my next book. I wasn't supposed to be fighting for my life.

One of the women assumed I was waiting for a space by the mirror and cleared out. I took a step closer and pretended to look for a lipstick. I needed to call the police. I watched as the other woman walked out. There was a very big problem. I couldn't tell the police what I knew without admitting to them that my friends and I had broken into his apartment. That would not only get all of us in some boiling water, but it would leave room for the possibility that we had planted the hatchet. I looked back up at the mirror. The room had taken on a surreal, nightmare-like quality. How could none of us have thought of that? I was in exactly the same position I'd been in before the evening began.

My cell phone rang again. This time it was Jason. "What the fuck are you doing in there? We have to get the hell out of here."

"I'm going to invite him to my place for a drink."

"What?"

"Marcus has a key to my apartment. Call him and tell him to go up there right now and hide. The bathroom—behind the shower curtain would be perfect. Tell him to bring the phone in there with him. He is in no way to make himself known to Anatoly. I'll find him when it's time."

"Are you mental? Time for what?"

"Just tell him, Jason."

"I can't believe—got to go." The line went dead.

I replaced the phone and dragged my lipstick across my lips. "This is it," I whispered. "The game ends tonight. That fucker's going down."

I made an attempt at fixing my hair before rejoining Anatoly. "I was just on the phone with my sister again. I changed my mind, I'll deal with her tomorrow. Tonight, I want to spend with you."

"Oh?" His eyes fell to my newly painted lips. "Do you want another drink, then?"

"No, no this place is way too packed. Let's go somewhere a little more intimate."

"I'm open to suggestions."

I reached up and lightly caressed his shoulder. "My place can be intimate."

Anatoly's eyes slanted. "You want to bring me up to your place?"

"Mmm-hmm, don't worry. I haven't sharpened the kitchen knives in ages."

"Good to know."

"So is that a yes, or are you scared?"

He cocked his head to the left. "I think I can handle myself."

"Good." I dipped my finger into my Bloody Mary and sucked the liquid off. "Did you bring your bike?"

"Yes."

"Then parking will only be a problem for one of us. Why don't you follow me? That way you won't have to wait in front of my place while I look for a spot."

"All right." Anatoly stood up and started to put on his leather jacket. "By the way, if you were worried about that crazy man who's been staring at you all night, I used the time that you were in the bathroom to speak with him."

I dropped my keys. Anatoly retrieved them for me. "What, um…what crazy man?"

"The one who felt the need to share his colorful views on art during Balardi's opening at Sussman Gallery. Didn't you notice him? I thought I saw you looking at him earlier."

I didn't trust myself to speak, so I just shook my head. Anatoly took me by the shoulders and turned me around so that I was facing Jason's direction. Maybe a vampire had found him, because all of his coloring was gone. He didn't look up. He just sat there studying the bubbles in his beer. I tried to relax underneath his grip. "He looks a little like him but I don't think he's the same guy. The other guy was skinnier."

"That's him. He's been talking on his cell phone all night. Kind of like you."

I tried to laugh but it came out as more of a gasp for air. "What did you say to him?"

"I told him that it would be very unwise of him to be following you if that was what he was doing. He claims that he's here waiting for a friend who's running late. The way he's been looking at me makes me think otherwise but it doesn't matter. I don't think he'll give you any problems, he doesn't have the same bravado this evening."

"Well, he's probably just embarrassed that you remembered him. God only knows what he was on that night." I linked my arm with his. "Come on, we have better things to do than stand around here talking about that freak." I led Anatoly out of the bar.

Jason didn't follow.

"My bike's right here—would you like a ride to your car?"

"No, I think I'll walk, I need the fresh air."

"You'll get plenty of fresh air on the bike."

I patted my hair. "I just fixed myself up. Besides, I parked pretty close. Just get yourself situated and I'll be by in a minute."

Anatoly pulled some gloves out of his helmet. "You're the boss."

God, I hoped that was true. For this to work I had to be the one in control, from start to finish. I started to walk away but Anatoly grabbed my arm and pulled me in for a deep kiss. "Have I told you how beautiful you look tonight?"

"Yeah, but it never hurts to be reminded." I cautiously removed my arm. "There will be plenty of time for that at my place."

When I got to my car I placed a quick call to Marcus to verify that he had gotten the new instructions. Apparently he had, because the instant he picked up he started screaming at me about my state of mind. I quickly repeated what I had said to Jason and turned my phone off before he could argue further. No one was going to talk me out of this, not now. As I passed Baja Cantina, I saw Anatoly pull in behind me. There was no longer even a choice.

Near my place I found parking and walked him up to the apartment. I opened the door for him and he slid past me into the living room. My eyes immediately went to the base of the cordless phone. The receiver was missing. Obviously, Marcus had done as I asked and was in the bathroom with the phone. I smiled and took a step closer to Anatoly. "Thanks for giving me another chance."

"No problem, I—"

I didn't let him finish. I laced my hands behind his head and pulled him down to me. The kiss lasted for what felt like a year before he finally came up for air.

"You're all business tonight."

"That's right." I leaned in and grazed the nape of his neck with my teeth. "All business."

"This is a side of you I haven't seen before. You're much more…aggressive."

"We've been close to this on a few different occasions." I was now nibbling his ear. "I haven't been with someone in over two years. I'm not interested in setting any new world records."

"God forbid." He kissed me again. This time his tongue explored the regions of my mouth while his hands slid down my back. Then lower.

"Let's go into the bedroom." I took his hand and showed him the way, casting a quick glance at the partially open door of the bathroom as we passed.

We were at the foot of my bed now. Somehow I managed to take a moment to turn on the radio. Anatoly's kisses were growing increasingly passionate. He used one of his hands to hold me in place while the other went to my inner thigh.

"Wait…" I whispered.

But Anatoly didn't stop. "Wasn't it you that said we've let this moment come and go too many times? No more waiting. I want you now."

I tried to push away from his chest. "I want you too, but we have to use protection."

Without missing a beat, Anatoly reached into his back pocket. "Got it."

I shook my head at a speed that should have given me whiplash. "I hate condoms," I lied. "I have a diaphragm in the bathroom. Give me just a moment?"

Anatoly hesitated. "I suppose if you prefer…"

"I do." I disentangled myself, then gave him a final gentle kiss on the collarbone. "It will only take a minute. Don't move a muscle."

Anatoly's expression betrayed some kind of inner battle, but he didn't stop me from leaving the room. I closed the bathroom door and pulled back the shower curtain.

Marcus was standing there holding the phone like it was a loaded gun. "What the fuck do you think you are doing?" he asked in a low whisper.

I took a step forward. "Hit me."

Marcus just stared at me.

"Don't question it, just do it. Give me a black eye now, and then go out the bathroom window. You scaled up

Anatoly's two-story building, you can scale down my three-story one."

"My God, you have finally lost your mind."

"Do it now, or he may kill us both."

Marcus's expression had changed from one of anger to one of bewilderment.

"Sophie, are you coming?" Anatoly's voice traveled through the door.

"I'll be right there. Why don't you turn the bed down?"

"Your wish is my command."

I exhaled and started to turn back to Marcus when I felt the back of his hand land heavily against my cheek. I suppressed a cry of pain and surprise as I staggered backward. Marcus caught me before I lost balance. His left hand went to my injured eye.

"Sophie…"

"Go." I pointed toward the window. "Tell the others to go home and not to call. Tell them my life depends on it."

"But…"

I pointed to the window again. Marcus shook his head and handed me the phone. He caressed my hair one last time, then climbed out the window. I dialed the three numbers.

"911 emergency."

"Please help me," I whispered. "He's going to kill me." I then pressed the mute button. They had all the information I wanted to give them for now and I certainly didn't want them to hear anything that would expose this for being the setup that it was. I covered the earpiece with my hand so Anatoly wouldn't be able to hear the dispatcher's questions. I exited the bathroom, leaving the light on and quietly closing the door behind me. I tiptoed to the kitchen and tossed the phone out onto the fire escape. They would have plenty of time to trace the call. I put my hands on either side of my neckline and tore my shirt open. Buttons flew everywhere. I heard Anatoly knock on the bathroom door, and then the creak of the door opening.

"I'm in the kitchen," I called out, "getting us some champagne." I climbed on top of a chair and pulled down an empty wine bottle that had been waiting to be recycled. Holding it I leaned against the counter and counted the seconds until he found me.

Seven seconds exactly. "Sophie, what are you doing?"

Before he could react, I kicked the kitchen stool over and smashed the wine bottle against the counter so that I was in possession of a jagged-edged weapon. I backed up against the window. "I know who you are, you son of a bitch. And I know what you've done."

Anatoly stood there in silence for a beat. Then he slowly reached down to his ankle and pulled a gun out of a hidden holster. I dropped the bottle.

"What the fuck did you do to your shirt and face?"

"Please…please don't do this. Don't kill me." Tears were forming in my swollen eye. How much time would it take the police to get here? A minute? Five?

"You stupid— I'm not going to—"

The front door flew open and two uniformed police officers burst in, their voices shouting out their identity. I heard the gunshot and fell to my knees. I saw blood on the floor but wasn't immediately sure of where it was coming from. It wasn't until I saw Anatoly clutching his wounded arm and the police apprehending him that I understood what had happened. A third police officer came in and started asking me questions, but I couldn't understand what he was saying. The room was spinning at a breakneck pace. I leaned over and threw up.

So once again I was answering questions for the police into the wee hours of the night. I told them everything, although I did allow a little poetic license over the evening's events. I told them that I had been suspicious of Anatoly for some time. I told them about the crimes I thought he had com-

mitted and the facts that had led me to believe he had opportunity. I also told them that Anatoly had asked to meet
me for drinks and had convinced me that my fears were un-
founded. I relented and invited him up to my apartment. But
then he got too aggressive for my taste and that's when things
got out of control. He hit me, I managed to call the police
and then threw the phone out the window so that he
wouldn't be able to hang it up before they could trace the
call…. I must have inadvertently pressed the mute button.
He tried to grab me but only succeeded in ripping my shirt.
I tried to defend myself with a broken bottle and it was then
that he pulled the gun on me.

Okay, so I took a *lot* of poetic license, and I completely
forgot to tell them about Dena's and Marcus's roles in the
whole thing. But they got the important part: Anatoly pulled
a gun on me and tried to kill me.

I declined the detective's suggestions to visit a hospital for
my injury, although I did allow them to take pictures of it
and my ripped shirt. When I was done at the station I went
back to my apartment, collected Mr. Katz (who had been
bravely guarding the dust bunnies under the coffee table
during the whole ordeal), and left so that the police could
collect evidence and dust for prints. It wouldn't be long before they would be searching Anatoly's place, as well. I called
Dena from my cell phone and asked if I could crash at her
place. I had never heard her so beside herself. Within fifteen
minutes she was there to pick me up. I put Mr. Katz in back
and climbed into the front seat.

"Where the fuck is your head?" she was screaming as she
drove toward Noe Valley. "There are risks and then there's
pure stupidity. What if he had raped you? What if he had shot
you before the police got there? Did you even consider those
possibilities?"

"I didn't have that luxury. I had to stop him, and this was
the only way."

"Oh, fuck that. We could have come up with *something* else. Anything would have been better than that."

"It worked, didn't it?" I asked. I turned and smiled at my annoyed pet, who was loudly protesting through the bars of his cat carrier.

"Only because you are insanely lucky. Jesus, Sophie, when Marcus told me what you were up to I almost had a heart attack and died. Died, Sophie. I haven't even hit my sexual peak yet."

"God help us all when that happens." I gazed at the rows of houses through the thin layer of dust that had settled on the side windows. "You know what's weird?"

"You, taking cavalier chances with your life?" Dena was changing gears with the force of a race-car driver.

"Anatoly pulled a handgun on me."

"Yeah, well that part actually makes sense, considering he was trying to kill you."

"None of the characters in my book was killed with a handgun. Someone in my first book was shot with a hunting rifle, and in my third book a woman was shot with a sawed-off shotgun, but no one was ever killed or even threatened with a handgun." I adjusted my position so I could take in Dena's profile. "Anatoly varied from the script."

"I guess seeing you dead was more important to him than recreating one of your novels." Her little Toyota groaned in protest as she tried to make it do zero to sixty in three seconds.

"Yeah, but that was his whole M.O., killing people in the manner they described in their entertainment medium."

"Sophie, you're not going to get this to make sense. The guy is crazy, and I mean Ted Bundy kind of crazy. Logic and consistency means nothing to people like that."

"I guess you're right." I closed my eyes to the blurred lights of the city. "Besides, I'm tired of trying to figure this all out. By tomorrow afternoon the police will have found the hatchet in his apartment and this will all be over. That's all I really care about now."

"Amen, sister."

The next day I was called into the police station and greeted by Detective Lorenzo, who was cordial if not downright friendly. The first part of the conversation went as I had anticipated. He offered some evasive apologies for not taking me seriously before—enough to partially pacify me, but not enough to get him sued. He politely inquired about my eye and if I had slept well. Then the subject of Anatoly came up.

"We found the murder weapon used in the Barbie Vega case in Darinsky's apartment. He's now being charged with that murder, along with the attack he made on you."

I sniffed at the coffee-like substance that had been offered to me. "Well, I guess you finally have your evidence, then."

"Hmm." He took a large gulp from his cup. He seemed to gain an enjoyment from the beverage that, as far as I could tell, was completely unjustified—it wasn't Starbucks. "We are checking into the possibility that he was involved in Tolsky's and JJ Money's deaths, but so far, we don't have any solids links."

"You have to find something." I scooted forward in my chair. "DC Smooth is in jail for one of those murders. You can't let an innocent man take the wrap for Anatoly."

Lorenzo put his hand up to stop me. "Don't worry. If Darinsky is the responsible party in that murder, he's the one who will do the time for it, assuming of course that he doesn't get the death penalty, which is a real possibility here."

I nodded and felt the beginnings of a migraine take up residence in my skull. I was not actively opposed to the death penalty, but the inescapable visual of Anatoly losing his life at the hands of a death-row correctional officer was more than a little unsettling. I sipped from my paper cup, then pressed my lips together so I could suppress the impulse to spit it out.

"I have to say, I never would've expected any of this from this guy. He's had a few minor scuffs with the law in the past but nothing major, and he has a history of being a pretty good P.I. I would have pegged him as one of the good guys."

I wrinkled my forehead. "P.I.?"

"Yep. That's his real occupation. He started as an investigator for an insurance firm, and then switched over to representing private citizens a few years ago. Get this, the last person to have hired him was Shannon Tolsky."

I spilled my coffee down my shirt. "But I talked to Shannon. We even talked a little about Anatoly—she never mentioned that."

"She says he told her to keep his employment a secret. A few weeks after taking on the assignment she fired him, didn't think he was making enough progress. I'd say there's not a lot of love lost between those two. She was more than willing to embrace the possibility that Darinsky is responsible for killing her dad."

"So, he's claiming he's been investigating the Tolsky murder?"

"Uh-huh. He says that after Miss Tolsky fired him, he continued the investigation on his own. He claims he had reason to believe that Tolsky was having an affair with a woman in the city, and he thought that she might somehow be involved in his death. He says he thinks that woman was you."

"Me?" I lurched forward, spilling more of my drink. This was getting too weird.

"You. In fact, he's clinging to the story that you set him up, that you staged your own attack, but that's a little farfetched for us. After all, you couldn't very well have punched yourself in the face—could you?"

I sat back in my seat. "No, that would be difficult."

"Plus, by Darinsky's own admission, you've never been up to his place and there doesn't seem to have been any opportunity for you to have planted that hatchet in the kitchen—so there goes that theory."

The hatchet had been in the bedroom. I recognized the trap. It was the fact that Lorenzo felt the need to set it that worried me. What would it take to get this man to believe in my innocence? I forced myself to drink what remained in my cup. "I can't believe he has the audacity to make up accusations about me, but I guess people will do whatever they feel is necessary to save their own skin."

Lorenzo offered a tight smile. "That they will. They'll need your testimony to get a conviction. I trust you'll be a cooperative witness?"

"Absolutely."

"Then I'll see you in court." Lorenzo stood up to indicate that the meeting was over.

I followed suit, smoothing my skirt before reaching out to shake his hand. "Thank you for taking care of this. It'll be nice to be able to sleep peacefully again."

He grinned and walked me to the door. "Just don't invite any more men up to your apartment that you suspect of murder, okay?"

CHAPTER 20

"'I swear,' Kittie said with a bored sigh, 'if I have to go to one more S&M party I'll scream.'"
—*Sex, Drugs and Murder*

I went back to my place, where I had dropped Mr. Katz off earlier. I bent down and scratched him behind the ears. "It's just you and me again, buddy." He tolerated my affections for a few minutes before going back to his food bowl.

I went over and checked the answering machine. Eighteen messages. I skipped through the first five from reporters before I got to Leah. She couldn't believe that I would put off talking to her about her marriage in order to have drinks with a psychotic. There were three messages from my mother. "Millions of nice Jewish boys out there and you had to take up with Bugsy Segal. Did I raise you for this?" Another eight from the press, and then there was one from Marcus.

"Hi, honey. I think a little celebration is in order. Let's do dinner at my place tonight. Jason's working, but Donato, Mary Ann and Dena can all make it. We'll drink, drink and drink some more until the whole thing's funny. Shall we say seven-thirty? Call me at the salon to confirm."

I dialed up Ooh-La-La to accept the invitation and to tell him about the information I had gotten at the police station.

"A private dick, huh? I've always wanted one of those."

"It's not funny, Marcus. In fact, it's really weird."

"Why, because you thought all P.I.'s were good guys? There are corrupt cops, so there have got to be a few bad-boy P.I.'s out there."

"I guess." I looked over to the spot where he had held me at gunpoint. "But we're not talking about corrupt. We're talking about nuts. I mean, what's the motive here?"

"You're not having second thoughts about his guilt, are you, honey? He's been sleeping on a bloody hatchet."

"Yeah, I know." I stretched my legs out in front of me. "Obviously he's guilty. I guess I would just like it if it was wrapped up a little more neatly."

"You can't always get what you want, but if you try sometimes, you just might find…"

"Goodbye, Marcus. I'll see you at seven-thirty."

"Ciao, Bella."

I called my mother and spent twenty-five minutes reassuring her before I finally cut her off with some excuse about having an appointment at the police station. I half walked, half crawled to my beckoning sofa. Mr. Katz jumped up on my stomach and curled into a little fur pillow. I smiled and rested my hand on his back.

"So what do you say, sweetie? Are you up for a four-hour catnap?"

At seven-thirty sharp I arrived at Marcus's. It was Donato who answered the door. "Ah, it's our heroine."

I laughed and scooted into the apartment. "I don't know if I qualify as a heroine. Maybe just a private citizen who isn't afraid to take stupid chances."

"Do not minimize what you have done. You have proven yourself to be an exceptionally brave woman."

Gorgeous and charming. If he was straight, I would've jumped him right then. "Thank you. But really it was a case of being forced to rise to the occasion. Where is everyone?"

"Mary Ann and Dena are going to be fifteen minutes late. Marcus is at the store purchasing more wine."

"More wine, huh?" I removed my jacket and hooked it on the coatrack. "If I didn't know any better, I'd say he was trying to get me drunk in order to have his way with me. Unfortunately I do know better."

I started to hang up my purse but my cell phone started doing it's *"Frère Jacques"* thing. "Hello?"

"This is Mrs. Tolsky. I want you to stop calling me."

"Oh, gosh, you caught me a little off guard. You don't have to worry—"

"Both you and that Anatoly person. I spoke to Shannon, and I know exactly what information you want and I'm going to give it to you now, but in exchange you both must stop harassing me immediately."

"Actually, what I was about to say—"

"My husband *was* having an affair with someone in San Francisco," she continued, "but much to my humiliation and complete disgust, it was not with a woman but with a man."

I took in a sharp breath. "Excuse me?"

"You heard me. I received a video in the mail, without a return address or a note. I can't tell you how disgusting it was. Alex swore that he didn't know he was being taped, but that's not really the point now, is it?"

"No, I guess not."

"The other man in the video—if you can call people who do those things *men*—was tan with dark hair—Latin, I suppose. That's all I know. I certainly didn't spend any time studying it for distinguishing characteristics. Of course, I destroyed the tape."

I started surveying the room. A table set for five, a fresh bouquet in a crystal vase, a CD tower...

"I would appreciate you not leaking any of this to the media..."

...a Japanese screen, an entertainment center...

"But at the moment that's not really my main concern. Just stop calling me."

...a new set of golf clubs...

I ducked just as the putter was swung over my head.

I whirled around and grabbed the other end of the club. Donato yanked it to the left with enough force to pull me off my feet, but I didn't let go. His boot went into my stomach and I gasped in pain. I still had the end of the club, but I wouldn't be able to hold on much longer. I pulled the putter as hard as I could, prompting Donato to do the same. Then I let go. He fell backward and the club went flying through the closed window.

I turned to run but he had my leg, and I came crashing down. He was straddling me now. I tried to evade his grasp, but it was no good. My arms were pulled behind my back. I heard Marcus's phone come crashing to the ground and then felt the plastic of the cord dig into the skin around my wrists. I screamed and cried for help. He flipped me over and stuffed a silk scarf into my mouth until I gagged.

"You have a choice about how you are to die," Donato instructed. "I can inflict minimum or maximum pain. I would prefer minimum. Please nod your head if you agree."

The feelings of panic I had experienced when Andy had attacked me, when I found Barbie, when Marcus had discovered the hatchet, couldn't compare to this.

"Nod your head, Sophie, or I'll start with the face."

I nodded.

He removed the scarf from my mouth, careful not to inflict any undue discomfort. His gentle touch was terrifying.

"Why?" I whispered.

"Why?" He crouched over me. "Sophie, you surprise me. I thought you, of all people, would understand."

"I don't."

He sighed and gazed out the broken window. "This is my art."

"Your art?"

"But can you not see it? I have, in fact, created a new art form. Just as Monet created Impressionism and Isadora Duncan created modern dance, I can now list myself amongst the greatest artistic geniuses of all time. And *my* art...my art is more powerful than anything that precedes it."

Had my fear affected my hearing, or was he truly this crazy? "Donato, this isn't art. This is murder. It's not revolutionary, it's not unique, it's...it's evil."

For a split second Donato's perfect face became distorted and twisted, then it smoothed back out to its elegant shape. "I thought you would see. But since you do not, allow me to enlighten you. Art is simply a creative way to recreate the world that we already live in. Picasso did not invent the female face, he simply put it together in a manner that caused us to see it differently. But the ancient question is still on the minds and lips of every man or woman who has read a book, listened to a piece of music, or viewed a performance—'Is it art that always imitates life, or can life be made to imitate art?' This last century has only served to make those questions more relevant. The child who shoots his schoolmates after seeing it done in a movie. Was the child violent because he was watching the film or was the movie violent because its creators had tapped into the mood of contemporary youth? I address this in my art. I take the more cerebral art of singers, filmmakers and writers like yourself, and make it more tangible, more passionate, more accessible. Surely you see the genius in that? The horrible beauty? Why, there has not been an artist that has had such a direct affect on the lives of people since Leni Riefenstahl."

"Leni Riefenstahl? Leni Riefenstahl made films for Hitler equating Jews to rats. How is that related to what you're doing now? Are you some kind of whacked version of a neo-Nazi? Are you doing this because I'm Jewish?"

Donato pulled himself to full height. "You are not listening to me."

I pulled my knees into my chest.

Donato ran his fingers through his hair. "Forgive me—" he was smiling now "—but I do not care about your religion, nor do I harbor any ill will against the Jewish people— neither did Riefenstahl."

The videos and the lectures from my college history courses began to flood into my mind. "Her art...oh God, she did it for her art."

Donato's smile widened. "Precisely. You do understand." He again knelt by my side. "Hitler gave her the opportunity to change the world through her art. To be allowed to make films so powerful that the citizenship of Germany was willing to stand by and applaud while the Nazis directed their dogs to rip apart the children of their Jewish neighbors.... How could any true artist not envy the ability to achieve something so monumental, so earth-shattering?"

I shook my head and tried not to hyperventilate. How had I missed it—it must always have been there, in his eyes. His eyes were insane. "You killed them—all of them—in the name...in the name of art."

"I assume you are referring to JJ Money and Tolsky. Yes I did. JJ Money was at a social gathering. He lived in the penthouse above the apartment of a collector, that is how we met. I was able to draw him into conversation and he spoke of his music, he claimed to be the voice of black urban youth. He defended the violence of his lyrics— after all, he was simply verbalizing an existing anger. He said the music was real, and that it was that reality that people were afraid of." Donato laughed quietly. "I am paraphrasing of course—the exact slang he used is beyond my ability to repeat."

"And that inspired you?" I knew it was a lost cause but I had to reason with him, I had to try. "Donato, don't you get it? The sentiment in the music may have been real, but he wasn't actually hurting anyone."

"Precisely." Donato's lips pulled back once more to display his white, glistening teeth. "He had not gone far enough. He lacked the vision, the courage. It was left to me to bring his message to the hearts of the public. When he died, the world stopped and listened, not just his fans, not just his critics, the world. Everyone was touched by his anger, by his magnificent rage."

"So, did you become his lover, as well?" It was a stall tactic. I just needed time to think, to come up with a way to do the impossible.

"The only lover that he truly desired had to be injected or inhaled. Those who love narcotics are easy to befriend and manipulate. I would visit my client, then travel up to see him, bearing gifts, always bearing gifts. I do not think he knew that it was my plan to call DC Smooth. He was too high to notice when I took control."

"And now DC is in prison suffering for your 'art.'"

"Ah, that was perfect, although the irony was missed. DC has a song that speaks of being unjustly accused due to the color of his skin. No one made that connection. Perhaps I made his guilt a bit too convincing."

I wriggled my wrists against the cord; there was no way of loosening it. I could try to keep him talking until Marcus returned from...from where? Not from getting wine. My breathing quickened and I forced myself to ask. "Marcus?"

"Marcus? You wish to know what has become of him?" Donato massaged his palm with his thumb. "He is at Ku-

leto's with Dena and Mary Ann, awaiting your arrival. I told
Marcus that you called to change the plans and he informed
the others. They know you may be late, so they will not be
concerned." He checked his watch. "But more time has
passed than I had expected. We must get on with this. They
are waiting for me, as well, and I must do what is necessary
to ensure that Marcus is given credit for this crime. I had
originally planned to seduce Dena, but after my research I
came to see that she does not allow men to enter her heart
as easily as she allows them access to her bed. Marcus was
more open, more…vulnerable." He sighed and stood up. "I
do wish I could sign my work, but I must accept my required
anonymity." He crossed to the clubs.

"And Tolsky?" I asked. Time, please, God, give me time.

Donato lifted a driver for his scrutiny. "You shouldn't have
fought me over the putter. I did so want to get the details right."

"How…how did you get to Tolsky?"

"JJ Money introduced us," Donato said, his eyes never
leaving the club. "Once I discovered the truth of his sexu-
ality, the rest was simple. Margaret only needed the tape to
end the marriage. I knew that she would destroy it, and once
I convinced Alex that I, too, did not know of the tape, it was
inevitable that he should turn to me for comfort. I vowed to
help him repair his wretched union. The gratitude he expressed was truly touching, particularly after I offered to dictate a letter to Margaret that he could send to her. 'To my
beloved wife, I can not live without you…' He wrote my
words and drank my wine. He could not taste the Valium by
his fifth drink. He only woke briefly when I made the cut,
just long enough to cry out in pain, long enough for me to
give him one last kiss." He pressed the club to his chest. "I
do think I loved him. He was beautiful in his suffering."

Donato started toward me, the club loosely balancing
in his hands. "But you know all this. You are stalling, and it
has become tiring."

"Please…"

"I wish you hadn't sent Barbie to the park that day, she interrupted my creative flow. My talent cannot be wasted on the insignificant. It was you who was supposed to die."

"Donato…"

"Shh." The scarf was in my mouth again. He caressed my cheek. "If I had not known that you would come to suspect me, I would have chosen you as my lover. It would have made this moment all the more poignant."

The tears were blurring my vision. I tried to make some last protest but choked on the silk.

"Shh…do not worry. Your art will now be given the serious attention it has always deserved."

I squeezed my eyes closed and tried to remember how to pray.

Donato cried out. I opened my eyes to see that the source of his vexation was Dena. She had somehow confiscated his driver and was swinging it at his head. He grabbed the club from her and threw it down, then he lunged for her, but I managed to kick my feet out in front of him and he crashed face down onto the ground.

Dena jumped on his back, her heeled boots causing him to howl in pain. I looked over at the crystal vase resting on the side table. She could use it as a weapon. I tried to tell her as much but the scarf made that impossible. I frantically started to push my bound form along like a snake, in hopes that by moving toward it I might be able to draw her attention to the vase. She took no notice and instead leaped off his back and dove for her tote bag, which she had dropped on the floor. Donato began to rise, his teeth bared. I looked up at the vase, willing Dena to do the same, but in the moment that my eyes were averted I heard a snapping noise and Donato's guttural scream.

I refocused on Dena. She was standing above Donato with a whip that she had apparently cracked across the side of his

face, hitting his right eye in the process. He was on his knees
clutching it with both hands. At last, she looked in my direction and realized my purpose. She skirted Donato's arm
as he flung it out in an attempt to grab her, and seized the
vase. The sound of the crystal breaking over his head echoed
in my eardrums, and then there was silence. Donato lay motionless on the floor.

She ran to my side, took out the scarf and started working on the wire. "Jesus, okay, hang on. Are you all right?"

"Yes!" I felt the wire loosen and I yanked my hands free
and threw them around Dena's neck. "Oh my God, thank
you. Thank you. He was going to…oh God, Dena. How did
you know I was here?"

"We were supposed to have dinner here, weren't we?" she
asked, pushing my hair away from her mouth.

"But it was relocated to Kuletto's. He said Marcus called you."

"Well, if he did, I didn't get the message, but the golf club
among the shards of glass on the sidewalk—that message I
got loud and clear." She pulled away from the embrace. "You
have to call the police now, and I'm not fucking kidding
this time."

I nodded and tried to wipe away the layers of tears from
my cheeks. I looked over at the whip, now lying motionless
several feet from Donato, but decided I wasn't ready to comment on that yet. "I'm calling, I'm calling right now." I didn't
wait for Dena to reconnect the phone but searched the floor
for my cell instead. It lay adjacent to Donato's body. As I
reached for it I saw his hand twitch.

"Oh God." I snapped back my arm and bolted for the
opposite end of the room. "He's coming to, I think he's
coming—"

"Relax, this isn't a movie. Even if he does come to he
won't be able to do much more than moan and writhe
around in pain. But if it will make you feel better…" Dena
went to her tote bag and pulled out a pair of handcuffs lined

with purple faux fur. "Ta-da!" She latched them onto Donato. "I have a matching blindfold too. Should we use it?"

"You…you carry those around with you?"

"I just came from Jason's. The whip's just for looks…at least it was until now."

"Okay." I tiptoed over to my phone and snatched it out of Donato's proximity. "I'm going to call the police now and, um, I'm just going to let you tell them about the cuffs and the whip. Cool?"

"For Christ's sake, it's not like I was carrying a concealed weapon or anything."

"No, no, that would be easier to explain."

CHAPTER 21

"Since the majority of domestic abuse victims are women, it seems appropriate that every woman be allowed to seriously injure one man a year in order to maintain a healthy social balance."

—*Sex, Drugs and Murder*

"L'chaim."

Mary Ann, Dena and I raised our glasses over our pizza. Sometimes the most traditional toasts are the most appropriate. Two weeks had passed since Donato's arrest, and this was the first time since then that any of us had felt emotionally stable enough to go out and celebrate his incarceration.

Dena swished the wine around in her mouth before swallowing. "So I read in the paper yesterday that Donato confessed to every detail of his crimes, including the planting of the hatchet in Anatoly's room, but he's still refusing representation."

"Why would he want representation?" I asked, pulling my second piece of pizza from the pie. "He's proud of the murders he's committed. He certainly doesn't want anyone to try to pass them off as acts of insanity. Now he's finally able to sign his work."

"I still don't get why he did it," Mary Ann said, putting a hand delicately over her mouth to hide the food that was still in there. The busboy clearing the next table smiled shyly at her. Mary Ann was the only woman I knew who could attract men while talking with her mouth full.

Dena shook her head slightly and lifted the wine bottle to refill everyone's glass. "For once I'm glad you don't get it. That man was beyond sick. Let's just be grateful that his last masterpiece was left unfinished."

"Yeah, no shit," I agreed. "You know DC Smooth called me last week to thank me? They let him out just in time for him to see his kid being born. Oh, and Mark Baccon should be thanking me too, since he no longer has to worry about getting the death sentence. Of course, he'll still do time in prison for drug possession and breaking Barbie's restraining order against him."

Dena laughed. "You can't ask for a neater wrap-up than that. *This* is what you should write a screenplay about, Sophie. It's got all the ingredients: drama, violence, a little romance, and three chicks who know how to kick butt."

"I'll drink to that." I drank half the contents of my refilled glass in one gulp. "There are still a few loose ends hanging around, though."

"Such as?" Mary Ann asked.

"Well, there's Marcus for one. He's taking this whole thing really hard. I've been over at his place every day this week and he's a mess. He's basically spent the last fourteen days alternating between crying and vomiting."

"Wow." Mary Ann's eyes widened in sympathy. "I can't even imagine what he's feeling. I'm surprised he agreed to meet us."

I glanced at my watch and then at the door. "He said he was going to be here fifteen minutes ago, so maybe he changed his mind." I shook my head in disappointment. "I told him he should see someone to help him through this."

Dena raised an eyebrow. "You mean like a shrink?"

"Yes, I mean a shrink. He just found out that his best boy-toy was a pseudo-Nazi serial killer who tried to bludgeon his best friend with a putter. In my book, that kind of revelation is worthy of a few therapy sessions...." I looked toward the door again. "Okay, Marcus just walked in. Just don't talk about it and try to look supportive, in case he needs to shed a few more tears."

Dena's and Mary Ann's heads turned in his direction. He was wearing a perfectly fitted pair of Calvin Kleins, a beautiful khaki shirt that he had picked up with me while shopping at Armani A/X a few months back and a smile that would stop traffic.

Dena shot me a look. "Oh yeah, he looks real depressed."

"He was!"

Marcus finally made it over to our table. "Hello, darlings." He pulled out the empty chair next to me and gave me a breezy kiss on the cheek.

"Marcus...you seem...um..."

"Refreshingly non-suicidal?" He adjusted the rolls on his sleeves so that they displayed his forearms in a more flattering manner. "Well, I took your advice and I went out and got myself my very own shrink."

"I gave you that advice two days ago, so you can't have seen this guy more than once. Is he a miracle worker or something?"

"Honey, you have no idea. I met him at The Stud. He's five-eight and has curly black hair and the most adorable wire-rimmed glasses. He got his master's in psychology at Stanford a few years back and he's just twenty internship hours away from getting his license. I'm telling you it was lust at first sight."

"Marcus, that's not what I meant."

"Who cares what you *meant*," Dena said. "Obviously this guy is exactly what the doctor ordered. Besides, I've always felt that sex therapy is underused. You'd be surprised how many problems can be solved with a good screw."

"You said it, girlfriend." Marcus pulled out the largest remaining slice of pizza and put it on his plate. "Daniel is very good at showing me alternative methods for dealing with my frustrations. Speaking of sex—" he shook a fork at Dena "—I read that little bit about you in the *Metro*."

Mary Ann groaned, but Dena grinned like the Cheshire cat. "Can you believe it? Talk about an image change. I've gone from being the girl your mother warned you about to the admirable heroine who can take down serial killers. And I loved the article's title." She moved her hands in the air as if she were spreading out the words in front of us. "'Thank God For Furry Handcuffs.'" She laughed. "Even I couldn't have come up with a better headline. You know since that came out my business has doubled? Everybody wants me to show them how to properly use a whip."

Mary Ann protested. "Some of us are trying to eat." She flipped her curls over her shoulder and took a bite of her fourth slice. "Have you talked to Anatoly yet?"

I lowered my eyes and readjusted the napkin on my lap. "Um, no, I've been kind of busy." All of the charges against Anatoly had been dropped. After the incident with Donato, my memory of what had happened the night before had become very blurred and confused. I didn't confess to filing a false police report or anything silly like that, but it quickly became clear that I no longer made a convincing witness. I hadn't talked to him since that night, and his silence was becoming increasingly conspicuous.

"You're going to have to do it sometime," Dena goaded.

"I will…I'm just waiting for…"

"For what?" Dena gave me a disdainful look. "An engraved invitation?"

"Guys don't usually send those out to women who frame them for murder," Marcus pointed out.

"Okay, okay, I know. The ball's in my court."

"So, go run with it." Dena reached down and retrieved my purse from the floor. "We'll take care of the check. You have another loose end that needs tying."

After standing outside Anatoly's apartment building for well over an hour, I knew exactly how many cracks were in the sidewalk in front, not to mention how long they were and how many jagged points each one had.

I bit my lip and looked up at the glass door. Maybe it wasn't a good day to do this. Plus, I really should call first. I nodded decisively. That was it then, procrastination was definitely the way to go. I turned on my heel, determined to go home and discuss the matter with Mr. Katz.

I heard the door open and close. I didn't have to look, I knew it was him. I could feel him glaring at me. I inhaled and turned back around. Oh yeah, that was the glare.

"Anatoly...hi. I was just finishing up a walk..."

"You've been standing here for an hour and a half. I could see you from my window."

"Really? Gosh, I thought it was more like an hour and twenty minutes." Not even a smile. "If you saw me out here, how come you didn't come down sooner?"

"Why should I do anything to make your life easier?"

"Good point." Okay, different approach. I clasped my hands behind my back, lowered my head a notch and peered up at him. "You look good."

Anatoly wasn't buying.

I sighed and threw up my hands. "Okay, okay, I'm sorry. I am. I am really and truly sorry."

"Not good enough."

"Oh, come on, Anatoly, can't you give a girl a break?"

"I have a bullet wound in my arm."

"Okay, that was bad. But, hey, it's just a flesh wound, right? And if you wear a short-sleeved shirt, you'll be sporting one kick-ass conversation piece. The chicks will be lining up to—"

"No one is more repulsive than a rapist, but do you know who takes a close second?"

"Donato?"

"Someone who falsely accuses a man of rape."

"Now wait. I never accused you of rape." I held my hand up in protest. "I told the police that you got a little aggressive during a make-out session, I backed out, you got pissed and tried to beat the shit out of me. Oh, and I said that I thought you had killed a few people, but I swear to God that was it."

Anatoly stared at me, speechless.

"Well, that's a little better, isn't it?"

Anatoly shook his head. "You are the most perverted and conniving woman I have ever met."

"Oh, now, hold on." I strode forward until there was only a few feet between us. "I thought you were trying to kill me, and I had every reason to think so. You may not be a murderer, but you *were* stalking me. You broke into my apartment, took photos of me without my knowledge, fed me a line of bullshit about your being a contractor, and then you pulled a gun on me."

"You were threatening me with a broken bottle."

"Uh-huh, right. The gun didn't just magically appear when I broke the bottle, okay? Tell me, how did you plan on explaining that one during my little seduction number, hmm? Didn't you think I would notice that you had a concealed weapon strapped to your leg when you took off your pants?"

"I could have taken it off without your being aware of it. If we had gotten that far, you would have been distracted by what else I had hidden under my pants."

"Oh, and what would that be, your brain? Because that's obviously where you keep it."

Anatoly was clenching his fist now. "I wasn't going to go into your apartment unprotected. Last time I was there you pulled a butcher knife on me.'"

"I thought…"

"I know what you thought, and I thought you were the killer. I have never met an innocent person who was more effective at making themselves look guilty."

"Me? I was the victim in—" I stopped myself. This was not why I had come. Yes, he was pissed, but if I was the one who had been shot and thrown in jail I might be a little ticked off too. I took a few deep breaths and tried not to grit my teeth. "I'm sorry. I know what I put you through and I can't imagine how I could ever make it up to you. I made a huge mistake, and you suffered for it. I did come close to losing my own life because of my little blunder, so maybe you can take some comfort in that."

Anatoly's shoulders relaxed a little. His gaze went past me to the parked cars on the street. "The image of Donato standing over you with a golf club isn't one that I find comforting." His eyes shifted back to me. "He didn't hurt you, did he?"

I broke into a broad grin. "Well, what do you know! You do care about me!"

"Don't be ridiculous. I was just curious—if you were a stranger I would have asked you the same question."

"Ah, I see. I didn't tell the papers this, but he did fracture one of my ribs."

"He did what?" Anatoly's jaw tightened and he clenched his hands into fists. "If I could get my hands on that son of a bitch, I'd have him begging for the lethal injection." He looked at me with concern. "How are you now? Do you need to sit down?"

"Actually, I was just messing with you. Thanks to Dena and her S&M toys I got through the while thing without a scratch."

By the way Anatoly was staring at me you would have thought I had grown a second head. "You really are completely insane, aren't you?" he asked.

"Maybe, but I think I proved my point." I leaned closer to him. "You like me."

"At the moment I'd like to throw you into the Bay."

I rolled my eyes. "There are easier ways to get me wet."

Anatoly burst out laughing. "I can't believe you just said that."

"Actually, I can't believe it either. I've been spending too much time with Dena lately." I put a gentle finger on the spot on his arm where he had been injured. "I really am sorry about this."

"I've been through worse," he said. His expression softened as he looked into my eyes. "After our first few encounters I was ready to take you off my list of suspects. At that point I was looking forward to getting to know you on a more…personal level." There it was, that sexy little half smile of his. "But then you forced me to reconsider. I'm glad my first instincts were correct. I'm glad you're not a murderer."

"I'm glad you're not a murderer too."

"So we can agree on something."

I took a step closer. "So does that mean you still want to get to know me on a more personal level?"

"No."

I laughed. "Okay, fair enough, how about on a professional level? You remember my mentioning to you that my sister thought her husband was having an affair?"

"Vaguely."

"Well, she's decided to hire a private investigator and, considering your experience, I was hoping you could recommend somebody."

Anatoly snorted and shook his head.

"Kidding. Really, I'd like to hire you. How much would it cost me to find out if my brother-in-law is a conniving rat?"

"For you? Six thousand for the first month's work."

"Six thousand? Is that how much P.I.'s make?"

"No, for the job you're describing I usually charge less than half that, but considering all you've done for me, I decided to give you a special."

"Gee, thanks." I tried unsuccessfully to push my hair behind my ears, and took in a deep breath of the crisp clear air. "Well, it's a hell of a lot cheaper than a civil suit. You're hired."

Anatoly took a step back. "For six thousand dollars?"

"You thought you priced yourself out, didn't you."

"Yes, I did."

"Guess you calculated wrong, huh? Can I introduce you to my sister tomorrow?"

"I..." Anatoly seemed to be at a rare loss for words. Finally he stuffed his hands in his pockets and stared up at the sky. "One o'clock at your place?"

"Sounds good." I started to leave, but Anatoly took hold of my arm.

"I have a condition."

"Okay."

"If either one of you threatens me with a sharp object, I quit. No refunds." Then he turned around and returned to his apartment.

I crossed my arms in front of me and watched until the door came to a complete close. "Oh yeah, he wants me."